RIVERBIG

RIVERBIG

A NOVEL

Aris Janigian

HEYDAY BOOKS
BERKELEY, CALIFORNIA

Heyday Institute would like to thank the James Irvine Foundation for their support of Central Valley literature.

Library of Congress Cataloging-in-Publication Data

Janigian, Aris.
  Riverbig / Aris Janigian.
    p. cm.
  Sequel to: Bloodvine.
  ISBN 978-1-59714-104-8 (pbk. : alk. paper)
  1. Brothers--Fiction. 2. Armenian Americans--Fiction. 3. Widows--Fiction.
  4. Farm life--Fiction. 5. Fresno (Calif.)--Fiction. 6. Domestic fiction. I. Title.
  PS3610.A569R58 2009
  813'.6--dc22

                              2008047296

Book Design by Lorraine Rath
Printing and Binding: Thompson-Shore, Dexter, MI

Orders, inquiries, and correspondence should be addressed to:
    Heyday Books
    P. O. Box 9145, Berkeley, CA 94709
    (510) 549-3564, Fax (510) 549-1889
    www.heydaybooks.com

green
press
INITIATIVE

Heyday Books is committed to preserving ancient forests and natural resources. We elected to print this title on 30% post consumer recycled paper, processed chlorine free. As a result, for this printing, we have saved:

    6 Trees (40' tall and 6-8" diameter)
    2,041 Gallons of Wastewater
    4 million BTU's of Total Energy
    262 Pounds of Solid Waste
    492 Pounds of Greenhouse Gases

Heyday Books made this paper choice because our printer, Thomson-Shore, Inc., is a member of Green Press Initiative, a nonprofit program dedicated to supporting authors, publishers, and suppliers in their efforts to reduce their use of fiber obtained from endangered forests.

For more information, visit www.greenpressinitiative.org

Environmental impact estimates were made using the Environmental Defense Paper Calculator. For more information visit: www.papercalculator.org.

10 9 8 7 6 5 4 3 2 1

For In Sun, Valentine, and Miran,
my three angels.

PROLOGUE

"UNSAN MUSHO," FRED TAKAHASHI SAID. "I will fade away from this farm like the mist."

He nodded his head in agreement with himself, dropped to his haunches, low as a frog, and then pressed his two hands on the ground.

"Don't write me, don't do nothin'. Make it like your own." He smacked his hands free of dirt, peered deep into his trees, and said, "When I come back we'll settle up with whatever needs settling."

Chamichian's mind was fixed on a picture of that mist, its drift poetic and lonesome but hardly comforting. What if Taki's house caught fire? What if the trees contracted some impossible-to-stamp-out-disease? There were a hundred what-ifs. Chamichian let them sit.

Sparrows rustled in the gray and naked branches, the tumescent earth faintly churned. In the dead of winter the orchard was fragrant, like a steeped bag of tea. Chamichian took a deep breath of it and said, "Damnedest mentality I've seen from this government yet."

Taki stood and took a large loop of keys from his back pocket and handed it to his neighbor. Chamichian accepted it with a nod.

"And these here are for the shed." Taki had pulled out another, smaller set of keys, three in all.

"The shed?"

He showed them in a palm. "Promise me you won't touch my machines. Lot of sweat and blood wrapped up in them machines."

Fred had dinked around with them for little over a decade. He swore that sooner or later he'd get them to do everything human hands could do in a tenth of the time. They had perturbed Chamichian all out of proportion since the first day he'd laid eyes on one. It was spring thinning, 1935, and instead of hiring a crew to get in there and knock some fruit off, Taki wobbled out of his shed a story-tall contrivance with oversized tractor tires and great big mechanical arms. Like the captain of some major seagoing vessel, he ferried it forward, gearsticks shifting this way and that.

Half a dozen or so neighbors, gathered as witnesses, watched it make a wide swing, stall, sputter, and grind until Taki got it lined up ever so illogically on a row. When it finally lurched into the orchard the Bible verse wherein the camel is made to pass through the needle's eye came to Chamichian's mind. Jimmy Souza, the neighborhood welder, cursed Taki's god-awful misuse of metal. Right away, the two mechanical arms began slapping ferociously at the trees. The stunned men waited for the result and, once the dust had dispersed, ten trees or so in, verily, it was manifest. Leaves were strewn everywhere, branches dangled by the bark, limbs had been lopped. Robert Markarian said last he checked it was thinning not pruning time. The men chuckled hazily and sidled over to the calamity. On the ground, baby plums, green, golfball-size, were scattered as far away as two rows. Chamich reached to pick a couple up. Souza kicked a few around. They each one shook his head at the ruinous senselessness of it all.

What with the time and energy Taki spent on the machines over the years his whole orchard—the one he was leaving now—was in a shambles. Plus, a poorly tended farm is going to infect farms that border it sure as flu gets passed from one kid to another at school.

"You know, Taki, we Christians have a saying: Don't jingle a money bag in front of a beggar. In other words, I say this respectfully, maybe you should pocket that set of keys."

Taki nodded, looked to his left, his right, and then put his arms around Chamichian. He knew Chamichian was the cleanest farmer in the district, in every particular meticulous as a watchmaker. Taki had no doubt he was the luckiest man in this most unlucky situation, but still...He started to sob, shuddering straight through his boots.

Chamichian patted him on the back. "Don't you worry. I'll take damn good care of your land. You go ahead."

Taki put himself together and went ahead. Chamichian watched him go.

"Don't you worry," he muttered to himself. "Don't you worry about a thing. You go ahead now, like a mist."

Within a week, he was at work cutting the cankers down. In no time, he marked where water was pooling, stretches where the trees were thirsty. He replanted wood that Taki had left for dead, dug new irrigation rows, straight as rulers.

It drove his wife, Marie, haywire. True, he was spending more time on Taki's piece than he was spending on his own, but he so enjoyed the soulful anonymity of an orchard that whether it was Taki's or his own proved moot. In winter, the feel of frosty earth crunching beneath his boots, the fog's quiet song, sheer in hand, up the ladder he'd climb, positioning his body to turn inside the thick of branches, snapping, snapping and clearing its insides out to let the tree grab what it could of the brittle sun.

Sometimes, walking among his trees, he felt proud as a prince surveying a city rich with monuments that he himself had erected. Yes, memories of the past would occasionally overwhelm him and he'd have to pause, sit on a berm, and cry, for his past, for his people's unfathomable fate, but even more often he found himself overwhelmed with gratitude. He had a roof over his head, two kids, and an orchard, debt free, to his name. His wife looked over what they had, wasn't into fancy purses or shoes, and raised their Lilit—a little slow in the head—without any prejudice. If Marie couldn't see or feel it, he'd just have to light a candle and say a prayer that one day she would. In the meanwhile, for however long, maybe forever long Takahashi would be interned in those camps, Chamichian would farm Taki's orchard no less than were it his own.

He did so for three years, and then one day Fred and his family came back. They were greeted by the neighbors with open arms, but the shame they were made to feel in those camps seemed to have followed them home. Vince, the kid, and old lady Takahashi must've stayed indoors for a good three weeks. Chamichian met Fred out in the orchard, where he tried to lift his spirit by showing off how he'd spruced up the trees, evened the canopies, repaired each and every ditch so that water ran down them without a hitch. "You been gettin' fifty boxes a tree. I figure another year you'll have yourself sixty-five."

Even with what he had recovered from the three harvests, Chamichian had still dumped a good two thousand dollars into Takahashi's field. Marie knew that her husband hated calling in a loan as much as most men hated to give one out, and she believed that if he let too much time lapse he might very well let it pass. She prodded and pushed until Chamichian trundled over to the Takahashi's with a shoebox of tags and receipts under his arm. They pulled one after another out, Fred scrutinizing each like an agent from the IRS. Had Chamichian really needed to do this or that? "Well, okay, it did need fixin', but…" "Looks like you gave Walt down the road there ten bucks to weld that hitch? Don't he regular do it for five?"

Takahashi said he'd like some time to review the expenses. Right then and there most farmers, especially any number of hot-blooded Armenians, would've taken a mallet to the man's head, but Chamichian was, as they described it from the pulpit, "patient and long-suffering," and so a week later the two men sat down beneath an elm tree in Chamichian's yard and with a bottle of brandy between them sized it up this way and that before they cut it down the middle: a thousand bucks, due a month after the upcoming harvest. Chamich didn't begrudge Taki, though by any normal accounting he'd been cheated by half. In fact, just the opposite occurred—he favored the man's land even more. In his three years as caretaker, Chamich had grown partial to Taki's twenty the way a wet nurse grows partial to a baby. He'd finish spraying his plums and then swing over to Taki's and spray thirty or forty rows of his peaches; when Takahashi's trees were thirsty he'd step in and give them a quick drink. With all that help, Taki found he had more time than ever to tinker with his contraptions. After that, Marie turned her nose up when her husband so much as uttered Takahashi's name, and swung her eyes away when she passed "those people" on the road.

Chamichian paid her no mind, and in time his friendship with Taki would grow. Indeed, at least so far as anyone in the valley could tell, never before had two men with such radically different roots and measures of the world taken to each other so well. They started cooking their own moonshine. Chamichian had sketched a still on a grocery bag, and with that sketch Taki had fashioned an apparatus that produced an almost perfect brew. The man was a shabby farmer but at welding was a master. His piping was coiled flawlessly as any snake and his copper kettle was smooth and seamless as a baby's tum. They'd hauled in raisins from Souza's and stacked the lugs in the shed. Two weeks later fire was spreading out beneath the kettle and they were listening to the sound of their mash coming to a boil. Drip by drip a mason jar they'd set there at the end began to fill. The anise aroma was heady.

"*Saki* is our name," Taki told him.

"In Armenian we call it *aragh*. It means 'sweat.' And when we toast we say *'anoush,'* sweet; in other words, 'Enjoy it.'"

"We say it *'kampai,'*" Taki told him. "Nothing in your glass."

They lifted their jars and clinked.

"Anoush," Taki said.

"Kampai," Chamich said.

Chamichian had been in this country since he was fifteen. He mastered English with barely an accent, but he never really felt like anything other than an immigrant and he knew that Taki felt the same. Both of them believed that whatever it was they were, it wasn't American—not by a long shot. Two or three days a week, they'd tote their fold-out chairs to Taki's orchard and with a crate between them they'd drink their moonshine as sunset swamped the rows.

It was out there that Chamichian's picture of America, his place in America, began to come into focus. He'd always seen America as a kind of high-class country club in which he was a gardener, temporary help for blue-blooded men whose roots ran beneath that property deep and wide. Now he saw a different picture, and it bore likeness to an Old World trading bazaar. Families from far-off places would travel there with donkeys and dromedaries loaded up with goods. They would pitch tents, set aside their differences, and barter: a rooster for a spool of silk, a bag of anise for a bag of salt, carving knives for hand-hewn spoons. There they would share recipes, strike up friendships. Their children would teach each other games. This is all that America was. So long as they observed the rules, anyone was welcome to this bazaar. No matter how far off from their homelands, every man, woman, and child was as entitled as the next to call it home.

Chamichian lifted his shot glass: "May your life be long and happy, Taki, and your cares and sorrows few." It was a traditional Armenian toast. "And let your many friends around you prove faithful, fond, and true."

Taki shook his head. "Them are a helluva lot of words for what amounts to a swig of Armenian sweat."

It would be the one of the last drinks, the last laughs the friends would share. In a few months' time, Taki would be struck down by a stroke. Chamichian would continue to farm his own trees just as he always had. He would continue to rack up ribbons for his Santa Rosas at the county fair. But that lovely anonymity he felt in his orchard would drift into a vague loneliness. The chirping of the birds would now feel muted, and no matter how fluently water flowed down the rows, it would run sluggish in his heart. After a while, Chamichian came to the conclusion that even the sweet and round succulence he'd come to expect from his plums would never be there again.

I

IT WAS A LITTLE PAST FIVE and the sun was flooding the vineyard rows so that the tall end posts cast scabbard-shaped shadows on the road. Andy was late for his appointment but took the last stretch languorously, letting the shafts of dark and light alternate on the side of his face. Takahashi's peach orchard was up ahead. From a recent pruning, all the way down the quarter-mile rows, branches lay in bundles on the ground, and from deep in that orchard came the sound of hundreds, maybe thousands of crows cawing. He drove over a short canal bridge, beyond the birds' otherworldly bawl, and shambled onto the bumpy shoulder.

Andy stepped out of the truck and leaned against its body for warmth. He took in Chamichian's gigantic piles: three Mount Ararats, he thought, of stumps and twisted roots, and he chuckled at the sad irony. The sun now lowered level with their crests, sending sparrows, hidden like tiny pilgrims in their tangles, fleeing in every direction. Roughly eight hundred Santa Rosa plum trees, perfectly spaced and handsomely groomed, once stood on those twenty acres, but, obviously, no more.

Chamichian was five years dead and now Andy was angling to rent that "open" dirt from his widow. She was a notorious crank and had already sent packing half a dozen other farmers who'd come there cash in hand. She even slammed the door in Vince Takahashi's face. Andy might not have bothered himself if the earth upon which those piles rose weren't some of the choicest on the valley floor. For a mile in each direction the water table was high enough that a man could damn near dry farm, and the dirt was so chock full of minerals that stray dogs stopped to chomp on it when they passed.

The week before Chamichian had pulled the trees, Andy had bumped in to him at the fairgrounds for the blessing of the grapes. Their portly priest, Reverend Jambajian, stood over a hundred lugs brimming amber-colored Thompson and blessed them with sprinkles of holy water. He said a brief homily, they all said amen, and when Andy looked up he discovered Chamichian had been standing there next to him. Chamichian was generally regarded as one of the best fruit tree farmers in the valley, and they knew each other from church but not much beyond that. Still, he took Andy paternally by the arm and said, "Let's go over here." They stepped beneath a mulberry for shade.

Chamichian asked how work was going.

"Work is good," Andy lied. He hoped he wouldn't ask about his brother, but then he did.

"It's a little complicated situation right now."

Chamichian narrowed his eyes and nodded sympathetically, "Go ahead."

"I don't know, but looks like one thing's for sure: that fifty acres we got out there won't cut it. Not with my brother's family and the one I've got coming."

"You're wife is expecting?"

"Yes."

"Affarem!"

"Appreciate it." Andy paused. "I don't know what's going to happen, frankly. I don't want to bad-mouth my own brother, but what I can tell you is we're at some kind of dangerous stalemate."

Chamichian repeated "dangerous" and sighed. "I don't know why we are doing these things. Forty years ago we flee the Turks, and now we are here, fleeing each other. Haven't we come to America yet?"

He reached into his side pockets and pulled a flask from one side and two glasses from the other, shaped just like those they use to take communion. "Here." He poured the moonshine into Andy's glass and then poured a shot into his own.

Before either could take a slurp, "How's the harvest turning out?" Andy asked. He knew the answer was "bad" and half wanted to take the question back.

Chamichian pursed his lips and shook his head. "I'm ripping them."

"That's some decision."

"I've had it. Four years—the same song. Comes a point enough is enough." Chamichian patted Andy on the shoulder. "It's enough is all. To the harvest. The last harvest," he said, and tossed the moonshine back.

"To your health, Baron Chamichian."

ANDY CHECKED THE TIME: fifteen minutes past the hour. When he looked up he saw the crows from next door start from out of the orchard. Piece by piece they rose and billowed in the air like some vast pirate flag. Since that talk with Chamichian, he had lost the stalemate with his brother over their farm, and he was on the verge of bankruptcy. On a haul of broccoli over the ridge route he'd dumped his brakes and, if not for the cop who'd cleared the road ahead of him, Andy most surely would be dead. He almost destroyed his marriage by hiding it all from his wife. The only blessing—a second child had come into their lives.

And now he was procrastinating, standing at the edge of that field, fifteen minutes late. He'd known people to lay back and watch the world pass, but he never counted himself among them. But then again, he had proven to be a mystery to himself more than once. What he knew for certain was that, at the age of thirty-five, he no longer had the luxury to wait.

"What the hell. Come this far, might as well give the old lady a visit."

Halfway up the walk, he heard a big dog bark. It cut the air into halves...quarters...eighths...and pushed him quickly up the steps. He rapped at the door. TV light flapped against the toile curtains: an old-fashioned maid, a cow, some overhanging trees, a boy pulling a wheelbarrow up a path to who knows where. She came to the door, asking who it was in a slightly hysterical voice.

"It's Andy," he said.

She opened the door. "Come in, come in."

"Thanks for seeing me."

The room was stingily lit. It smelled of parsley, Vicks VapoRub, the gray must of age.

"Sit, sit." With a hand she motioned him toward a couch upholstered in green velour. Andy took a seat and waited for her to turn off the TV. As his sight adjusted to the dim, he noticed on the wall in front of him an oil painting of Ararat. Beneath it, on a half-moon-shaped table, a portrait of JFK, two unlit candles standing like sentries on either side.

He waited for her to get comfortable in her chair and then asked how she was doing.

She told him, in Armenian, what things were available to the eyes on TV. It made her heart quake, how wild the world had grown. He nodded and reached for a few pistachios from a server. This country, America, she said, is like crabgrass left to its own. Her daughter was living in town and hardly paid her any attention anymore. Thank God she was doing well, but as for herself, it wasn't easy since her husband had died. Sometimes she wondered where her next meal would come from, which made Andy wonder by what other means than eating she might've gotten so plump. He dropped his eyes and shook his head in sympathy. Her stockings—the color of old rubber bands—garroted her calves just below the knee. The way her bloated feet were shoved into her slippers reminded him of water balloons.

He opened a pistachio and tossed its nut into his mouth. The meat was chewy, its oil rancid, and he wanted to spit it out, but where? On the table? Into his open hand?

Andy swallowed and asked what she was doing with the land, politely, as if the question came from a good neighbor, not a potential renter. She grunted and started out of her big chair. Andy wondered if this meant he was going to be out the door too, and with him the deal. She turned toward the kitchen huffing and puffing. Then she asked him if he cared for some tea.

"That would be nice."

"Nice," she echoed in a super-American voice. "Very nice."

What a pistol, he thought. She probably feared a renter would steal the land from her like a piece of furniture. He decided, in this case, that contracts, agreements, those kinds of things would only heighten her suspicion. Gaining her confidence the old-fashioned way was the only way. Be patient, he told himself. The logic of old folks is childlike. And don't be surprised if at any second the straight line you draw going from A to Z jigs back to D.

No sooner had she set his cup of tea on the table than he told her it was a shame that such a fine piece of land should be left idle, that the only thing getting any value from it was weeds. He told her that he'd come to rent.

"Surely you didn't come to play pinochle?" She flipped her handkerchief to one side, all of a sudden her old eyes sharp as a diamond cutter's.

"Have you considered how much you want for the land?" he asked.

"Of course."

"Well then, good, we got a starting point."

"They think I am a stupid old lady, especially this What's-his-name, next door. This Takahashi boy. How dare he come by wanting to rent my land? Has he no shame?"

"Maybe you're asking too much? The times aren't good."

"How old are you to know when times have been good and when times have been not good?"

"Don't get me wrong."

"I am fine," she said, "don't worry about it. I take care of myself. Thank God. But my daughters must have something too. The one, thank God, her husband has a good job. But how about my poor Lilit? How is she to live after I am dead? I stay alive only for her."

"How is Lilit?" he asked.

"She sits in her room. I have no idea what occupies her mind. Lilit!" she yelled. "Sweetheart!"

Andy lifted a pack of cigarettes from his shirt pocket.

"You see," she said.

From beyond the tip of his cigarette a dog appeared, low to the ground and in the dark of the hallway.

"She fails to tell the difference between night and day. Sometimes when the moon is bright she wanders the house like a ghost. Like she is looking for someone. But who?"

Andy was still trying to bring into focus that dog. Its head was so big it might've been cribbed from some cartoon.

"My eyes are muddy. I can hardly watch her anymore. I am afraid that she will disappear or get run over by a car, I don't know what. They tell me last week a car hit a woman as she tried to cross the street, and the driver drove away. Was this woman a squirrel? Is this a country of Turks? I wonder sometimes. Look what they did to this poor boy, this handsome young man. Cut down like a stalk of corn. For what?"

He could see Kennedy in those stills, sitting proud and presidential one second and doubled over dead the next. Every man, woman, and even many children had mourned, but the grief of old women, he'd observed, seemed especially deep.

She paused to dab her eyes with that handkerchief and said, "The things our eyes are made to bear."

"How old is she now, Lilit?"

"How old? She is coming on thirty years. Her mind is a child's, what can we do? Maybe someday some good Armenian boy will see how good her heart is. Do you know anybody?"

"I'm afraid I don't."

"If they only heard her play the piano. She has never taken a lesson."

"I'll be damned."

"On the record she hears something, and after three or four times it is hers. Her mind is like a tomb. Whatever song goes in, she rolls the stone over it." She cupped her hands together with a pop. "Do you play an instrument?"

"The trumpet. I've played since I was a kid. Mostly classical. At college I was in the orchestra. She should play at the church."

"I don't know why, she fears the priest, especially the deacon. The censer, when he whips it. I tell her, 'He is not angry, sweetheart; he is sending up prayers to God.' Easter and Christmas we must sit in the back. Have you seen her paintings? Lilit!" she screamed.

Her daughter came out and stood at the threshold, her head lowered. She was skinny but her black hair fell over her face so that Andy couldn't say much else about how she looked.

"Come, come."

Andy stood.

"Play something. This is Andy. He wants to rent the farm."

Lilit sped headlong over to the piano, sat down, and started like a windup doll.

"The Girl with Flaxen Hair," a Debussy song—one of Andy's favorites, but at such breakneck speed it was barely recognizable, a kind of musical smear. When she was done she marched back to her room.

The old lady smiled. "Isn't that nice?"

Andy, frankly, was rattled.

"She paints like she plays the piano. Same thing. God has given her something, a gift. Anyway, until she finds a man she has her mother's love. You are married, yes?"

"Yes, and two sons."

"What a blessing. If only we had a boy we would have no such problems."

"What did Taki offer you for the land? If you don't mind me asking."

"I might as well have handed it to him for free. Anyway, I won't do business with that Takahashi boy. Do you know what we did for those people?"

Andy thought. Old man Takahashi and his wife had been dead for years and she's still bashing them over the head. "Your husband was a good farmer and a good man. We were friendly."

"God rest his soul," she said, "he *was* a good man. But blind—blinded by his goodness. Is such blindness a virtue or a sin? Why did he tear out those trees? I still ask."

"Well. What do you think would be a fair price? You must've had a chance to think about it some. In your opinion."

"Fair? What is fair? What do *you* think would be a fair price?"

"Well, I was thinkin' about that. The land is in sad shape right now."

"Why sure, but don't let that trouble you. It will clean up easily. A few trees is all."

"Not by itself. It's a concern, that's all."

"Okay, so it is a concern. What else concerns you? Words like 'concern'…You went to school, I hear."

"I have a college diploma."

"You see? Our people need educated people. I wish my Lilit could find someone like you."

"And then there's your equipment. I would need it. Not much. A tractor, discs, maybe some other odds and ends. I see you've got a flatbed."

"Whatever we have," she flung it all to him, "it is yours. Everything works like the first day we bought it. Like 'brand new,' the way the Americans say. What else?"

"Well…"

"That's enough. You tell me what is *fair*."

"I don't know. I guess I figure seventy, eighty dollars an acre." He had planned to lowball her, but not that low. Maybe the reality of his circumstances cut him off at the knees. "You have twenty acres, so what are we talking, fifteen hundred or so?" Maybe the absolute number would play a little different. "I think that's fair."

"Why don't I just pay *you*. Here," she reached for some make-believe money from the pocket of her dress.

"I don't mean to insult you."

The conversation paused and then the woman said, "Twenty-*two* acres. Who told you twenty?"

"Is there twenty-two out there?"

"Around the barn there is two acres that can be used. Nobody sees it. Maybe they don't want to see it?"

"If it's ground I can maneuver a tractor around then, okay, twenty-two. Whatever it is."

"It's none of my business, but what will you plant?"

"Tomatoes. And, might as well put it all on the table, I would not be able to pay you until after the harvest," he said. "But I will sign a note guaranteeing that you would be paid directly by the packing house people before any money came to me."

"Your pockets are light."

"I will need what I have to plant. Many people are in this position these days, not just me."

"Fine. Let me sit on your offer."

"I'll be frank with you: you have good earth. I hope we can strike a deal that is fair on both ends."

"What is fair? Is it fair that I am getting old, that my eyes are poor? Is it fair that my husband died and my daughter goes unloved? Let's not talk about fair. It is too late for fair."

Andy nodded his head.

"What are we to say? *'Eeshteh, pachtes eh;* anyway, this is my fate.' Let us just pray to God that tomorrow is better than today."

"Well, thank you for your time."

"Watch the roads. It is getting dark."

"I'll do that."

"And I will let you know."

Back at his truck, Andy found he was in no mood to go home. The sky was darkening all around, but the horizon was still suffused with a dusty yellow light. The few inky clouds left over from the rains looked like rends in a rawhide shade.

His mind turned back to Vince, a.k.a. "that Takahashi boy." "She's a tough nut to crack," Vince had carped. "All them years we've been neighbors, and when I went over to make her a deal she just about run me off."

The two families had farmed adjacent each other for going on twenty years, and Vince's old man and Chamichian had been as close as two men could get. But no sooner were they dead and gone than the bitterness, rippling beneath the surface, burbled back to life. It was an old story. From one end of the valley to the other was chapter after dumbfounding chapter of friendships or kinships gone south over a harsh word, a favor unreturned, a handful of disputed dirt. Just down the road farmed the Silvas, cousins Tony and Joe. The boys grew up together, raised row crops side by side, until one day the county shows up to mark the true property line for a barn Tony wanted to throw up. The surveyor determined that half an acre actually fell on his cousin's property. One thing led to another. Fifteen years later they'd pass on their respective tractors and not so much as tip hats hello.

Things kindle, Andy supposed, spread inch by inch, until all of a sudden the situation goes *boom*. In his own neighborhood, Nelson and Schaeffer, Volga Germans, had come from the old country on the same boat. There wasn't a day passed they didn't stop to share a jug of water, a gallon of diesel. Then one day Nelson accused Schaeffer of siphoning off canal water. Again, one thing led to another and voila, the one was threatening the other with a gun.

And then there was Andy himself. He had his own mind-boggling chapter in this book. Yes, the Takahashis and Chamichians went back a long way, but sometimes, Andy reckoned, too much history is worse than no history at all. Sometimes the fuse is a generation or more long.

Now the two men were gone. The widow needed money and she expected Vince to pony up an offer with a few extra dollars tacked on as compensation for her husband's charity. In her mind, the dud Vince lobbed her way was insult added to injury. But Vince, if truth be told, didn't have much room to maneuver: a good many farmers were trying to stay afloat by renting open dirt on the cheap for a seasonal crop. The idea was to throw up some winter cukes or cauli or brock, pray for a sweet spot in the market, and parlay that money to cover the harvest of your permanent crop. Nobody was any more in the position to cover anybody else's ass.

They were on the tail end of what they called a "bad trend." After the war there was a boon: what money a farmer made, he planted; that's all a farmer knew to do with his money. Bonds, stocks, or apartment buildings in town, what others called "diversification," never occurred to a farmer. As a result, though, too many acres got planted. Tree fruit, vines, nuts—all long-term investments, nothing you could tear out on the run. When the trees came into production, the market shook and prices, they tumbled one year, two, a third. Farmers went from making a barn-load to tucking away a few shillings to break even. The situation, impossible to get worse, got worse. Harvesting and packing expenses cost more than what anyone could fetch for the fruit all pretty in a box. The question became when was this trend going to end, and how long could a man sustain such shocking losses? And what should a farmer to do—sell insurance, doughnuts, shoes?

Those trees had been Chamichian's bread and butter. They had borne fruit year in and year out—weathered staggering heat, frost, bitter hail, and stunning storms—and had the scars, literally, to prove it. So, pulling them was no small decision. Indeed, it was a once-in-a-lifetime decision, a step of such irreversible magnitude that a period of calm reflection was advised: a month, two, or three after the harvest, after consultations with other farmers, packers, accountants, God and, of course, kin. But Chamichian—again, one of the most celebrated, levelheaded fruit tree growers in the valley—had decided to do it mid-stride of the harvest.

Chamichian had delivered what he thought would be the first— but turned out to be his last—run of that season's plums to the packing house and watched as they were dumped onto the conveyer, washed, sorted, packed and stacked, and shuttled into the icebox. Charlie Mushigian told him it was the sweetest looking fruit he'd seen so far that year. "You're a damn good farmer," he told Chamichian. "Too bad it's the damnedest year for plums."

Chamichian gave it a week before he rang Charlie up. Seeing that his fruit had fetched three golds in the last ten years at the county fair, the pack-out was pretty much what everyone expected: 92 percent. Though the smaller-sized plums were still sitting in the cooler, the buyers were all over his twenty-four count. Who wouldn't be at two bucks a box? It didn't take a genius to conclude that another disaster was in the making if the market didn't shape up.

It was just a few days after the call to the packer that he was getting the bins lined up for the second pick when, through the choking and blinding dust of the harvest, Chamichian was stopped by a sudden and stunning clearing of the air. Usually a farmer works head down, plowing every possible obstacle out of his path in his march toward a dubious future, but now Chamichian's vision was riverbig and he seemed to be peering down at the scene from above. Way above. From up there it was obvious: his fruit had been humiliated, their nine months' labor spat upon. From up there, the way the farmers looked for the approval of the packers like little boys to their fathers—it disgusted him. Hoping against hope, praying that they would survive…it reminded Chamichian of how the Armenians laid their necks out for the Turks, waiting for God Almighty's mercy that never came. If he let those trees stay, he "couldn't live with himself" is how he finally explained it. It was enough. Enough was enough.

That Wednesday, after the blessing of the grapes, Chamichian stepped out of bed, made himself breakfast of *soujouk* and eggs and, without a word to his wife, hitched his field wagon to the back of his pickup, placed on that wagon a one-and-a-half-inch auger five feet long, a lug of dynamite, a sack of ammonium nitrate, and a big ball of twine, and shuffled it all to the far end of the orchard, away from the house.

At the base of each tree, he sunk that auger and began turning with two hands until he had bored the length of that auger down. Then he unwound a long piece of twine, lowered it into the hole, put his foot on the near end, and dropped in half a stick of explosive and, for good measure, a pound or so of fertilizer. With the wooden side of his shovel he packed it all in. Marie saw him move from tree to tree with these implements and figured he was going for gophers.

The series of booms jerked folks from their work all the way across the district line. Clods shot up and rained down on the tops of the trees, and a gaudy coil of dust and smoke exuded from those small holes for minutes afterward. In one massive action, the hardpan beneath those trees broke into bits like a china dish smashed at newlyweds' feet. Marie was probably still thinking gophers.

Only when he took a chain and looped it 'round the trunk of one of his Santa Rosas, only when he took the other end and hooked it up to the rear of his John Deere and straddled the tractor seat and punched the peddle, tugging and tugging, and then all at once feeling the tree pop from the ground like a rotting tooth, only then did the whole picture come into focus for his wife.

The huge bunches of dirt stuck between the hoary and twisted roots threw up a bitter cloud as he dragged them one by one through the orchard. It was a terrible and now public spectacle. The farming equivalent of genocide. This pushed Marie to nervous ruin. Halfway through the month-long ripping the market rose fifty cents. She petitioned family and friends to step in, as though there were some way those trees, already blown to pieces at their roots, stood a chance of being restored. At one point, her hysteria out of control, she waved down neighbors as they passed in their trucks, pleading for help. They paused only long enough to shake their heads in sympathy. To Chamichian nobody dared utter a word; a man who'd come to those terms with his farm, and his very wife, was sure to be volatile as gasoline.

Scratched, split, bruised, and squished plums lay scattered along the twister-like path Chamichian had cut down the middle of the orchard to give himself maneuvering room. On the slowly starved branches, plenty were left hanging; round and succulent, meat the hue of cognac, some still dusted with blush.

Poor Marie frantically went at that pitiful lot like a woman goes for heirlooms at the low point of a flood. She picked, picked, picked, and stacked the brimming boxes on any open surface. Outside and in the house gnats and fleas congregated over the boxes, so thick that a person had to move around waving a hand as if to shoo smoke away. Day and night she canned, who knows, hundreds of bottles? Off twenty acres of trees comes nearly two hundred tons of fruit; the woman barely made a dent.

Chamichian was in no hurry to clean up the mess he made out there. For the first several weeks, it would've been a shame to tamper with the trees since fruit still hung on the branches and was obviously free. Those who decided to go on in and fetch a bucket or two did so sheepishly. Maybe they felt a little like grave robbers. On the other hand, maybe the measly five cents a pound they could pay for the same thing at the market hardly made it worth their time.

After a month or so the fruit that still obdurately hung began to turn prunish, and the tens of thousands dropped to rot. Across the orchard, geysers of gnats pulsed. From half a mile down the road you could smell plums turning to mush. Heaps of maggots were born. Birds—sparrows and jays and robins, but mostly crows—came to pick at them in droves.

Half the winter passed, and it wasn't until February that

Chamichian got around to cutting the trees into pieces and hauling the wood out. He might've just burned them, but he felt it a disgrace that such good wood go to waste—at least that's what he told Sammy of Sammy's Shish Kebob in Sanger. Five cords or so went to him for cooking his lamb. He put a six-foot-high stack for firewood against the backside of his own barn. Lord knows how many cords went out on the side of the road. "FREE" the sign said. He would hardly be out an hour cutting and loading before he'd plod back to the house. Exhaustion fell upon him thick, like tule fog.

He kept at it a little over a month until all that was left were fifty, sixty trees plus the roots—worthless as firewood, impossible to cut to any regular size. The trunk, the branches, the limbs were one thing, but those roots...in their thirty-year hunt for water, they'd turned, lick by lick, into a corkscrewing, bundling, bulging, promiscuous mass, a physicality that defied any orthogonal reckoning. All a person could do was study them and grunt from amazement.

Admiration aside, Chamichian had to get rid of them, and only setting them on fire would do the trick. So he got on his forklift and one by one piled them into heaps as high as the forks would go. He'd built three mountains out there, each about fifteen feet high and twice that many feet in diameter, when he suffered a heart attack. "Massive" was the word that they used. A massive heart attack. Chamichian was a good man, and at the shish kebob luncheon that followed the funeral, nearly a dozen people eulogized him with beautiful turns of phrase and solemn vows to never forget his good name.

Andy looked up from his thoughts and watched the horizon dim. Crows wheeled in the last luminous gray of sky like ashes, like the thousand aimless aspects of some tattered darkness. He stamped out his cigarette, hopped in his truck, and made down the road. But he was staring down another road entirely, the one that Chamichian took, and he spoke now as if beseeching him: "You did what you had to do. Okay. Listen. If you give me this piece of dirt," he told Chamichian, "I promise to do you right. I promise. I promise to do your wife right.

I'll clean up that mess. You told me 'enough is enough,' and you made good on your word. By golly you did—but now it's my shot. It ain't about me, and it ain't really about you—it's about that earth lying there. It's good earth. I see something growing there. It would be a human shame to let it go to waste."

2

IN ANTHROPOLOGY 101, Andy had learned the strangest thing: he'd learned that some primitive people believed the dead must discover that they are dead—it isn't obvious to them. The whole seismic notion of being separated from their kin is so painful, so unthinkable, that for weeks, and sometimes months, the dead act as though they're as hale and hearty as ever. There he is, the pathetic ghost, chatting it up with his wife, sitting next to the mother-in-law at supper, rollicking with the men on a hunt.

This puts pressure on the survivors. On the one hand, they pity their departed and they miss them, but on the other hand, they want to put some commonsense distance between themselves and the dead. They want to remember, but they also want to forget. When the dead refuse to accept their new accommodations in the afterlife, the survivors have a hard time readjusting to theirs. Still, they go easy on the departed, at first ignoring them or making certain to speak about them in the past tense: "It's too bad Uncle Reggie is gone," or "Remember the way he caught minnows with his eyes closed?" They take away his sleeping mat and retire his favorite spear. If the deceased still doesn't get the picture, the living resort to more extreme measures: they coax him onto a boat without oars and send it downriver or, hoping to bamboozle, they lead him into the forest and then scatter in every direction, abandoning him. They keep at it until the guy comes to his senses: Hey, I must be dead! I have no place here anymore!

Since the rift with his brother, five years ago, Andy could relate to these primitives. His brother had considered him dead well before he'd made the pronouncement. Even now, five years passed, there were moments Andy still couldn't grasp that the land, and the brother, that he'd inherited were no longer his. He felt just like those dead primitives, and maybe even worse, since one of the benefits of being dead was you could also turn a dead ear to bill collectors and the like.

HE AND HIS BROTHER HAD FACED what all farmers had faced, the same future Chamichian had been made to face: a seemingly neverending hole. But they'd dropped into it even deeper when they'd decided to roll the dice on a tomato crop they put up in Perris, California. The crop was a beauty. While Abe held down the fort at home, all by himself Andy had brought it right around, but a week before the harvest it was ruined by a windstorm: the worst kind of luck, at the worst kind of time.

Seriously short on operating cash they scrambled for a loan, but the banks sent them on their way. They were this close to going to relatives when Andy tracked down a government program available to GIs. Abe, having served his country, qualified. The interest was near nothing, too good to be true. Only there was one hitch: Abe owned half the land, and the government would only loan on that half. If Abe were the sole bearer of title, they could get double the money—and they needed double to keep things going. So, they fudged the facts. Andy signed over to Abe his half of the land, his twenty-five acres. They did an end-run on the government. Deal done, they were flush with money.

The loan was a reprieve, or so Andy believed. But soon he began to notice that far from dampening Abe's anxiety, the money seemed to stoke it. He started talking nonsense, about how he and his wife were now at risk should they default on that loan. He started bossing Andy around, scrutinizing how he spent "Abe's money." Before Andy knew it, Abe was blaming him for the tomato fiasco down south, as though he had struck some devilish deal with Mother Nature to bring them to the brink. He and his brother started trading accusations, back and forth, playing a game of "you do that to me, I'll do this to you," all through the winter, the set, and the harvest. Andy drafted in his own hand a letter that put down between them the truth behind the lie: that the land, in spite of what it said in the hall of records, was half Abe's, half his. He put it in front of Abe. Abe signed it. But it wasn't worth much; no court in America was going to entertain a complaint that was based upon finagling the feds.

Andy was in the middle of pruning. This was late January, and fog had settled in. All around him in the rows lay switches of vines and dying leaves. He heard distant footsteps through the white silence of the fog, and when he turned he saw a figure standing at the top of the row. It took a beat for Andy to make out that the figure was Abe, and that he held a shotgun off to his side. Andy's father's shotgun. Like the land, he had inherited it, to kill rabbits, badgers, or a trespasser that meant them harm. "What's up, Abe?" he'd asked. Abe answered by lifting the gun and pointing it at Andy. Then, right there in the drifting fog, Abe said, "You have no place here anymore."

ANDY WAS BORN ON THAT FARM, raised on it. Except for four years at college, he'd lived nowhere else. He knew it better then he knew just about anything, better, for sure than he knew his brother, and far better, as it turned out, than he knew himself. *You have no place here.* Exactly what the Turks told the Armenians. Told to a people who'd had a place there for over twenty-five hundred years, more than a millennium before a Turk had ever set eyes on those legendary mountains. *You have no place here*—exactly what the Turks told the Armenians about fields that they had cultivated for generations on end. *Leave this place,* they said. *It is ours now.*

But who will care for my vines?

We will tear them from the ground.

And our *khatchkars,* our thousand-year-old crosses carved into a single slab of stone?

The sand will bury them as time will bury you.

Who will bring flowers to this ancient grave?

We will use the headstones to pave your way to your heaven.

And our books?

We will erase them, like you, from the face of the earth.

Our tongue?

Imagine a fallen leaf.

IN THE FIRST FEW MONTHS after Abe ran him off the farm, Andy'd now and again drive by it, strangely stoking the pain in order to clear the air of his immobilizing confusion. On the far side of the acreage, he'd cut the engine and study the very spot where Abe had pulled the shotgun on him. He'd live it over, add or subtract a scene, edit Abe's words or splice in a few of his own. He'd wonder if he'd done right by running away. He might've charged Abe, forced him to pull the trigger. He might have barreled through the gunshot, taking with him to the grave whatever portion of Abe's flesh he could.

Cruel that the house, the barn, the fence was all there, the same as it was the day he'd had to leave it all behind. It was as if the universe had failed to register the breach, as though God were telling Andy that he must move on and wait for justice to be served in another place, in a more damning, otherworldly way.

Then, about four months after Abe had leveled that shotgun at him, Andy got a call from one of his sisters. It was a Saturday afternoon, and he'd just returned from a haul of lettuce to Los Angeles. Abe was in the mental hospital, she told him. She didn't know much beyond that.

Andy sat on the news for a week. It occurred to him, of course, that

Abe's "nervous breakdown," as his sister had called it, was the moral payback Andy had been looking for. He was satisfied to finally know that a part of Abe's brain, the sane part, the part that had loved him and that he loved in return, was revolting in protest to the point of splitting his being in two. But another part of him, bigger still, hoped that Abe wasn't beyond being brought back to wholeness—for Abe, and for their brotherhood.

He went to see his brother with that hope. In a padded room, with chicken-wired windows, he found Abe sitting in a corner, his body half in shadow and half bathed in warm light. They sat across from one another and talked, not quite like the old days, but pleasantly enough, and absent any malice and conceit. In the end they agreed to repair what had been sundered—once Abe got out, that is. But the minute he got out, he walked straight back into his wife's lair and their promise to make things right evaporated.

Andy's two boys, they helped him get through it. He'd watch with wonder as they tried to master their wobbly world. When he hugged them he'd tremble from the bigness of the feeling, and as they got older he'd lie on the ground and let them climb over him, the load and industry of their little bodies upon his own filling him with a joy he hadn't known since he was a boy. But then the babble and chatter, all that hectic motion, their drilling screams would get him dizzy and he'd have to step outside for a breather.

On the porch chair, he'd light a cigarette to steady himself, but no sooner had he gathered some traction than he'd begin to totter, from worry, about taking care of his family, about how, with no income to speak of, no farm to squeeze or equipment to leverage, he aimed to pay the bills. The couple of thousand he'd borrowed from family and friends was one thing, but the bill collectors were another.

They showed up, by his wife's accounting, every week. Kareen claimed it had gotten to the point that her heart quaked whenever she saw someone she didn't know pull up in front of the house. When he came home, her scared and angry face told him the whole story.

LIKE THAT PRIMITIVE confronting the fact of his death, the depth of the schism between Andy and his brother didn't hit him all at once. He spent money like he had the next season to count on, as though there was a kitty to dip into. Farm bills kept showing up at his house, for sulphur, trays, stakes, and wire, and weirdly, he kept paying them, not all at once, but a few dollars here, a few dollars there. Maybe he believed that so long as he paid those bills the land was still his. Before he knew it, ends weren't meeting, so he started hauling produce from Fresno to L.A. with the only hard asset to his name: a tractor-and-trailers.

Sometimes overcoming the lion's roar of the engine, the flabbergasting heat or cold, the wildly jostling cab, like being in a Parkinson's patient's brain, and the transmission, the way it bellowed beneath him as he downshifted and yard by yard lurched the twenty-ton trailer up the Grapevine's grade, sometimes all this amounted to a kind of epic challenge. There were other hauls that proved less epic than Catholic: sitting in that cab for six hours at a stretch was a kind of purgatory, a lonesome room where you were made to reckon with your sins, mull over the state of your soul, account for the turns you took and missed.

One day he had loaded up his doubles with Santa Rosas and had pulled out onto the 99 about nightfall, an hour later than usual. From early in the morning the sun had screamed and his cab was hot as an Indian sweat lodge. He hoped, he prayed, the air would cool by the time he reached Bakersfield, but it never did. As though the sun had simply morphed into the moon, the temperature at nine p.m. was the same as at noon. The way a sailor submits to the seas, he had learned to submit to the heat, but that afternoon it agitated and then tore at him, so much so that he shot past his regular truck stop right through to Gorman before he pulled into a gas station set up for cars.

Through a big window, Andy could see a high school kid, blond hair, sitting in the booth with his legs kicked up on the desk, flipping through a magazine. His summer job. It was well-bottom dark, but there was still no chance the kid could miss a set of doubles loaded up with peaches ten yards from his window. A little fan next to his feet was blowing his hair this way and that. Andy let a good minute pass, which equated in that cantankerous heat to half a day, before he honked his horn to get the punk's attention. The kid dropped the magazine and made a face like he'd been asked to clear the shit from an outhouse. Through the window the kid and Andy locked eyes, and then the kid lifted the magazine and picked up where he'd left off. Andy might've just given up—was this really worth a fight?—if the next gas stop wasn't on the other side of the hill. He felt this swarming pressure in his chest, like roaches were building an empire in there.

He hit the horn again, and kept his hand on it.

The kid bolted from his seat—his bravado half amusing Andy. But the other half of him wanted to smash the kid's face in. Andy pushed open the cab door and stepped out. The fury he'd felt continued to rise in him like Turkish coffee in a *jezve*. The kid came through the door and stopped. In the glow of the truck lights, Andy saw fear in the kid's face. Fear of Andy. He'd always wondered how one man could stop another man in his tracks just by the way he stood, or stared. Now he knew. Now he was one of those men. He grabbed the gas hose, walked it to the tank, screwed the cap off, and sunk it in the hole.

"You can't do that," the kid blurted out.

Andy laughed; it was the laughter of someone for whom laws had all of a sudden become trifling. It was very near the feeling of someone who'd become a law unto himself. He'd never really felt that way before.

"Fuck you," Andy answered.

The kid ran back inside and grabbed the phone. He spoke rapidly—to his daddy or the cops, whichever. Andy watched the numbers on the gas pump tick by. When he'd filled up, twenty-three bucks and change, he casually hooked the hose back up, got in the cab, and drove off.

That was the start of something, in part—the start of a feeling that he didn't owe anyone shit anymore. He'd learned, as people must, to put a leash on his anger before it got out of control, but now it seemed running of its own rabid accord, dragging the rest of him with it. It was freeing, to run that way, to not have to pause and confer with the world, and when he did pause, he noticed that his anger had condensed the swirling mess inside of him to some shocking essence. He'd always upheld the notions of dignity, patience, self-respect, however much he failed to live up to them, but now they seemed like the knickknacks of the well–to-do. He was rescinding his compact with society to join a dark and exclusive club, a kind of cult, whose other members ironically disgusted him. Did that mean he disgusted himself? Probably.

Drink, and plenty of it, proved to be part of the profile. If it was late enough in the day, 2:30 say, he'd go to Sammy's bar and knock down three whiskeys in quick succession, do a beer or two, top of it off with a bourbon, why not? and get home at eight or even later. Kareen felt repulsion and pity for him at the same time. What is going on? she wondered. From the doorway she'd watch him limp across the room in his saggy underwear and collapse obliviously into bed. He was like some pathetic animal. When she got into bed she avoided him like a pile of soiled clothes.

Andy doubted he'd slept so well his entire life. After three years of agonizing insomnia, popping up in bed electric with worry, he had finally arrived. To where he could not say, except he slept well there, mysteriously tranquil, as though the omnivorous inferno inside of him had devoured most everything in its path. There, in this clearing, he was turning into something new—from something that was complex and faceted, that strove and struggled, to a something that merely repeated itself to a closing point, where no light or beauty could leak in, but neither could disappointment or pain.

He was a college graduate, but he had developed the mentality of a high school dropout. On the one hand, he hadn't much ambition to work, but on the other, no work seemed beneath him, as though wrecking his body with exhaustion or dozing all day was one and the same. To satisfy that part of him, between hauls he took a day job side by side with a small crew of Mexicans clearing out three old barns in no-man's-land way the hell west of Kerman.

One evening after work, this crew started drinking, tequila out of the bottle, a bottle to each man. They made a fire with some of the old wood they'd torn off the side of the barn and they sat around it getting smashed, telling jokes, about themselves, then each other, then each other's moms and dads, until one of the Mexicans—Jose or Henry, something like that—produced a jackknife from his back pocket and held it steady over the edge of the fire till the blade turned chalky and then he asked which of them was man enough, and he wagered not a single one, and then he pressed this knife, the flat edge, against his forearm, and without wincing burned it until the flesh started to smell. The other Mexicans laughed, feverishly, and nominated him "loco," and then one of them who had been staring in the fire all night said, "Give it here." It became a kind of game now, and they started falling in line like votaries, one after the other, each taking the knife and holding it over the edge of the fire and branding himself. They shook their heads and cackled and cried in some vile enjoyment. Andy was so drunk the whole world was a kind of hysterical blur, and he was hard-pressed in that state to admit consequence, so when the knife came his way, he followed suit. And then he passed out.

He'd heard of guys waking up in a pool of their own vomit, but he always figured this a figure of speech, some cowboy-book concoction, but there it was, he could smell it before he saw it, a few inches in front of his face, liquidy bits splattered on the dirt. He was still drunk, that's how much he'd drank, and when he stood the world shimmied from side to side. When he took his first step forward the pain hit him in the head like a tack hammer.

The other guys had passed out on the ground like so many gunnysacks of maize. Smoke dribbled up from the fire. His throat was cauterized from the alcohol, and he could smell tequila oozing from his body. Except for a dull stinging and a blistered image of the blade, the burn might've not been there at all, but it was also possible that this one pain just couldn't pierce through the din of the hundred others.

Home was only a half-hour drive but it seemed to take half a day, as though he were repeating the same stretch of road three, four times over and over again and he couldn't remember frankly how he got from one crossing to the next.

Andy looked like he'd been in a major brawl, and that is what he told his wife when he got home around seven a.m. Her heart was torn up from worry. His eyes were red like poached tomatoes and she could smell the ugly tequila on his body. She bandaged his arm and put him to bed.

Her mother, who lived two blocks away, came over. She'd been up most of the night with her daughter, but unlike Kareen she was hardly ready to put Andy or his dereliction to rest. From the bed he heard the door slam and knew he was in trouble. "Beast!" Valentine shrieked. "What was he doing all night? Measuring the streets?" He could hear her light a cigarette as she began to march back and forth across the living room floor, cursing in multiple tongues, especially Turkish, which she reserved solely for such execrable occasions. "*Cacnem sooratut,*" she concluded, for causing her daughter worry, and, frankly, he had to agree with her, he deserved no better than a "shit in the face," and he had indeed lowered himself to the makeup of a beast—the worst sort of beast, a beast that harmed himself as much as he harmed others, a beast that fouled his own nest.

He fell wildly asleep. When he woke at dusk, he found himself crying over the whole god-awful nightmare of his life, crying at how bizarrely he'd turned out, how within nine months he'd gone from a guy who even his rivals would agree was confident and good-natured to a guy who even his closest kin would agree was mean and confused.

For the next couple of weeks, he kept his head down, his voice low. He'd more than hit bottom; he'd burrowed through to the other side of the earth. And there, he'd forfeited his humanity, and he wasn't sure exactly how he was going to get it back. Who was there to petition? His soul was like a village burned to the ground, emptied of its inhabitants. He'd waited and waited, praying for something to step in, whether it went by the name of God, Justice—any Thing capable of correcting the wrong. When this Thing didn't show up he'd taken it out on himself. If God didn't think he was worth saving, then by God, he'd prove Him right!

Abe had busted him into pieces. But it was Andy himself who was pulverizing what was left.

3

THE LAST TIME ANDY HAD VISITED an attorney was to consult about the transfer of title to Abe, and he'd learned from that experience that attorneys don't mince words, they don't read between the lines, or use images and metaphors to convey the meaning of those lines. In short, there is no poetry in their opinions. Saroyan, the attorney he and Abe had consulted, flat out told them how things would stand after the title of land had been transferred. He told them Andy would have no claim on the property, that Abe would be the one who was financially exposed should the operation go south.

Now, as he pulled up in front of David Polladio's office, Andy reminded himself that he should listen to this attorney as though he were a scientist explaining the inviolable laws of physics.

A little bell, like that at an ice cream shop, tinkled when he opened the door. Polladio sat behind a large mahogany desk to the left.

Andy doffed his hat. "Good afternoon. I'm Andy, Andy Demerjian."

"Mr. Demerjian." He put out a hand. "Take a seat."

"Thanks for seeing me, sir."

Andy remarked on the number of books lining the walls. It never failed to amaze him how many books there were in the world and how few of them he'd read. He wondered if it would make a difference if he had.

Polladio took off his glasses and rubbed an eye with his fist. There was the other possibility: a man flat out exhausted by all those books.

"How can I help you, Mr. Demerjian?"

"Like I kind of told you over the phone, I'm in a bad way, financially," Andy said. "I've come to a point I think it's smart to talk to somebody about it."

Polladio rocked vaguely back and forth in his high-backed leather chair.

"I had a farm and lost it. I guess you can call it a long story, but my brother, he took it. Actually, I signed it over to him. I've already talked to an attorney about this, so I won't waste your time or my dime. Anyway, the farm, it's his now. As result, sir, I've more or less lost my livelihood and I've got bills piling up higher than my head. To cover them, I've borrowed from just about everyone I know."

He grew emotional saying this, as though he'd just discovered how calamitous his circumstances had turned.

"Let's see what we can do," Polladio said.

Andy liked that he put it that way, "we," as though, if need be, a team of folks was waiting in the wings to help. It made him realize how alone with all of this he had lived.

Andy took a deep breath.

"Tell me now, where do you put your liabilities? How much do you owe, Andy, and who do you owe it to?"

"That, I figured you'd want to know." Andy reached into his jacket pocket and pulled out a neatly folded paper. He unfolded this paper and with two hands smoothed its creases out on the desk. In a column called "owe," one set of numbers was penned, and in a column to its right, "own," was a set of numbers ridiculously short by comparison.

"In dollars and cents, eight thousand, give or take."

"May I?"

"From what I figure, anyway." Andy slid the paper across the desk.

Polladio bent up close to study it. "Do you have any assets?"

36

"What I own?"

"That's right."

"A car and a tractor and a set of double trailers. Frankly, it kind of boggles my brain to see where, after twenty years working like an *esh*, I've ended up."

"Esh?"

"Sorry. It's Armenian for jackass."

"Tell me, Andy, do you use the rig for a livelihood?"

"Off and on. Yes, sir. But hauling has been scarce."

"Call me David."

"David."

"You have here, I see, a thousand dollars in a bank account."

"That's right. I've been saving that. I need that money on some farming deal I'm putting together right now. If I get the land, I gotta have something in the bank to work it."

"Any regular sources of income?"

"I'm a farmer by trade. But no. To answer your question: not at this time. But like I'm said, I'm working on something."

At this point, Polladio dragged a pad of legal paper toward himself and jotted down a few notes.

Andy remained deferentially quiet, as though a doctor were probing his body with his hands.

"These people you owe…"

"Yes, sir. There's plenty of them."

"Friends? Relatives? Who?"

"All of the above."

"Sure. I see here a chemical company, a packing house, a box company. Here's what looks like a parts and tire shop." Polladio underscored it with a finger.

"They've given me plenty of time. More than plenty. Best I could I chipped away at the debt, but now, the bottom line is they are starting to pound on my front door. This is my main concern. I've got a wife, you see. It's shaking her up pretty bad, these collectors and the like coming around. She just can't take it no more. I need them off my back."

"No money owed to a bank?"

"No, sir."

"You own no home?"

"We rent."

A minute passed in silence.

"You see," Andy said, "I was thinking maybe bankruptcy." He flipped a hand over to show that it was empty.

The attorney nodded sympathetically.

"Right up front, Andy, I've got to tell you, bankruptcy looks like an option. But the money you owe friends and family...it might complicate the picture—that is, for you personally."

"You mean shorting them?"

"They would be listed as creditors same as the others."

"I was thinking about that. I was thinking maybe I could cut a separate deal there. I mean on the side. Frankly, I was hoping this could all be done hush-hush. You know. Get rid of the bill collectors and proceed to take care of the people I personally know. I mean, I hate to say this, but I don't even want my wife in on this."

Polladio nodded, then proceeded to make clear the mechanics of liquidating one's assets against one's debts. It would be, among other things, a public affair. In summary: If you'd hoped to safeguard your dignity—forget it.

"I see," Andy said.

"It's not a simple process. But, believe me when I say this, I've seen many men go through it and come out the other side."

"Like hamburger meat, sounds like."

He left the office with all the facts, the whole ugly lot of them, and pulled onto the 99 going north. When he passed the Fresno County line he veered off the highway and cut down toward the river. It was terribly cold, and so before he stepped out of the cab he slipped his gloves on. In his boots, buffed to a shine for his meeting with the attorney, he winded step by step down the slope, his breath leaving him in boll-like bursts. The river was calm, black, and lustrous as a pool of crude. Floating over its surface were wisps of white mist. He sat on his haunches and tapped out a cigarette and watched the water convey a naked branch downstream. He had waited a good year to go to an attorney, afraid, probably, of what he'd hear. Now, he'd heard it.

Several beer cans and a couple of amber flasks of whiskey were littered along the bank. Schoolkids, whooping it up. He shook his head at their stupidity and at his own not so long ago. He recalled that half a dozen kids over the years had committed suicide there. Fed up with the world and seeing no way to change it, wanting a say and having no voice, they'd declared, I never want to feel this way again, and threw themselves in. As a method for forever drowning the pain, he allowed, the river—above and beyond a gun, or rope, or bottle of pills—had an intrinsic, almost poetic appeal. He imagined the cold's jolt, the drop and drag, the sound of the world gone except for the river churning, the glowing numbness as you sank, tumbling and tumbling deeper and deeper into it, no more top or bottom, just water, darkness's swift and inexorable surge.

There were only two choices, life and death. On the life side of things, two options again: bankruptcy or beg. "Discovery," attorneys called it, that period between the claim and the trial when all that was hidden got brought into view. The word had always mystified him, but now it made perfect and common sense. There was nothing to discover beyond what he had already discovered. It was all there, on that sheet of paper, folded in his back pocket. He wanted to ball it up and pitch it into the river, but then thought better. He walked over and picked up what he could of the teenagers' litter, climbed back up the slope, and emptied the bottles and cans in the back of his cab. It was nearing three p.m., no time for a man to be drinking, but after all the pummeling he'd taken that day, he felt he owed himself one.

"HOW YOU DOIN', ANDY?" Sammy tossed a paper coaster in front of him.

"Most ways same as yesterday. Other ways, worse."

"Double?"

"Let's start with a single."

"Hell, it's early yet."

"It's already been a long day, my friend."

With one hand Sammy reached back for a bottle, and with the other he pulled a short glass from beneath the bar. He set them both there, jiggled two, three ice cubes from a scoop into the glass, and poured it.

Andy took a sip, let it warm in his belly for a few seconds, took one sip more, and then peered down the length of the bar. Two guys, looked like bankers, sat at the far end with martini glasses in front of them, tossing beer nuts into their mouths.

"Fancy suits."

"I caught something about farming. But neither looks like they'd know what to do with a shovel."

Andy grunted.

One of the men was bald; the other had black hair, slicked back and shiny.

"Italians," Andy figured.

"Or Mexicans with money."

The one with hair turned his head. Andy caught his eyes and nodded, then said, without really caring one way or another, "How things goin'?"

The man answered by lifting his martini glass, nodding. He looked familiar.

"One helluva martini, ain't it? Sammy here brews that gin in his backyard."

Sammy smiled. With a little towel he made a pass in front of Andy's glass and left to attend to three other customers who had just sat down.

Andy asked, "Where you guys from?"

"L.A."

"Business bring you here?"

"Doing what you might call a little research," said Slick.

Research, Andy thought. There was a word he'd never heard in conjunction with Fresno before.

"What kind would that be?"

"Farming. Crops, on the Westside."

He could see in his mind's eye the eternity of cotton out there. "That's some area."

The two men looked at each other and then the one without hair said, "Okay we join you?"

"Sure." Andy glanced at his watch to indicate he had to be moving on soon, and put out a hand.

"I'm Andy Demerjian."

"Zero Torrentino." They shook. He had a huge Adam's apple looked like one of those hammers the doctor checks reflexes with.

"Eddie Rizzo."

"Rizzo? Shit." He slowly put out a hand. "I thought I recognized you." Eddie gave it a quick shake. "I think we went to school together. Central?"

"Class of forty-four."

"I was three years behind you. Sammy there was a year behind me. Hell, we all went to school together."

Eddie rapped his fingers against the bar and shook his head.

"Demerjian? Don't ring a bell. But you remember me, huh?"

"Just barely. You know how it is—that three-year difference in age might as well be thirty. But your dad I remember like it was yesterday. Giorgione. Giorgione Rizzo?" The thought of that Italian lightened Andy's spirit.

"That was my old man."

"Was?"

"Had some cancer or something, ahh, gotta be five years now."

"Sorry to hear it. It's sad to see them go, that generation. They took a lot of tricks with them to the grave."

"You still farming, Andy?" Eddie asked.

"By hook or crook."

"Grapes?"

"Actually, I'm shifting my emphasis a little bit. Right now I'm looking at tomatoes." Andy paused, then wondered aloud, "So what've you been doing, Eddie?"

Eddie shrugged his shoulders. "This and that. Here and there."

"That right?"

Eddie explained to him that a couple of years after graduating from Central High, he'd headed for Chicago and got himself into business.

"So you were never really into it with your dad. The man made a damn good dago red from what I remember."

"The old man was a *vignaiolo*, huh, Eddie?" Zero smiled, a little drunkenly.

Andy said, "In fact, my dad grew some grapes for him. I think it was Alicante, just a piddly bit."

Eddie shrugged. "'Piddly bit.' That's the problem with farming, the way, you know, your dad and my dad did it. They threw up a few acres here, a few acres there, threw up a crop and a prayer, and then they sat back, stupid-like, and waited."

Zero slurped his martini and nodded.

"Those days are over. It's what you call a 'wrong strategy.' Got to do things different now," Eddie said. "Scale. Everything is scale."

"Interesting." Andy tossed back what remained of his whiskey and admitted, "There's days I think maybe I should've skipped town for awhile. I went off to Cal Poly but, sure as a homing pigeon, I ended up right back here."

"You see shit you don't see, that's all."

"Expand your horizons, huh? Chicago. L.A."

"What're you drinkin', Andy?" Zero offered.

"I'll pass."

"How about we get together sometime this week? Pick your brain a little, if you don't mind?" Zero asked.

"Sure. But I wouldn't count on much to pick."

They nailed down Wednesday, six o'clock. Andy lifted a few bucks out of his wallet.

"Let us take care of it for you."

"Wouldn't think of it." He dropped two bills on the bar. "But thanks anyway. And welcome back to Fresno."

WHEN ANDY GOT HOME Kareen was standing at the table driving her fists into a huge wad of bread dough.

"Mrs. Chamichian—that old lady in Sanger—she called."

"What did she say?"

"That she wanted to talk to you."

"I guess I better drive out there."

"You know, Andy," Kareen said, "Levon, across the street, I saw him today. He said that that boss of his has some work at the gas station. One of the men who worked there left. Maybe you should talk to him."

"Pumping gas, huh? Anyway, it's nice to know my neighbors're thinkin' about me. I'll give him a call to thank him."

"I was thinking too…maybe I should work."

"How can you work? You got the kids, honey. Where are they anyway?"

"Where they take care of children."

"The kids are in a nursery?"

"With my mom. But maybe I can work at a nursery. I can bring them with me."

"It's something to think about."

Andy went over and held her by her wrists, just above where the dough clung to her skin.

"Nobody's going hungry here. We got plenty food on the table. Roof over our heads. Let me handle it. Let's see what the old lady has to say."

THE SHEER THOUGHT OF HIS BOYS sitting in a room jammed with kids killed him. He pictured them wondering why their mother was tending to these crying and snotty-nosed strangers while brushing aside their own needs. He could pay off these bastard creditors himself, or at least chip away at the debt with the little money that he had at his disposal. But then where would he stand? Come to think of it, where the hell would he stand even if he got hold of twenty acres? What the hell are you thinking, Andy? Even if you plug some tomatoes in tout de suite, you'd be looking at three, four months of living in a fucking tunnel, watching these rats come and go.

He cut up, south, toward Chamichian's, rolling down the window to get a few gulps of air. He thought of the old-timers, back in the forties, the kind of shit they pulled off when things got tight.

There was Leo Hamalian and this Jewish broker, some big shot from San Francisco who was short on grapes getting on October. Anyway, he drives by the Armenian's ten and sees they're still hanging. Hungry for those Thompsons, he pops out a check based upon an eight-ton crop, some five thousand bucks.

Deal done, the next day, this Leo cashes the check and the Jew shoves a crew in to quick-pack them for table. He sets them up and drives away. A few hours later he returns, licking his chops, only to see half a dozen pallets, and the entire crew—at barely ten o'clock—sitting on its ass next to these pallets. At first he figures they're heating up tortillas for lunch, until he notices the packing tables are lined up parallel to the row, ready to move on out.

"No grapes," the crew boss tells him.

"What the hell do you mean 'no grapes'? There's ten ton an acre there. Eight at least." He starts frantically up the row, the crew boss trailing him. No grapes to the left, none to the right, the shock deepening the deeper into the row he goes.

"*Medio. Nada.*"

That old fox Hamalian had rightly wagered that nobody, especially a broker with shiny shoes, would plod more than a few vines in to check the crop in advance of the harvest, which, in this instance, he'd completed two weeks earlier, leaving ten, eleven vines on either side off the avenues as bait.

In other shady dealings, there was a time when every other farmer was "getting stolen" a piece of equipment to collect on insurance. Andy's cousin Manoog, after two years of crop loss and his wife banging on his head, decided to torch his double-insured barn. Aram Beldikian was in such dire straights he did the unthinkable—set fire to his very home—but because he wanted nobody to be party to the crime, he had kept his plan hush-hush, even to the wife. One evening when she's off to say her prayers at church, he puts a match to the place. Imagine the hell that broke loose when he learned that for ten years the woman had been stowing money in coffee cans up in the attic.

None of these people was a criminal. Some were stupid, sure, but all together they were honest, hardworking men who showed up regular at church, put their 15 percent in the dish, bowed their heads and took communion and sung with emotion the "Hyer Mer." But they also had a natural understanding of the ultimate rights and wrongs that no accountant or auditor or human judge was going to trump. In other words, not the law that governed Fresno County nor the State of California nor even the goddamn federal government had the right to demand a man sit back and starve. No—there was a higher law, and it held that he who works a ten-hour day, drinks only now and then, and gambles just for fun should not be forced to forfeit his land because nature had turned hateful three years in a row, or grocery shoppers were partial to soda pop rather than peaches that season. The law meant nothing to them. If truth were known, just a generation before, they had watched such a law, one that was supposed to protect their land and limbs, butchered by Turks and fed to street dogs. They believed in the Good Book, but there were two orders of lying and stealing and cheating: one that belonged to the oppressed and another that belonged to the oppressor.

But those days were over, Andy thought. In one generation, the Armenians had turned from growling lions and wily foxes to poodles licking society's boots. Of course, society had gotten shrewder. The insurances companies, they'd figured these Armenians out. Couldn't blame them for that, but it had gotten so that even the goddamn government—whose stockholders supposedly *were* the people—had an agenda not all that much different from the Wall Street gang's. What with the way McCarthy had chased after them Reds, the whole country had been cowed into a corner. The feds, they had their eyes everywhere. What kind of fucking America is that?

It occurred to Andy that being decent didn't count for much anymore. A good man, a genuinely good man, and a bad man, rotten to the core—they were judged only in so far as they obeyed the law or dictates of those in power. In other words, it didn't matter how dirty you were on the inside so long as your shirt was starched in public.

Andy pulled up to Chamichian's, stepped out of his truck, dropped the cigarette, and put it out with a boot. When he looked up, he saw the daughter Lilit on her knees in the vegetable garden working some weeds with a hand shovel. Her faded flower-print dress reminded Andy of old bedsheets. He watched her for a spell wondering about her, the mechanics of her dimwittedness.

Andy raised a hand "hello." When she noticed him, she jerked up and, holding down her skirt, bolted toward the house like bullets were whizzing over her head. Andy was bothered to think she might have judged his intentions as anything other than neighborly, and then he saw the dog.

It had been lying in the late afternoon sun next to Lilit and now rose and stood, taking Andy in. It was about as ugly a dog as Andy had ever seen. Medium height, white, barrel-chested, and with a strangely large heart-shaped head. If a dog could be mongoloid, maybe this dog was one.

"*Parev*," hello. The old lady was standing on the porch.

"*Parev*," he said.

"I called your house. I think it was your wife who answered."

"Yes."

"She sounds like a nice girl."

"Very nice. Sorry I came so late in the day."

"There is still light."

"Little left out there."

"Come in, come in."

He took off his baseball hat and stepped inside, spontaneously sighed, then caught himself and smiled.

"I saw Lilit outside."

"She likes to garden," she said. "She weeds when there are no weeds."

"She must be in heaven come summertime. I think I might have scared her. She ran inside."

"What are we going to do?" she said.

"And that's some dog you got."

"It is Lilit's. We found him running the streets. After my husband died, we felt it would be good to have a dog. A guard dog."

"He'll do the trick. He's built like a sumo wrestler."

She started toward the kitchen.

"Would you like some *kufte*? I've just made a batch this morning."

"Please. Please. Sit down."

"They're delicious."

"I'm going to pass."

"It's up to you. They're starting to use beef in *kufte*, you know. I don't trust cows. Not even for milk. We didn't even know beef until we came to this country."

"Damnedest thing, isn't it?"

"I came forty years ago and still sometimes I feel that I have just arrived."

Andy nodded his head.

"I was left in an orphanage in Lebanon. We suffered many things there. I did not speak of it for years. But I am an old lady, and what do I have to be ashamed of anymore? The orphanage, it was another kind of desert; our dreams always took us very far away...Paris, London, but most of all America. But when we saw America in our dreams, it was not this."

"This country has its goods and its bads, I suppose."

"Good. Bad. Like this, you throw them around." She made as though she were juggling balls, and then set her hands on her knees. "Maybe you've been in this country too long."

"I was born in this country."

"Look what they did to this Irish boy," she said, gesturing to her shrine of JFK. "You talk to his wife, this Jackie, have you ever seen such a lovely face!" She threw her shoulders back. "Proud. A princess. You ask this woman, sick with grief, about 'this country has its good and bad, I suppose.'" She wagged her head.

"You're right, there."

"Of course I'm right."

"That was a crime against this nation's soul. We're on the same page."

"Same page." She laughed at the Americanism. "Anyway, let's turn to the next page. I have considered your offer. You have offered me eighty dollars an acre."

"I think I said seventy, eighty. Something thereabouts."

"Eighty, you said."

"Okay. Eighty then."

"This is not enough. Give me one hundred dollars an acre and it is yours."

Andy lowered his eyes and folded his hands between his knees, buying himself a few seconds to think it through.

He thought it through. It was worth that much, he told her. In different times he could imagine the land renting for twice that much. But the market was in as sad a shape as he'd seen it in years. He was struggling to get back on his feet. It wasn't no sob story, just a fact: one hundred dollars per acre was a little pricey. He'd be willing, he said, to go ninety dollars, tops.

"What is ten dollars more? Come now."

"Let's do it this way: If I have a good year, I'll flip you your ten more. How's that sound?"

"You sound now like a packer is how you sound."

Andy swung his hands in, pointing at his faded denim shirt, and said, "Does this look like a packer sitting across from you?"

"Agheg, agheg," she said, "all right. That's enough. Let's not bicker over ten dollars. But I want you to know how many people I've turned down. Who knows, if I would have had my head together I might have gotten one hundred and twenty."

"I appreciate it. It's a terrific piece of dirt."

"I trust you." She pointed a finger at him.

"I promise I'll pay you first thing."

"You will give me a signed contract telling me all of this. I want it all down on paper."

"You'll get it."

"Now, what are you going to do with the trees left out there?"

"Can't plant tomatoes over them. Gotta get rid of them."

"Good. Good."

"I guess I'll get started tomorrow, if that's all right by you."

"Or the next day. Whenever you want. You take your time."

"To be frank with you, I don't have no time to waste."

UP UNTIL THIS POINT, he had avoided his creditors because he couldn't face the humiliation. Two orders of humiliation—being betrayed and being broke—the one, as they say, indivisible from the other. He'd known many of these creditors for years, and they'd known him and his brother as a team. He had shot the shit with them ("How's Abe doing, Andy?"), joked over a smoke ("Remember that time when Abe...") as they packed his grapes or placed a lug of peaches ("It's on the house, Andy") on the gate of his truck. After the betrayal, Andy expected that he'd turn around and tell them all ("Can you believe what Abe did...?"), but that wasn't how it went down. If they knew, they might've even written off part of his debt—but he had no appetite to talk about it in any detail. Not a single word of the millions the dictionary contained, no combination said how he felt. The cold hard fact of that shotgun, the concussion of those words, "You have no place here," addled his brain so mightily he withdrew into silence. He bore the betrayal like some hideous sin that he himself had committed.

He would now need these people's help. Bud Kaprelian, the packer, was first on the list. He owed him, supposedly, the most, and he braced himself as he walked into the office. Bud was working up some numbers on his desk.

"How ya doin', Bud?"

"Andy. Here to settle your debt?"

"Kinda."

He felt like a child as he excused himself for not answering letters, telephone messages, ignoring Bud's collectors. In the course of what amounted to a confession, Andy must've said, "I'm telling you this man to man here, Bud," half a dozen times. Bud kept silent, tapping a knuckle every now and then on his desk like he was keeping time to a dirge in his head. When Bud rudely asked him what the hell he then proposed, Andy was relieved: "Bud, it ain't much, but I've actually got you something by way of a proposition."

Here's what it was: Andy's debt would be levied against his take on the upcoming vegetable crop, which Kaprelian could both pack and broker. All Bud had to do was advance him the harvesting costs.

Business being business, Kaprelian had a note drafted on the spot securing the agreement, and note in hand, Andy headed off to the chemical company. There he promised Doug Jackson, whom he'd known since a kid, 'round about the same deal: Doug could put a lien on Andy's tomato crop, if he would kindly supply some spray and fertilizer. DJ, as they used to call him, sat way back in his chair, allowing Andy plenty of room to drag his honor through the mud before he told Andy his offer was a no-starter. Andy then tried what amounted to a left hook: he told Doug that he had no money, so it was useless to keep pounding at his door. "There's got to be a way to settle this here, Doug, but a lawsuit, frankly, ain't it. I've got one thing to my name—my kids and wife—and seeing how the old lady's been beating on my head about the debts, you can take her."

"Who do you think pays my bills, Andy?"

"I imagine you do, DJ. Maybe your secretary."

"Not without you paying me first, I don't. I got family too, Andy."

"I understand that."

"Same as you."

"All I can say is when a man is broke he's broke. You can wring me a hundred different ways, but I don't got no juice."

"I'll let you know."

"Appreciate your time."

Andy had betrayed Doug, though out of no fault of his own. Doug felt betrayed by Andy, and Andy felt betrayed by Abe, and Abe felt betrayed by his stepfather. Everyone felt justified heaping the hell that had been heaped on his head onto the head of the guy in back of him. Where did the heaping start? When would it ever end? With this imponderable, he walked into the box company, and the tire and parts shop, with similar proposals. Where they bit, he felt he'd bought himself up to six months; where they didn't, a month to six weeks for the effort alone. By the end of the day Andy felt woozy.

"I took care of things, sweetie," he told his wife. "You let me know first thing if anybody else comes by."

"How did you take care of it?" Did he pull money out of his hat the way magicians pull rabbits? Who could blame her for doubting?

"We'll be all right. Everything is more or less even steven now."

He had told her that before.

"Don't worry. These tomatoes are gonna pull us out of this mess once and for all. I got a feeling."

"You apparently have a feeling for everything," she snapped.

"It's my personality, I suppose."

"But have you paid everything?"

"One or two people left. I'll get to them pretty soon. Important thing is the bill collectors won't be comin' around."

Her eyes said she didn't believe a thing he was saying. How could he blame her? He didn't want her to feel that way, but what was his defense—that he'd never lied to her before?

4

WHEN THEY WERE COURTING, Andy had driven Kareen out to the farm to show her that he was a man of means. That's our farm, he'd said as they approached the fifty acres. Touring the vineyard, Andy explained, "When my dad came over from Turkey, he met my mom. She was a widower—there's why five of my sisters and brothers got a different last name. Anyway, they married and bought this acreage. After our mom died, she left it to us. Me and Abe farmed it together ever since. See that house? We built it from the foundation up." Andy pointed to a cement platform. "Once upon a time a water tower sat on it. Just a kid, I was sleeping in a little room up top of it when one night a fire caught. I jumped down through the flames what amounted to two stories, and landed with barely a scratch."

She asked him, coyly, how much the land was worth—his half of it, of course. He answered with a promise: enough to assure them a decent living. Hard years would come, a hailstorm or late rain, but in the long run, that farm would keep giving surely as an annuity. They would always have food on their table, more than enough, as long as they had that farm. That promise played no small part in her agreeing to marry him.

He knew she hailed from the beaches of the Mediterranean, and he treated her like some exotic and spellbinding thing that he'd been blessed to find. But over the next few months, as she told him who she was and what she had come from, she would gain depth in his mind. Her mother, Valentine—a green-eyed beauty who loved more than anything a good joke and a strong cigarette—was a survivor of the massacres. She had escaped almost certain death when a Turkish army officer, mesmerized by her blonde hair and stunning eyes, plucked her from a pack of girls being auctioned off to Kurdish tribal leaders. He took her for his own. She was only twelve years old. With this man she had a child, and with that child she'd made her escape from him and Turkey, on a boat headed across the Mediterranean. The child died on the seas.

In Alexandria she married a man twenty years her senior. Who could say if, on her end, love was involved? Who in those days, Andy assumed, had the luxury to ask? He owned a successful shoe factory and the couple had three daughters and a son, but then World War II came to visit Alexandria. Night after night, the Italians bombed the city, the air-raid shelters stuffed with people. One morning they emerged and found her husband's factory blown to bits.

The family moved from Alexandria to Cairo, then back, living here and there like gypsies, finally settling in the outskirts of their hometown in a bomb shelter on the beach. The father cobbled together a living and moved them back into their apartment after the war ended. He was barely getting back on his two feet when cancer cut him down. Kareen was fourteen years old. Valentine pulled her three girls out of school and set them to work as beauticians: massaging and manicuring feet, prettying up fingernails, applying henna dyes to women's hair. Valentine was keen to get them married off to well-to-do men, and she sent letters to America, asking relatives who had established themselves there if they knew any eligible men. One showed up; his name was Arsen. Within a month, her eldest daughter married him and off to America they went.

Arsen was Andy's friend. He had introduced him to Kareen.

Now they were in America—Fresno, America—which, compared

to the beaches of Alexandria, was a kind of swill. But it mattered little. Though her son, middle daughter, and extended family were still in Egypt, Valentine had taken her youngest daughter, Kareen, a world away from hunger and danger, and, knowing that history, Andy was certain, right from the start, that he would play no small role in making sure it stayed that way. With the security that his farm, his inheritance, brought, he believed he could live up to that obligation.

Then, the shotgun showed up in that bitter fog. His brother standing behind it. The promise he made to Kareen ripped to shreds—but how was he to tell her the truth? (Hell, he hadn't quite told himself.) They had just gotten married and were going to have a baby.

He left in the morning and returned late afternoon, just as he always had. When she asked how he was keeping his jeans so clean, he told her he'd found a newfangled way to pull water out of the ditch, not that he'd been driving aimlessly up and down Kearney Boulevard just to burn time. When she chided him for downing a six-pack of beer every night, he told her that the stress of the farm, of not getting booted off it, was the reason. And the unpaid bills, thirty, sixty, one hundred and twenty days overdue? That's how it is in farming; creditors don't really expect you to pay until the harvest is in and settled.

He hoped upon hope that things would straighten out, but they only kept going south. Harvest came, and went. The creditors started showing up at the door. The right time to tell her was no time. The only question was how to bring the news. In his head, he'd practiced a hundred different ways; most were shaped like a corkscrew. The arguing between he and Kareen got ferocious, like his drinking. They were quarrelling about why their rent hadn't been paid when Andy came out with it, straight as a dagger: "I ain't got the money."

"When are you going to get it?"

"I don't know."

"How much money don't we have?"

"A lot."

She sat at the kitchen table, her body turned away from him, and asked a few questions: "Is this why…" "Is that the reason…" He answered her, straight up, sinking deeper and deeper into shame. Finally, she swung her eyes around and howled, "You lied to me. You lied! You lied!"

A sledgehammer. He'd been expecting it, but that did nothing to pad the shock. *Bam bam bam.* He went wobbly, speechless. He wanted to say, "I did lie, but not to deceive you; not to harm you but to keep you from harm," but the words were too small—like crystals of salt they dissolved in his mouth. Instead, he studied his own image in the mirror of her eyes. He watched himself turn from a trusted if troubled figure to a twisted and deceitful beast.

With that beast she had moved from a ranch-style home on the swanky part of town to a shack in old Armenia: rent, sixty bucks a month. There was rust in the pipes. Mice populated the closets. The carpet was so threadbare in spots the hardwood showed. The heater knocked all night, and after running a few hours the swamp cooler got spasms and shut down. He'd sometimes lie on that old carpet and ponder the patterns the winter rains had made on the ceiling, as though he might read his future up there. They'd gone from paradise to purgatory, that fast.

In time, though, Kareen beat the pain back. He'd sometimes watch her scrubbing the floor or ironing the drapes or going at the grout in the tile and think that if her focus and energy had been channeled for combat the woman might've been some Patton. That's how fierce was her determination to turn their little box house into a home. Still, for the longest time he wondered if he'd be asked to stay once her work was done. He wondered whether after her enemies—confusion, frustration, humiliation—had been vanquished she'd vanquish him as well.

He reached Chamichian's farm, pulled onto the dirt road, and puttered the truck past the house back to the shed. The sun was starting to peek over the mountains and he sat there for a spell, watching it, feeling anxious. Maybe about the thousand things that could go wrong before he'd even driven down the first stake—or maybe, just maybe, it wasn't panic but excitement at the prospect of having a piece of dirt other than his backyard garden to work for the first time in five years.

He doubted a soul had stepped into that shed since old man Chamichian had died, and so he walked open the big double doors reverently. Straight ahead he made out the '47 and '52 John Deeres. He flipped on the overhead light. To the tractors' right a forklift and two Gustafson rigs, and on the other side and against the wall Chamichian had leaned his ladders, buckets stacked next to them. All told, the shed was clean and well-organized as a dentist's tray. Andy approached the tractors feeling a little shy for disturbing their slumber, but nonetheless settled right in to the seat of the '52 and leaned over to pat it on the hood like it was a horse whose confidence he hoped to win. When he turned the key over, the tractor drowsily coughed before it opened into a basso, the sound knock-knocking against the wooden barn holy as some church organ. He let it limber up until he could smell the diesel exhaust, and then he jiggled it into low gear and nudged it out into the first light of day. There was a big onionskin moon sitting waist high on the horizon. He steered the Deere toward it.

After a few minutes on the tractor, his body settled in and he understood that what he'd earlier felt was neither panic nor excitement but rather worry that once he'd stepped back into farming he'd be thrown back into the sinkhole of loss that he'd struggled so hard to climb out of, like a ballplayer might initially feel stepping back onto the field after a hideous injury—excitement and worry all wrapped into one. He maneuvered the tractor, focusing his attention on the uprooted trees, the mess of work he had in front of him. The leaves, the fruit, and the seeds, the bark of the trees—all of it had disintegrated into the earth, leaving only bare trunks. After an hour on the tractor, he counted close to fifty trees still on the ground.

He hopped off the tractor, pulled his gloves on, grabbed a large branch, and rocked one of the Santa Rosas back and forth until he heaved it over. On the rotting underside were beetles and spiders and maggots and worms, turning the tree to mulch. Thinking of the money he would save on fertilizer gave him a boost. A little after noon, he pulled out Chamichian's chainsaw and went at the trees with a vengeance. They were just wood now—something to be cut up and gotten out of the way. Only the mulch they provided for the new planting counted for anything.

THE ITALIANS WERE WAITING for him in a corner booth with martinis—looked like their drink of choice. They smiled and stood and Zero put out a hand and Andy apologized for being late and took the spot nearest the aisle. He was a little shaky from the saw work and he figured a thick drink might help steady him. "Do me a double," he told Sammy. "In fact, put that bottle on hold."

"Hard day, Andy?" Zero asked.

"Nah."

"It'll be sittin' *there*," Sammy said.

"Appreciate it, friend."

Andy watched him go back toward the bar, picking up coasters along the way.

"He's a good man, Sammy," Andy said.

"That right?" Eddie said.

"One helluva ballplayer to boot. One of them guys, you know, never shit with nobody, but on the other hand nobody you want to shit with either, know what I mean?"

"Tough guy, huh?" Eddie said.

"Only when it's called for. Anyway, you guys into sports?"

They talked a little about baseball, football, college, the pros, speculating on what team was up, what team was down for the upcoming year. Andy hadn't much of an opinion on the matter, liked to play ball more than gab about it, which made him wonder why he'd asked the question at all.

Sammy returned with his drink, a bowl of beer nuts.

"Thanks, barkeep," Andy told him.

When Sammy was out of earshot, Eddie asked, "Who bookies around here?"

Andy dusted his hands of the nuts and chuckled. The only bookie he knew in town was Peter Boyajian, who also happened to be one of the most notorious lefties in the county.

"I'll be damned," Zero said. "A bookie two-timing as a Red."

"Only in our fucking Fresno," Eddie guffawed.

Andy said, "Saturday he'll be reading that manifesto and Monday he'll be collecting on bets."

"What a fucking town."

"Sammy run numbers?" Zero asked.

"Naw. Maybe a game here and there." Andy didn't frankly know. "I'm not much of a gambler myself," he said. "Any kind of farming is gambling enough." Andy turned to Eddie. "You know, I forgot to tell you something the other day, Eddie."

"What's that?"

"So, your dad buys my dad's Alicantes, like I told you. But that Allie is a finicky little grape, thin-skinned, and for whatever reason, it didn't like the dirt. Three years into it, thereabouts, the crop yield drops and the color—that blood red—it's turned a little pink. My dad was kind of upset. It wasn't much to speak of acreage-wise, but dollar per ton it was a helluva lot better than what he was getting on his Thompsons. I mean raisins, for years, were in the doghouse."

"Up and down, raisins, huh?" Zero asked.

"Like a rolley-coaster. Anyway, so my dad calls Georgione, your dad, out. He wanted the man to see for himself. Georgione comes over and has a look. 'Don't worry about it, Yervant,' he tells my old man. 'We'll do something with it.'"

Andy chuckled. "I remember this because my old man, when he told us kids the good thing your father did, he got a little emotional. And he wasn't the kind of guy who got emotional much."

"What the hell did my old man do with those grapes?" Eddie wondered.

"What he does is he makes a vinegar."

Eddie nodded his head and smiled, like the image of his father was finally coming to focus.

Andy said, "I'll be damned, it wasn't some of the darkest vinegar a man had ever seen, molasses color, but damn good. My dad used to keep it in a special bottle and use it only now and then, like some holy communion juice."

"Yeah, he was all right," Eddie said.

Andy recollected, "I don't know, maybe Armenian, Italian, they were both used to being bent over and taking it in the rear. But that was an awfully nice thing what your old man did."

Eddie sniffed the air, like maybe he was drawing up a tear.

Zero was thinking business: "Andy, we thought you might be able to give us the scoop. We're looking for someone to help us grow crops out on the Westside, near Corcoran. We're lookin' for someone who can work with us. Do the job straight."

"You're not sure quite yet what it is you want to farm. Is that your question?"

"We're lookin' into that part too," Zero said.

Andy went down the list of crops that might grow out there. He named a few names of farmers in the area who might be able to manage it for them.

"We're not talking rocket science," Andy said. "Growing wheat, corn, cotton. It's not like trying to throw up tomatoes or cukes, much less a long-term deal like peaches or grapes. But still, you can't wing it."

"You think there's a market for corn, Andy? Could we go local with it?" Zero asked.

"There's always a market for corn. It's one of them staples, for mush or feed, you can't do without." He'd finished his first double. "Boy. I was thirsty."

Andy got Sammy's attention over behind the bar and motioned with his finger to indicate they needed drinks all around. Sammy nodded.

"Good thing about corn is it's a low-risk deal. You get headwind on a sweet market, you can cash in big, but if you lose, what're you out—seed, water, not much."

"That's the game we want to play," Zero said.

Andy had never thought of farming as a game, and he didn't care to think about it that way now. "Let me ask you this, if you don't mind: What the hell interest you guys got in farming anyway?"

Zero said, "Couple of years now Eddie's been pushing us to expand our business to California. Ain't that right, Eddie?"

"Thing is," Eddie said, "you get too caught up in one thing, the house blows down and there ain't nowhere to move to. Right now we've got operations going in Florida, Kansas, some alfalfa in Arizona."

"You want to branch out to California, in other words."

"Exactly right."

"Well, bottom line on which crop you choose, I suppose, depends upon how much you're willing to risk, and how long you're willing to be at risk. That and how deep your pockets go."

"Like anything else," Zero said.

"Like anything else."

"But know-how too, huh, Andy? Not anybody can farm two hundred acres. We've found that out the hard way."

True enough. Andy had seen plenty of men who claimed they could throw up a crop fall flat on their asses. But it could all be boiled down to a principle, and now he told them that principle: "It's about farming that one acre correctly. If you can farm that one right, you can farm a thousand the same."

Zero said, "Andy, I gotta tell you. We like you. We liked you from the minute we met you."

"Thanks. I appreciate it."

"Maybe you'd like to come out and take a look at this land. Maybe it would be the kind of deal that would interest you. More than anything, we want a guy who can do the job and do it right."

Andy nodded.

"Sounds like you guys want to build something big out there. I can see that. That's fair enough."

"I like the way you think, Andy."

Andy liked them for liking the way he thought, though in truth he hadn't been doing all that much thinking, just talking. But after the drumming he'd received over the last five years, he was flattered that someone with no prejudices one way or another should recognize his talents.

"Your father farm other crops than grapes, Andy?"

He was touched that they cared enough to ask. "Actually, his forte was the watermelon. Brought them up big as boats. But we're talking the thirties, now, and nobody knew what it was, and if they did, they were embarrassed to have to spit out those seeds."

Eddie laughed.

"I'm not shitting ya. Year after year he tried to establish a market, but it only sold in a few Armenian and Jap markets."

"Italians didn't buy it?"

"Now that you mention it, maybe a few. Probably Eddie's old man took a few off his hands, but basically what you had back then was an immigrant FOB mentality: if you can grow it in your backyard, why pay more than a few pennies a pound at the store? So, to make a long story short, my dad—who they called the Watermelon King, I kid you not—he went belly up. Years later, the watermelon makes a comeback, see, but this time it's farmed by a huge outfit, the Minassians. Now these people have muscle—piggyback it on their other produce. Way it always is. Now people can't get enough watermelon, and I'm talking about where American people shop, people who pay, in Frisco or L.A."

"Scale," Eddie said. "Scale."

"Every time you say that I keep seeing a round face and a dial."

Zero laughed.

"But the point I'm makin' is"—though, in fact he'd just then decided that he was making a point at all—"a good idea ain't enough."

Andy let his eyes drift away from the men, to give them a few seconds to digest his exposé. Zero tilted his head to the side toward Eddie, who talked in his ear. Andy came back from wherever it was he'd gone off to and politely smiled.

Zero said, "Why don't you drive out in the next few days and have a look. At the land. See what you think."

Just then Andy was feeling good enough he'd drive out there simply to take a piss.

Zero said, "There's some good guys we'd like you to meet."

"Sure. Why not? But look, whether or not you guys like me, I'm happy to give you a hand."

EVERY TIME ANDY DROVE OUT that way, he felt that he wasn't traveling forward through space so much as backward in time. West of Fresno, beyond the fruit trees and vines, all you could see was things growing low—cotton and barley and alfalfa—that extended to the ends of the eyes. Beyond that, the earth began to roll again, hills swept smooth by wind, rivers bone dry, and spans of dirt white as talcum, a calciferous terrain that made a man feel very close to a speck of quartz.

Like some navy fleet, gray clouds toured east, heading out over the Sierras. To the north hung other clouds; Andy counted six, shaped like jellyfish. That sky and its big melodrama, it reminded him how one lazy Sunday afternoon his dad declared he was headed out to those very parts and that Andy would join him. It was a first, because Yervant rarely breached the boundaries of Fresno County, except to go up to the mountains once or twice a year. (Beaches to the west were a wet and shadeless waste.) Andy remembered they packed a jar of iced tea and nuts and some dried fruit in a burlap bag, headed up the 99, and cut off around Delano and then shot clear past it. They were in June, Andy was only ten years old, and he thought his father and he were going on some kind of field trip. The weather was fair, the roads long and sleepy, and so he quietly sat for mile after mile past places called Pond and Lost Hills and Devil's Den. Where were they going? Pretty soon, Andy felt, they'd reach a place that petered out to perfect quiet, whiteness, and dust.

Yervant had gotten it in his mind to head out that way a few weeks before, after attending a lecture at the Asbarez Club. On Saturdays farmers would drive in from the country to spend a few hours with their compatriots in the city at that downtown club: a single room and kitchen, dimly lit with small wooden tables and around them fold-out chairs. There was a rack for Armenian dailies, a wall closet full with games. In twos and threes men would sit and slurp thick Turkish coffee or sip a water pipe. Between the flick of cards and the click of the wooden discs, men might parse the news of the day or openly admit their fate.

Scholarly books in Armenian were scarce in Fresno, but a handful of men were proficient in the American or European languages and possessed tomes in these tongues that told of recent scientific and philosophical trends. As a result, nearly every Saturday afternoon, the club would become a makeshift lecture hall where these men would speak on everything from Einstein's mind-blowing discoveries to the genesis of the whooping cough to the pessimisms of Spengler.

It was there, one fall afternoon, that Yervant heard Peter Minassian, an attorney by trade, tell them the history of the place where they had in fact arrived. What is it made of? Who lived here before us?

With a stack of books on the table in front of him, he told of what was once an inland sea, called Tulare. This eight-hundred-square-mile wonder had great stretches of wetlands where swans and billy owls nested, and mile after mile that teemed with wildflowers and vernal pools. Elk, antelope, and deer came to cool down there and drink. He had them picture massive migrations of geese from Canada in winter, the atmosphere thrumming like a tornado from millions of wings all flapping at once.

Yervant sat transfixed. And Minassian had just begun. He told them, next, of the natives, Indians called Yokuts, who had lived there among the tall reeds like the marsh Arabs where the Tigris and Euphrates meet, and how they fished the shallows with their hands, or with a single sweep of their nets raised hundreds of trout and bass. In winter, the canoes, he claimed, were fashioned to cut through the foggy shallows like a spoon through yogurt.

How many of them lived there? This was hard to know. Thousands, it is thought—and for thousands of years and happy with their lot, of a single piece with the earth, until they were ripped from it by disease, starvation, or murder. "By whom?" he asked, and from the rapt audience paused for an answer.

Who could blame half a dozen men for wondering if the perpetrators were Turks, even if they were half a world away?

"Catholics," he answered.

There was a chorus of "Of course." The Catholic Crusaders had done the same to them in 1204.

Then Yervant stood, shook his head at the magnitude of these Yokuts' loss, and asked of the remnants, "Where had they escaped?"

"*Cheegah,*" Minassian said, "there are no more," and he dusted his hands.

Not a single man could contradict. They'd been in the valley for some twenty-odd years and none of them had met a Yokut yet.

Yervant asked, "*Paitz, hech cheegah?*" But there are none?

"Scattered here and there, perhaps. Like sterile seeds."

That evening, Levon Simonian, Aram Topalian, and Yervant gathered at the house. The men took chairs on the front porch and continued, over a bottle of *raki*, the conversation, marveling at the ravenous and eden-like scenes Minassian had rendered. It was after harvest, late in the summer, and the ground was dry and the air hot and mostly motionless. Every now and then they would pause to savor the *raki*'s warmth and a cool breeze that shambled by.

When the sun died, Calipse brought out plates of cheese and bread and sliced meat and green onions, and they folded it all into little packets and ate. Soon the moon appeared fresh as lately fallen snow. From its case Levon lifted his fat-bellied *oud* and began singing, a quavering call. It was Turkish music, and though it was taboo, they sung, all of them, for the first time in many years in the Turkish tongue. Then Yervant got up and began dancing, by himself, or with a spirit the *raki* might have conjured, and down the steps he went to an open patch of dirt and in circles he turned. Then he stopped and announced, "You know, there was on this land a *'medz yeghern,'*" a "great cataclysm," as the survivors called the genocide. "We sit here and we eat and drink. We have found solace here, but let us not forget that we walk and sleep and work on the bones of 'Yocoots.'"

"YOCOOT," HIS FATHER WOULD SAY, hosing down the avenue, shooing a moth out the door, finishing up his soup. Every once in a while he'd pick up an English word and sporadically say it until he'd got it out of his system, like a man hacks until he's worked up the phlegm, but this was no English word Andy had ever heard, and he must've repeated it half a dozen times more as they drove down those unknown roads.

Finally they arrived there—in other words, to nowhere—and Yervant got out of the car and stood studying whatever it was that he'd come to study. Andy was awed by the breathtaking expanse of the sky and the sheer emptiness of the terrain, but Yervant seemed less awed than unnerved. The man was breathing deeply, his jaw faintly trembling, as though he were mustering courage for some once-in-a-lifetime work. Is something wrong? Andy asked. His father shook his head no, opened the trunk, and pulled out a shovel and a two-by-two frame of wire mesh and a bucket. "Follow me."

On and on they marched, and then his father stopped and punched a hole in the ashy dirt with the heel of his boot. *"Hos,"* here, he said and began digging. After he'd gone about a foot deep with that shovel, he started dumping the dirt into the bucket. When it was full, he had Andy hold the mesh while he himself poured the dirt onto it and his son jiggled it around. Andy figured his father was searching for gold. They stood out there digging and shaking, going from one dumb spot to the next. Nothing came of it until they hit upon a spit of earth that looked like it'd long ago been worked over with a gigantic rake. There, when they poured their first bucket onto the mesh, a strange article surfaced—a shell, then two, then three and more. Andy jumped up and down with delight, figuring they'd got what they'd come for. Though hardly gold, this thing must be equal to it for the strangeness of its setting. He watched his father take one, no bigger than a thumb, give it some spit, and buff it on his shirt. Then he put this shell up to his ear and listened. Andy imagined he heard the sea.

If that trip when he was ten or so gave Andy scope of what was out there, it was during college that he got a sense of the scale of man's efforts at taming it. This land was once a dish into which the Pacific Ocean sloshed, before a great tectonic shift pushed the earth up and sealed the ocean in. Bounded by mountains, a sea hundreds of feet deep formed and then over the years slowly seeped and drained, leaving a vast two-hundred-mile bowl with a mineral-rich floor. From high up in the Sierras came water, wild rivers that wove beautiful and fickle, ran headlong then trickled, in turns flooded and dried. For thousands of years men lived this way, treating the water like it was some fanciful god who accepted no petition. But this god was meant to be controlled, and control him men did. An army of scrapers was deployed to take those gently rolling hills and shave them into a flat and irrigable immensity the likes of which the world had never seen. A sea of money and an ocean of concrete, levees, canals, and culverts were built to channel water from a massive dam to hundreds of farms.

Andy was now on the western tip of the basin. In the middle of the road, two vultures were taking apart a badger or maybe a rabbit. They looked up from their repast and then rose. Andy drove past the pink meat and mangled fur, leveled his eyes through the rearview mirror, and watched the birds drop and pick up where they left off, at peace with their ruthlessness.

There were no markers out there, no decent way to sense distance except using avenues and roads, and without this, that, and the next thing to situate him, he barreled right past the corner of Avenue 66 and Road 88, where the ranch was located.

He did a U and, lo and behold, staring him down was a sheriff in a sheriff's car. Where the hell did he come from?

Andy pulled off to the side of the road and brought his car to a stop. The sheriff pulled off too and came within a few yards of his front bumper. Andy had no idea whether he was speeding; his speedometer had gone kaput some time ago. He pulled his wallet out from his back pocket.

"Morning, Sheriff," he said.

His face was bloated and red and he had a cauliflower nose.

"Morning."

"Is there some problem, Sheriff?"

"Your speed is a problem. You got any idea how fast you were going?"

"Be honest with you, it would be only a hunch." Andy rapped his dashboard with a fist. "This speedometer is on the blink."

"You need to get that fixed."

"Sure as hell. I guess I just get used to feeling the speed, but out here you kind of lose your orientation."

"Out here there's vehicles like anywhere else."

"I was born in the country. Yessir."

"Your license?"

Andy pulled it out of his wallet and handed it to him.

"Mr. Demerjian."

"Yessir."

He tipped his head to the side and looked behind Andy's seat.

"Step out of the truck, if you will."

Andy did as he was told.

The sheriff pushed the seat forward.

"Just a few tools back there," Andy said.

The sheriff reached in and pulled out a whiskey flask. He brought it to his nose and sniffed. He looked back there again and shook his head.

"Maybe this here is the reason you're losing your orientation." He held the bottle by its neck.

"No, sir. Those aren't mine."

"They just grow back there?"

"It's a long story."

The sheriff tossed the bottle back behind the seat and further scrutinized Andy's license. "Class A."

"Yessir. I'm now and then a trucker. I'd sure appreciate you lookin' the other way this time around."

"Where you headed?"

Andy pointed to the avenue. "Just making a U-turn to get there."

He looked over his shoulder. "That your property?"

"No. Some men I might be doing some work for own it. They should be there now."

"I'll be patrolling this road regular for the next few months."

"I'll make sure you won't have to bother with me again."

"Consider it a warning."

"I appreciate it."

He handed Andy's license back.

"How fast was I going? Mind me askin'?"

"Get that speedometer fixed and you won't have to."

"Fair enough."

He waited for the sheriff to go on ahead, then pulled up slowly and made a left down a dirt road, steering around a few potholes until he came upon a big white barn. Two cars were parked in front of it, a cherry red Cadillac convertible and a green Hudson Hornet. Four men, all of them in suits, none of them with hats, stood in the shade. He pulled up a good ways away so as to not smother them in dust, opened the door, and walked toward the men.

Zero and Eddie came up to greet him as the other two men lingered, probably sizing Andy up.

"Hey, hey, you made it," Zero said.

"You got to be half-coyote to navigate out here, but yeah."

"There's a couple of guys we want you to meet."

"I can see that. Looks like they travel in style."

"Oh yeah," Eddie said. "Big-time style."

Zero introduced Andy to the men, all of them Italian.

"What do you guys got out here?" he asked. "Two, three hundred acres?"

"Two-twenty," one of the men said.

"I assume you're renting."

"It's ours," Zero said.

"So, Andy, the boys said they like your style. Said you know your faming."

"Yeah, these guys are sharp." Andy winked at Zero.

"Are they?" asked the guy who looked most how a bookkeeper might look.

"Good-lookin' standpipe," Andy said, moving toward it.

"What do you think would grow out here, Andy?"

Andy pivoted and stood to give it a serious look. "Like I told Zero and Eddie here, cotton's a natural. Myself, I like this Pima cotton. Nobody here, as far as I know, has tried it. You might look into that."

"Pima?"

"It's an ancient cotton, goes back to the Egyptians. Bears a very fine, silky thread, but it's a little delicate to farm."

They asked a few questions and Andy answered them all without hesitation.

"You can be the market leader on Pima, though there's some risk there too."

"How's that?"

"It's a supply issue. It's got to be there, day in and day out. Say you're a company, start making bedsheets out of Pima, and you only got one supplier. What happens if that supplier goes bust, or his bolls go south one year? See what I mean?"

The Italians shook their heads.

"What's a farm manager cost in these parts, Andy? How much dough?"

"On average, for something this size, I'd say five bucks an acre for the season."

"Couple of thousand dollars?"

Andy said, "Might be a little low."

"Or a little high," the accountant said.

"That's sounds in the ballpark," Zero said.

"Look." Andy pointed out to nowhere. "A coyote."

It was so far away it was hard for the others to see.

His heart always stayed a spell when he saw a coyote passing from here to there all alone.

"They're the damnedest animals," he told them. "I ran over one once, when I was farming some tomatoes down south."

Eddie raised an imaginary rifle in his arms and took aim.

"Whoa," Andy said, lowering the weapon with his hand. "They're no harm. I'd just leave 'em be. I hate to say it, but you should know better than that, Eddie."

"We shot plenty as kids."

"True enough, but there ain't nobody raising chicken or hogs out here. Even in town, I doubt they're as dangerous as folks make them out to be. Fact, some old Armenian in Fowler made one a pet, just like a dog, though in truth they're nothing like a dog. Up close, you can feel their wild."

They all now watched it disappear.

Andy said, "Usually, they travel in packs, see, but what with the way the land's been cut up and fenced off, they get orphaned. But also, maybe his kin were shot down. Plenty of people are willing to play 'em like a sport."

Andy dropped to his haunches, scooped up some dirt, and let it sift away through his fingers.

Zero asked, "When do you plant cotton in these parts, Andy?"

"You got a shovel around here?"

Zero said, "Eddie, I think we got one in the barn." Eddie walked off to fetch one.

"In general, you gotta have a little heat. When you're talking seeds, you got to watch out for extremes. Not too hot, not too cold. They like it the way we do."

Eddie came back with the shovel, holding it out in front of him like a stinky rag. Andy wondered whether he'd ever used a shovel. Maybe he was one of them prissy farm kids shied away from mud and dust. Maybe that's why he'd left for Chicago.

"Thanks," he said, and took it from him.

He took the long handle expertly in his hands, angled it just so, and threw his foot down hard and fast, *cssh*, pulling up six inches of dirt. He dropped to his knees and put a hand down into the hole. A few seconds passed.

"I figure it's about forty-five degrees," he said.

Zero wanted to feel it too. He put his hand down in the hole.

"Need fifty-five, sixty or so. It's what you call an art more than a science, but in general, late March it should be heated up enough to support a seed."

"So you just keep testing the temperature?"

"Well, that and trying best you can to find a window where the weather is steady. You want it at a constant for a week or two after you seed. It's just like seeding a woman. When you plant it in there, if the woman's stressed out about this or that, the seed won't take."

The Italians nodded, chomping on the metaphor.

"And even if it do take, with a lot of stress that baby will shoot out with problems, you know, a harelip or retarded or something. Sometimes it's cosmetic, other times it's more serious. There's work, believe me, got to be done to prep the soil and get everything lined up just right. To be honest, if you're planning on going cotton, or any field crops really, you need to start getting your ducks in order right about now."

"That's what we understand."

"Whoever told you that told you right."

"What do you think of corn, Andy?"

"I'd grow whatever the hell you want me to. It's not my land, and it's not my money. You call the shots: I'm a farmer not no diva."

"We appreciate you coming out here, Andy."

"It's my pleasure."

"Does Zero know how to contact you?"

"I believe he does."

5

IT TOOK ANDY A WEEK to carve up the remaining fifty-odd trees. At the end of each twelve-hour day, there was sawdust in his hair, on his arms, in the cuffs of his jeans, in the pockets of his shirt, stuck to the stubble of his beard. His body was so shaky from the vibrations of that saw he was afraid he'd fumble his kids when he lifted them in his arms to say "I'm home."

For the first two days, Kareen forced him to take hot baths to ease his muscle aches, but when he slipped into that tub he felt ill at ease, as though it was too much sumptuousness all at once, as though his body might dissolve in that water like an Alka-Seltzer tablet. The sound of the saw buzzed in his ears for hours afterward. The boys' harmless outbursts rattled him like sonic booms. Their house was so tiny he had nowhere to escape, so he spent more and more of the evening on the front porch with a glass of whiskey on the armrest of his chair, thinking.

He hadn't heard back from the Italians. Sure, a part of him was hot and heavy to manage such a large patch of earth, but another part of him questioned how he'd fare as a so-called farm manager. Every nickel he had made in farming he'd made more or less on his own. He remembered his father dropping him off at the corner of Ventura and F Street with a cart brimming with produce they'd grown on the farm. He could see his little person, limping from one home to the next, peddling peppers, okra, fava beans, persimmons, and pomegranates to old Armenian ladies until sundown, when his father, who spent the day playing *tavloo* or pinochle at the Asbarez Club, came to pick him up. He remembered squirreling away his money to buy his first transistor radio, a baseball glove and bat. Both of his parents were dead by the time he was in high school, but he was so accustomed to pulling his own cart it was then just a matter of pulling it a little harder.

Outside of four dreamy years in college, when he had the leisure to read and write under a table lamp till midnight, all he'd done was pull. Even in college, he'd be on the road right after Friday classes to help pull on the farm until Sunday afternoon. He took a sip of that whiskey and remembered the kids with blond hair and chinos, how Friday afternoons they'd toss scarves around their necks and pack into cars and caravan up the coast to Santa Barbara. On Monday, they'd tell of girls, necking, bonfires and beer on the beach.

He wanted to be their friend. They wanted to be his friends. They became friends—sort of.

It wasn't just that his dad quaffed *raki* and theirs quaffed martinis; that his hair was black and theirs dirty blond—differences that were obvious to everyone. No, the disparity was that they believed they were entitled to this country whereas he felt kind of lucky to be part of the club—like, if they wanted to, they could boot him out. The difference was that where they felt betrayed if things didn't turn in the expected direction, he felt blessed when they did. They feared losing what they had; he always presumed loss is where you started. Aside from a bump here and there, they expected to glide into a future that was already theirs.

Being American meant you only looked back occasionally: July 4, Thanksgiving, Washington's birthday. Stories you told yourself about the cherry tree and Honest Abe. Being Armenian, though, was like driving a truck where your brain is split between what's ahead and what's in the rearview mirror. In fact, it's fair enough to say that history for an Armenian wasn't even history yet, it was a kind of past that you hadn't passed.

He'd have it easier than most Armenian kids changing that. His parents were long dead, and by the time he went off to college, the girls were out of the house, married, and getting on with their lives. Except for Abe and Zabel, nobody looked over his shoulder. When he returned to the farm on weekends, holidays, spring and summer breaks, he'd learned to hold his tongue. His sister-in-law would say, "You are becoming just like the *odars*." (There was no better way to translate it than as "the others.") "Damn right," he'd say to himself.

He spent longer and longer time away on break "becoming an *odar*." Quietly, he planned a future that had nothing to do with that farm. Maybe he'd be a football coach, a businessman, a fruit broker, say. It bothered his brother. He saw betrayal rather than an American in the making. How could Andy tell him that he just wanted to breathe? How could he tell him, "I want to be an American"?

He could blame Zabel, Abe's wife, sure. Superstitious, jealous in an Old World way that might have been comical if it weren't so deadly menacing, for years she'd worked on Abe, undermining and at the same time coddling him, until the man was left doubting whether taking a piss was within his purview. Abe never said what Chamichian said, "Enough is enough," so he got a share of the blame. Then again, maybe he got it all, by letting the frustration pile up to the side like cords of wood,

enough is enough
enough is enough
enough is enough
enough is enough

to eventually dump at his brother's feet. Maybe he'd been hording it longer than Andy had ever imagined.

Abe was only nine years old when his natural father perished, and then into his life had come Yervant, a tormented refugee from

Turkey. He married Calipse and inherited her five children, Abe the oldest and the only boy. Together the couple had two more children, a girl and Andy, the youngest.

His mind drifted back to the old farmhouse. He must've been five years old; Abe, then, would be seventeen. Yervant had just yanked Abe out of school, claiming he needed help on the farm. Abe would watch the girls and Andy shuffle out to the school bus every morning, trying to muster a smile. "See you when we get home, Abe," they'd sadly sing. Maybe four, five months passed before Abe's excitement about them returning home began to wane. When they came shambling up the avenue, or racing through a vineyard row, he'd stand or look up dumbly, like a hired hand. He was too young to deliver his world to the vagaries of fate, but also too young to take fate into his own hands.

Poor Abe, poor Abe, poor Abe. Andy said it enough that in some respects Poor became Abe's first name. In a world that had gone lopsided, with a father he loved on one end and a half-brother he loved on the other, Andy tried to square the injustice in his head. His dad couldn't do it on his own. His dad had to pull *someone* out of school. It wasn't because Abe was his stepson and Andy his real son; Abe was the oldest, the strongest. That's why he was chosen. Abe's sacrifice was a sacrifice for them all. They got schooling and, in exchange, Abe should get their honor and respect.

Andy tried to make everyone see it that way. When he'd get home from school, he'd hop into his work clothes and rush out to labor next to his brother. During harvest, he would push his sisters to put in an extra half hour lying down or turning trays to make Abe's day a little easier come morning.

When Abe got in an argument with one of his sisters, Andy would take his brother's side. If there were an extra slice of pie, "Give it to Abe," he'd say. There were even days when Andy would draw up a scale in his mind, putting his polio on one end and Abe's downtroddenness on the other. "Look, brother: You have that burden! But I have this!"

The thought would ease his conscience for a spell, but it did nothing for Abe.

Andy watched him drop deeper and deeper into himself, his solitude frightening.

One evening, dinnertime, Abe, who had been working since before the sun came up, sat, eating nothing. Andy wanted to lift his spirits, would have lifted his fork for him if that's what it took, and asked, "What's a-matter, Abe?"

Abe leveled his eyes at Andy. His look said, "What do you care?"

His mother jumped in. *"Inch gah?"* What's wrong? Maybe he was feeling ill.

"Hech," nothing, he said.

"Then eat," his father said.

It was a command. Abe picked up a fork and shoved it under the pilaf.

A minute passed. The fork sat there.

"Are you sick, boy?" his mother asked.

"Goozem mereeh," I want to die, he said.

All the utensils slowed and then came to a standstill.

Next, his brother was cowering on the carpet with Yervant swinging his belt down on him over and over, like that belt was a shirt he was determined to beat a stain out of, bellowing, "You want to die?!" It took the whole family, all seven of them, to pull the frothing man off the boy. He remembered how Abe stood, finally, sideways, his black eyes dead, dry. Then Abe bolted out of the house. Andy ran after him, but his father stopped him dead with his voice: "Sit!"

Abe disappeared. Later Andy would discover that he'd gone from one relative's to another seeking refuge, but at the time he had no idea whether he'd done that, hitchhiked to Mexico, or thrown himself to the river. Yervant seemed hardly to notice and kept turning those words, *"Goozeh mereeh?"* (He wants to die?), this way and that. *"Goozeh mereeh?"* he'd guffaw, he'd taunt, he'd mock. What gives him the right to kill himself? he was saying. He asked his stepdaughters at dinner, his sister on the front porch: *Goozeh mereeh.* Life was freely given, something you neither rejected nor chose. But only he who had endured pain and humiliation and suffered life's mocking indifference could claim death before death claimed him. They shook their heads lamely, painfully, the question a kind of molestation. "He said something is all," their mother answered. "He didn't mean it." "He said something…" his father echoed. "Well, in my house, if he ever says that something again he will get his wish!"

Goozeh mereeh? Abe hadn't lived long enough to suffer enough. The right to die wasn't his. It was a kind of cheating. He wanted to take a shortcut there, get to the finish line on the cheap.

Five days later Abe returned. No relative, all of whom were afraid of Yervant's timeless ire, would dare take him in for more than a day. That was Abe's last stand, at least from the outside. From that point on, like a blinkered horse, Abe rose in the morning and lay himself down at night, with no future, it seemed, beyond the endless series of chores Yervant set in front of him. Instead of a horizon, Abe was left staring in a mirror, a warped mirror.

Only after Yervant died and Abe went off to war did things change for him. Fighting in the trenches, he'd found himself. "He is a different man," some said, and yet others said that in the trenches he'd *become* a man. The hate that roiled inside of him like smoke in a bottle, he'd finally had a chance to uncork it. Andy had never stopped wondering what it said about a man whose only way to become a man was killing another man. He never stopped wondering about a man who only came to life when he was warring under another person's command.

More than five years down the road from the betrayal, Andy still could not decide if Abe had taken that gun to him or if what he saw in that fog that day was a twisted image of his brother. His father had asked, "What gives him the right to kill himself?" Now Andy was asking, "What gave Abe the right to try to kill me?" In that mirror, those two questions more and more looked one and the same.

6

THE OLD LADY WAS WAITING for him on the porch steps. He pulled up and sat in the truck.

"What are you going to do with that wood?" She looked to have been up all night formulating that question.

"Good morning."

"Good morning. But I want to know about that wood."

"I figured start burnin' it today."

"Burn it?" There was alarm in her voice, as though the first and only option in Andy's mind was the last in hers.

"Well, I ain't gonna make sandwiches out of it. You've got two dozen cords still sitting at the back of your barn; you want another couple?"

"I thought you would sell it and give me the money. That was our agreement."

"I don't remember nothin' like that."

"My husband sold some to some people." She flung a hand toward town twenty miles away. "Why don't you see if they need any more? There is a lot of money in firewood."

"I'm happy to sell it, but I can't go knocking door-to-door. I don't have that kind of time."

"You have plenty of time!"

"If you say so, I got plenty of time, but I don't have the time for this in particular."

"You've got time for this too."

"It'd take me to next Christmas to get rid of all that." Andy laughed at the whole insane notion, and then, since he was in that frame of mind, asked, "How's your daughter doing?"

"Why do you worry about her so much?"

"Maybe cuz I'm a decent guy."

"Don't rub your own back; it doesn't look good. We will split the money. I'm not stingy."

"I'm more worried about getting those tomatoes in."

"You'll have time for that. Don't worry."

Andy massaged his forehead with a hand.

"You plan on helping me plant 'em?" he said, and with that same hand showed how seed by seed they'd need to be plugged into the ground.

She gave him a look.

"Okay. Okay. I'll do my best."

"*Affarem.*"

"Hold the hooplah till we see how it moves."

"Everyone will want some. You'll see."

He backed up the bobtail to a pile. The tree was cut the random way that a tree is cut when nothing other than burning it is the aim, which meant Andy had a helluva time stacking it in the truck bed in some decent order. When it was full, he turned the rig around, lumbered it toward the yard, and tooted his horn so that the old lady would see he'd made good on his word. He cut the engine and heard a torrent of piano music—Rachmaninoff, sounded like—of such intense and unbridled vigor it was as though the piece were a kind of revenge on Rachmaninoff for having had the audacity to write it.

The old lady came out, wiping her hands on an apron, and stopped a few feet from the truck, nodding favorably.

"See how good it looks?" she said, as though Andy had just prepared a basket of fruit for some honeymooners. "How much money do you think that will bring?"

"How much? How much you water your trees middle of winter?"

She narrowed her eyes, "What's your point?"

"I'll do my best. That I promise."

"I worry about your sour face. How can you sell anything with a face like that?"

"I ain't peddling vacuum cleaners."

"Make believe you are and see how far you get."

"I'll take your advice."

"Believe me." She told him to try this place and that.

Loaded down with logs, he drove all the way into town to Richard Topalian's sandwich shop. He showed Rich the wood and Rich said he had no room to store what he already had. More or less the same story at the other sandwich shops in town, though at one of these shops he did happen upon an old Armenian who claimed he'd been lookin' for hardy wood to carve the figure of Jesus-hanging-on-the-cross out of. Andy decided it sinful to charge money for wood intended for such a saintly end. He drove the old man home and lugged half a cord, two logs at a time, into his alleyway garage for free. If Andy couldn't fulfill his economic duty, at least he'd make a dent in his religious one.

He wanted to shave a little more off that truck or else the old lady might conclude he'd just parked it for the day, so he unloaded fifty logs or so in an abandoned field just off Elm Avenue.

Half the truck was empty, and he hadn't made a dime. He had twenty dollars in his wallet and figured he'd claim he'd fetched ten for the wood, half of which was his to keep. A five-dollar net loss— well worth it.

He was done peddling then, and with a few hours left in the day, he went home to see if his wife needed a break from the kids.

"What am I going to do? *You* take a break," she said. "When was the last time you had a break?"

"Why don't you go shopping or something." Andy pulled ten bucks out of his wallet. "I sold some of that wood there."

"Are you sure?"

"Go buy yourself something. You deserve it."

"I was hoping to get new sandals." She lifted her left foot to show him a hole in the one she was wearing.

"Ten bucks should cover it, no?"

"Yes."

He kissed her on a cheek and told her to take her time; he didn't need to head back out for a couple of hours.

She bundled up, and he watched her walk down the sidewalk. It made him happy, and it made her even prettier than usual that she was on her way to take care of herself.

Marky was napping on the couch, and Yervant was sitting on the floor surrounded by Tinkertoys. Andy watched him try to articulate one piece with another, again and again, until he tossed the parts away and looked up to see what more doable thing there was to do. Andy put his arms out. The boy looked around the room, like "Where's mom?"

"Egoor, hokees," he said, "Come, my soul," and he did come. Andy lifted him and made a swing of his arms and swung him back and forth, just like when he was a baby. His young body warm against his own acted like a compress for his soul. He closed his eyes and sang a song and Yervant laughed and squirmed, but after a few moments, to Andy's surprise, the boy started to doze. They lay down together on the bed. He was amazed at how he'd gone from a bachelor to this—a family man. Piece by piece, the invisible family engineer had disassembled and reassembled him into something utterly new. It reminded him of the way a soldier, after boot camp, looks up to find that his body, his mind, his soul has been manufactured to plug into the war machine. He was, at times, proud, and at other times petrified by this new organization of his person, but just now, in the soft afternoon light, he was mesmerized, the boy's breathing a kind of lullaby. Together they napped.

The phone rang. Andy pressed his boy against his chest like a shopping bag and headed up the hallway to the kitchen phone.

"Hello?"

"Andy, what's going on, *campano*?"

It was Zero.

"Hey, hey. How things going?"

"We're moving."

"Back to Italy is what I thought."

Zero told him he'd been in Los Angeles. Would he be up for a drink, say seven-thirty?

Andy noted the friendly tone of his voice, but he wasn't aiming to expand his society. He wanted to know if they were going to talk business or bullshit, and he put it to Zero more or less that way.

"Let's just say we got ourselves a proposition for you, but the way we work, a little bullshit is always part of the deal."

Andy chuckled and told him he'd see them there.

The call gave him a jolt. He'd almost written the Italian deal—as he'd come to refer to it—off.

It was getting on three o'clock. He put the boys in front of the TV and stepped outside on the porch for a smoke. He wondered how he would play the Italians; under what circumstances he'd accept their offer, under what he'd up the ante, under what he'd fold.

But here came his wife, sashaying up the sidewalk with a Gottschalks bag over her arm. He whistled to get her attention, to let her know how pretty she was.

"How'd you make out?"

"I think nice," she said, reaching for a box in the bag. "I hope you like them." She flipped the top open.

"Pretty."

"Something simple," she said.

"Enjoy them, sweetheart."

"Are you sure we can afford this?"

"Remember I was telling you about that Italian deal?"

"Yes."

"Well, the head honcho just called. He wants to talk business tonight."

"You have so many deals, Andy. I forget which one."

"Cotton. They might want me to manage some. Two hundred acres or so."

Her eyes perked up. "That's a big farm."

"We'll see."

"But it's a good job if you get it?"

"I'm not counting my beans yet. I don't want to say one thing and do another."

She nodded, and then a worry struck her.

"How would you do it with the tomatoes?"

"If it's money in our pockets, I'll make it work."

"You'll kill yourself."

He kissed her and said, "I gotta get this truck back to Chamichian's."

HE PULLED INTO THE YARD as quietly as the bobtail would allow. As soon as he opened his door, she opened her door at the back porch.

"Look! Bravo! Half the truck!"

"I can't do this another day."

"What do you mean?!"

"I mean I'm not in the wood-peddling racket. I worked ten hours today, and what did I come up with? A lousy fifteen bucks."

"Not bad."

"In total," he said. "Splitting that with you puts me around a buck an hour, and a backache to boot. It just ain't worth it. If it was in your head that we had such an agreement, you figure what them logs are worth and I'll make it up to you after the harvest."

"So you are going to pay me and throw it away?"

"If that's what it takes to make your day. And next round we'll put it in black and white so that we don't have no last-minute surprises on either side."

"I don't want you to do that."

"But you do want me to work until Jesus returns to get rid of it. It just won't fly."

"Was it that hard?"

He didn't want to talk about it. "I'll unload this tomorrow back out in the field." Andy opened the pickup door and got inside. Through the open window he said, "No hard feelings. I want you to put your mind to rest; just consider it like I bought the whole shebang myself."

"What's your rush? Come in and have some mint tea. Let's talk about it."

"I gotta get going."

"You're upset with me."

"Naw." He lit a cigarette and took a puff. She hadn't moved.

"You go home. Sleep on it and see what you think in the morning."

Andy shook his head. *"Adíos."*

This woman was like a meat grinder. He'd seen it before, how these *mayrigs* sit home doing up *kufte* with their chubby hands while mentally they are digging tunnels, laying booby traps, intercepting messages, and sending out others. And the children for all that food—the *sarma* and *lahmajoon* and kebobs—stop moving emotionally. Andy had known untold number of Armenian men who never left home, who at forty were coddled the same as when they were six. They were scared shitless of women on the one hand, and worshipped their mothers on the other: a weird combination. And how about Lilit? She was closed in on herself like a roly-poly, like at any second someone was gonna come around and step on her. Maybe her mom had made her afraid. Why did the other daughter choose to stay away?

Andy had seen versions of that too. Out of nowhere, one or another of the kids would stage a revolt. He'd known many an Armenian man first thing out of high school pack a suitcase and hit the road with no more than a few dollars in his pockets. Along the way he might reinvent himself, change his name from Sulahian, say, to Michaelson, shack up with a blonde-haired girl named Melissa and disappear into the underworld of Vegas or Reno.

ANDY WALKED INTO THE BAR and just like last time the Italians were sitting in a corner booth, for who knows how long. They smiled, stood to greet him, and slapped him on the back. Andy ordered a scotch and for half an hour or so they passed the shit this way and that before Andy looked at his watch and told the Italians he had to be moving and, not to force the issue, but if they wanted to talk business, now was as good a time as any. The Italians liked to drink, that was a fact, and they liked to throw their arms around and cackle, but when they got down to business they sobered up lickety-split.

Zero bent over and said in a hush-hush tone, "Andy, here's what we like to see. We've been thinking about it good. We'd like to see you farm this acreage. The bottom line is we want you to be part of our team." He winked at Andy.

"Kind of catches me off guard, to be honest with you guys."

The Italians nodded, sympathetic.

"Not that I'm not interested in your proposal…Anyway, go ahead. I'm listening."

"But are you interested?"

"I'm listening. I'm listening good."

"Nexts. We want you to farm corn. That's our determination."

"Corn. Okay." Andy wasn't sure himself whether that "okay" meant "I hear you" or "I'm happy to sign on the dotted line."

"I like this Andy," Zero said to Eddie.

Eddie said, "Hey, we were neighbors."

"The rest of it: it's up to you," Zero said. "From there on. You call the shots." He threw his hands up to show they were empty of decisions.

"I'm glad I've got your confidence."

"And we need your, what you call, confidence. There's nothing we like more than confidence. You see."

"It's what oils everything. That and money."

"So far so good, huh?"

"Like I said," and to emphasize it Andy took a big gulp of scotch.

They were pleased with themselves. Everybody was pleased all around. Except they hadn't come there for pleasure.

"Now there's the dough: how much, when, this and that. Here's what we propose on that front. We put the money up. All of it. Whatever it takes to make it happen. Whatever you need."

"You'll need equipment. A combine, a seeder. You could buy it or rent it."

"Again, Andy, whatever you decide. This comes from the top. Not just me and Eddie talkin' here now."

"You mean the money people. The financers."

"That's right."

Andy laughed a tad. "Let's take care of that when we come to it. But as a way to start the conversation, I think you make sense."

"Does this sound like it makes sense to you, Andy? Tell me. Be honest with me if it doesn't."

"I'm being square with you. But who do I answer to? I assume you guys?"

"You answer to us, we answer to them."

"Lines of credit I assume you guys'll establish with the suppliers."

Andy's credit was zero—shit, less than zero.

"We pay everything with cash. See. We don't believe in lines of banks, lines of credit, none of that."

Cash? Who ran his operation on cash anymore? On the other hand, if he had taken that approach—his father's approach ("You want something, make sure you've got means to pay for it right there and then"), the approach of all those old-timers, he would have been forced to stopped spending long before he was broke; he might not have shit-tanked with *his* creditors.

"Gonna be a little clumsy, but I suppose we can make it swim."

"Then there's what we pay you. That too is an issue."

"In any deal I've signed on to."

"You gave us a figure, ballpark. We discussed it. But we'd like to propose a kind of partnership. We'd like to see you more than just a hired hand."

"I'm listening."

"And in a team the kind we're thinkin' here, we don't pay you, we don't hand a check to you like a punk. That would be an insult. No, we see the picture something different. We see you taking a cut of the nut."

"So, you're proposing a deal where I get money on the back end, depending how the deal rings up."

Eddie said, "That's how we divvy it up with all our farm managers."

Andy studied it for a beat and said, "I've got to tell you, if paying me a salary amounts to an insult, I've known worse. No. I need something more regular. Maybe you can consider a different picture: part partner, part hired hand."

"You're thinking maybe we'd take the money and run?"

"Nothing like that," he said, though in fact the thought had occurred to him. "I just need, you know, money to live on. It's simple arithmetic from where me and my family stand."

They went back and forth like this for another few minutes and finally agreed on a deal that would give Andy five hundred bucks a month. On the back end, Andy would capture 20 percent of the net profit off the crop.

The whole time, Andy had to suppress his happiness because he didn't want to let on to the Italians his desperation.

On his way home, he thought of the goddamn people he owed money to, he pictured walking into their air-conditioned offices and tossing a wad of dough on their fat desks. "Here's your money," he'd tell them. He'd thank them for their patience, their goodwill, telling them just the opposite of the facts to better rub it in their faces. "Our worries are over," he'd be able to tell his wife. The sweetest words a man ever said.

THE NEXT MORNING, ANDY GOT OUT to Chamichian's a little later than usual. It was chilly and clear-skied. In his boots, he trod over the frosted dirt, diesel can in hand. At four points around each of the piles he poured a gallon or so of fuel, lit a scrap of rag, and tossed it on.

From deep inside white smoke rose through the flames, and in no time that smoke began to pile up and stretch across the sky the color of dirty snow. Andy walked between the bonfires, satisfied that finally he'd be free of those trees and the whole uncanny history they were tangled up with.

The old lady stayed in the house, but Lilit stood just off the road on the south side of the field, apparently mesmerized.

As he made toward her he could feel the infernos tugging at his shirt, giving a sense of the ocean of oxygen they were leaching from the atmosphere. The dog was lying off to the side, underneath a tree. Andy watched it raise its big head and look Andy once over before it went back to dozing.

"*Parev,*" hello, he said.

She jumped, as though Andy had approached her from behind. The poor thing was skittish as a jackrabbit. He could almost see her heart beating against her chest.

"Hello," she answered.

"What do you say?"

"It's nice," she said, about the fire.

He nodded his head in agreement.

"It turns the world upside down." She shifted her hand at the wrist to show him how. "It wears many masks and never the same one twice."

He nodded his head again, as though this were perfectly obvious, and then paused, and nodded again, because it was in fact perfectly, even profoundly, obvious. He sized her up for the first time now, up close. Her hair was long, chaotically cut, and it dropped on either side of her big black eyes in licorice-thick twists. Her narrow brow was furled, nearly frozen that way, as though she were solving some interminable riddle in her head.

He turned his attention back to the fires. He had always been intrigued by human oddities—the old ladies with humps on their backs, men who lived alone with homing pigeons their only friends, the mentally lame like Lilit. In a way, he himself was one such oddity: from polio, his right leg was tapered to the semblance of a baseball bat, and his ankle, from several operations, had lost its definition, as though it had been fashioned from wax and left out in the sun for too long.

The dog stood now and trotted to Lilit's side. He cocked his head to take Andy in.

"Come," she said in Armenian. "I have something to show you."

He paused, wondering what.

"Something nice," she said.

"Sure," he said, but he wasn't sure at all. She was harmless, almost painfully sincere, but he wasn't sure he wanted to follow her anywhere.

"*Egoor,*" she said, come.

In the house, he could hear the old lady snoring. After all that tumult surrounding those trees, amazing, Andy thought, that she was now napping through their immolation.

"*Hos spaseh,*" wait here, she said.

He didn't like waiting in the parlor with that ugly dog. It sniffed around the furniture, then stood, staring at him.

"What the hell do you want?!" he told it.

Maybe he'd feed him those rancid nuts.

He had reached for a handful when she came out holding a cardboard sheaf, dressed up like a birthday present with two blue ribbons.

"*Nesteh hod,*" sit there, she said, and he did, on the couch.

Then she handed him this present. Her black eyes were deadly serious, as though he was her longtime friend to whom she was about to divulge some longtime secret. He untied the ribbons respectfully as possible and flipped opened the sheaf.

It was a watercolor of a little girl, dressed up in a purple gown, standing on toe with her other leg extended stiff as a broomstick behind her. The dancer's chin was pointed regally outward, and one white arm was stretched in front of her, the other dramatically raised above her head. The finger of that hand bore a shiny silver ring. That was something, but nothing compared to the backdrop: a kaleidoscopic world made of whorls and balloons and curlicues of different hues—the stuff of dreams.

Andy studied it for a good two, three minutes, struck over and over in that short span of time by this woman's otherworldly imagination.

He looked up at her. She was sweating. Her face, from the strain on her nerves, was jumping like a bowl of water hit at the rim with a stick.

"It's pretty," he said, and he meant it. He asked if he could look at another.

"Yes," she said.

He put that one gently aside for the next: the same girl, apparently, against a similarly rich background, sitting on a floor with a red box between her legs. Its lid is flipped open and her head is flopped to one side. Her face is a China doll's—slanted eyes and all, white skin glowing like snow. Her hair is straight and black and it reaches the floor, and her perfectly shaped lips are a weird, phosphorescent green. In one hand she holds a blue toy block, in the other a white one. She is neither studying the blocks nor seems ready to drop them; she is just holding them, oddly, as though she were set there for precisely and only that mysterious purpose.

Andy heard the old woman grunt, like a startled pig, and then groan.

Lilit reached over and grabbed the pictures from off of Andy's lap and started in a panic with them toward her room.

"Lilit?" her mother asked.

Andy had no idea what to do next. Would it be rude if he just left like that?

"Lilit."

"Hos em," I'm here, she said from the hallway, a tremor in her voice.

Andy's own heart picked up a step. He stood and went through the kitchen and then quietly opened door. It was getting on early evening. The fire had settled down, burning in piles quietly as lanterns.

Andy drove slowly down the road. The long shadows of the palm trees extended in front of him like the rungs of a ladder. He felt disturbed by that innocent visit, like he was on the threshold of some transgression. Where was the law against admiring a painting? Why did he feel that way? The mother, she was the reason. An admonitory odor seeped from the old woman's room; he could smell it all the while there. He rolled down the window to get some fresh air. The figures, he tried to pin down the gist of them—a haunting amalgam of porcelain and flesh, a girl imprisoned in some misbegotten game.

7

ANDY COULD FEEL THE EARTH oppose him as he ripped it with the disc; he could almost smell the mineral-rich sea welling to the surface. He had just made a turn on the tractor and was diving back in when an old pickup, from a distance a '37 or '38 Studebaker, looked like, came wobbling up the main road. Who the hell? The truck came up on the shed and stopped. Andy lifted the till and pulled off the field.

Out of the truck stepped a tall, rail-thin black man. Andy parked the tractor, hopped off, and nodded. The man doffed his straw hat and nodded back. He'd either recently lost a shitload of weight or inherited his wardrobe from some fat kin, because his loose jeans were cinched up by a leather belt that was several notches too long, so that it draped over his side pocket.

He stood kind of sideways, as though any second he might bolt. "Howdy," he said. He rubbed his throat, like he was fixing a necktie.

"Howdy to you. You folks lookin' for something?" Andy acknowledged the man still in the car.

"Yessir. Looks like you're working it up good and all."

"Uh-huh."

"Fine stretch. Mind my askin, you puttin' up cotton?"

"Corn."

He flicked at his white-dusted lip with a finger. "Reason: I'm lookin' fer work. Any kind'll do."

Andy shook his head, we ain't got none, sorry.

The man nodded sympathetically.

But seeing as how he'd come a ways, "Where parts you from?" Andy asked.

"Town a Corcoran."

"You a cotton-picker by chance?"

"All my kin clear back to Oklahoma."

"Used to be a lot of black Okies these parts back, huh?"

"Yessir. We done all the pickin'."

Andy knew what had happened, but he asked anyway, "What happened?"

"Machines. Done put us outta work. Pickin', I'm fast as a jackrabbit, but not fast 'nough. Thas what happen."

"Huh."

"I can do more than pickin'. Do just 'bout anything come farmin.'"

"That right?"

"Yessir. Thas right."

"I'm Andy Demerjian." Andy put out a hand.

"Thomas Jefferson."

"That's some name you got."

"Yessir. That'd be third president this here country."

"You related?" Andy asked in fun.

"Somes says we is."

Andy laughed. "Who's your friend?"

"Oh, he no friend; he my brother. Any kinda work, cleanin' up, 'paring fences, I'd be mighty 'preciative."

"You're sure hungry."

"Yes, I am."

Andy wasn't thinking of that kind of hunger. "You got a family, Thomas?"

"Yessir. Three little 'uns, not counting the missus."

"I got myself two kids, plus the wife. You drive a tractor, I imagine."

"Like a cotton gin gins."

"I hadn't really planned on it, and to be honest, I'm just a farm manager here so I'm barely squeezing by myself, but maybe I can use you a little."

"'Preciate it."

"Here and there, that is. I can pay you minimum, four bits an hour, as I need you."

"Whatever you got to spare in your pocket."

"I can't promise you any kind of salary, now. And definitely I don't got 'nough work for two men."

"He go where I go. Don't mean he's lookin' fer wages, though."

Andy looked over at the brother.

The brother nodded.

"You want me to finish that up?"

This was all going down pretty fast, but then again, for a man who is famished, fast isn't fast enough.

"All right. Go ahead."

Tom straightened that tie for a second time, obviously a kind of tick when he felt in a pickle, and asked if Andy might be able to pay him at the end of the day.

Andy had twelve dollars in his pocket. He'd counted it that morning.

"I'll make things good by you. Let me see how you ride that tractor. I want it deep but not too deep on that tiller."

"I'll work it up pretty as frostin' on a weddin' cake."

"I'll be watching."

Tom hopped on, sure-footed as a rodeo star.

Andy was particular about how to farm, even something as elementary as corn: from tilling to leveling to seeding and all the rest, he just couldn't stomach sloppy work. Probably too particular, he admitted. It had troubled his brother. Abe was satisfied to space the vines "more or less" three feet apart, or leave "more or less" three spurs at pruning, or just throw the tools in the barn and shut the door. Twice a week, Andy would spend a few hours correcting Abe's shabby work.

Tom rumbled out, swung the tractor around, and pulled the till in smooth as an alligator levels his tail into a swamp. He watched Tom, one hand on the shift and the other on the wheel, turn to get a good look at how it grooved in behind. Andy scrutinized the dust that flared up and the tractor's speed. He watched the till bob and took notice how Tom eased up nice but not timid where it grabbed. The brother sat in the car. Andy thought maybe he was a dimwit under Tom's care. He let him sit.

Tom pulled to the end of the drive. To save a few seconds or to show off, plenty of drivers would barrel on through, stress the tranny or brakes, risk a flip or overshoot their next drive. Plenty of men would do that, but not so Tom; he lifted the till, geared down, and instead of swinging it around fast like a big shot, he threaded the tractor back in with a nice, neat arc. Plenty to learn by the way a man drives a tractor.

Now Andy felt a tad bad for the brother. He walked over with a jug of water and offered him a drink.

"Thankee."

"Welcome." Something was up with the guy's left eye. It was jittery, out of sync with the right one, like it was suspicious of its twin.

"Your brother there is a decent tractor driver."

He shook his head and said, "Oh, he damn good. The best. Everything he do he do good." Unlike Tom he spoke rapidly, nervously. "Thas the way he is."

He took the jug and poured some into his mouth.

Andy wondered if he'd done time; maybe he was on parole, under his brother's watch. He flat-out asked him.

"You on parole?"

He flat-out answered, "They give me one year."

Andy nodded.

They turned their heads to watch the dust rise angrily from the back of the till.

"Sorry to see you sittin' here like this, but I just ain't got enough work for two men. Barely enough for one besides myself."

"No, no, no. Thas awright. I juss be sittin' here."

Andy swatted a fly away from his nose.

"But if you got extry work, I be happy givin' you a hand. No charge. Just for the exise."

"I couldn't do that."

"Just for the exise. Blood flow."

Andy thought about it.

"Well, if you want to get your blood flowing, you can help me out sweeping that barn. Get you outta this sun a little too. But as a matter of principle, I don't care to have a man sweat on my behalf without some measure of pay."

The man hopped out of the car.

"I'm sorry, I didn't catch your name."

"Woolie," he said, but Andy assumed he meant "Willie."

"All right, Willie."

The Italians had outfitted the barn with a cement floor, but they hadn't bothered to sweep it since the day it was poured. From beneath the door dirt had blown in and settled an inch thick, black as pitch. He handed Willie a big push broom and set him loose. Willie got in there and started working that broom like he was stoking some fire to keep from freezing. From the black fog it threw up you could barely see him anymore. Andy's lungs were starting to feel it, so he stepped outside, shaking his head at the vast difference between the two men. One moved around like a ballerina, the other like some big-time wrestler. Brothers, he thought; sometimes the only thing they got in common is a last name. Sometimes not even that.

Tom had idled the rig and was walking toward Andy.

He waited for him, taking account of his unhurried yet economical pace.

"This here broke off." He handed a bracket to Andy.

"Rusted. Must've come off the weigh box. Left or right side?"

"Left."

"Was it bouncin' around?"

"Some."

"It should work, but we gotta be a little delicate with it until I find the part."

"Git it made, faster."

"Think so? Probably right. I'll go down to the foundry first thing."

"Yessir."

"You want to finish up?"

"Yessir."

"You're a good tractor driver, Thomas."

Thomas blinked and nodded his head, like he'd been waiting since the day he'd last picked cotton to hear it.

ANDY HAD PLANNED TO WORK the corn and tomatoes by himself, hiring whoever he needed come harvest. He had steeled himself to swing back and forth sixty some-odd miles two times a day, split his time and brain in half, until he'd dropped from exhaustion.

It was money out of his pocket, a few less dollars at the end of the week, but he just couldn't let Tom go. If he were just an extra hand, that would be one thing, but as it turned out, Tom was an extra brain. He saw each step that needed be taken as clearly as Andy saw it. He had this picture in his head of the dirt, this picture in his head of the crop, and knew exactly what needed to happen to bring those two pictures together. Most farmers put one foot in front of the other and hoped they'd end up in the right place at the end of the season. Tom was the kind of man that cleared that very path so that the men he worked for might not lose a step.

Willie, the brother, didn't have the same genius; he was a body needed to be moving. Once he got moving, though, there was no stopping him, like there were three men inside of him all waiting their turn. So he hired him too. More money out of his pocket.

He gave Willie the job of knocking the weeds down around the perimeter, a more or less endless chore. "Go at it, Willie," he said, and handed him a hoe. Tom he put on the tractor. His goal was to break up that earth, give it room to breathe and means to drain before leveling it with a scraper and smoothing it with a plane.

Not that Andy took his eye off their work, or the ranch. He was out there every single day even when he didn't have to be out there. Even if he did nothing more than sweat a little under that particular patch of sun.

By Saturday they'd broken up all but thirty acres of dirt. Andy had gotten used to going out, Sunday was the same as Wednesday, and so when he should've been saying his prayers at church he found himself barreling his truck toward the corn. As he approached Avenue 6, he saw from out of the unrelenting flatness a great plume of dust 'round about what looked like the middle of the ranch. By God, it *was* the ranch. The till was throwing up a spectacular cloud of dust, big as a cumulous. He'd been pushing 80 mph on Avenue 26, but now he punched it up to ninety to faster see what the hell.

What the hell was right.

It was no till, and it wasn't Tom or Willie. It was a scraper operated by two chalk-white men: one on the tractor, the other on the ground twenty or so yards in front signaling with two hands like he was directing a jumbo jet. He had no idea what they were doing. From either side of the scraper the dust flared and ferociously tumbled.

Andy drove up just close enough to make them think he might be appointed to size up their work, waited for that tidal wave of particles to pass, and stepped out of the cab. Ground control saw him first and put his two hands up and pumped the air. The operator cut the engine.

With the machine dead, the dust rocked forward and over-whelmed them.

"Howdy," Andy said.

The two men came out of the dusty tumult squinting. "Howdy."

"Looks like you guys are scrapin'?" Andy asked.

They turned around to gauge their progress.

"Look plumb t'ya?" the operator asked.

"Looks just fine."

"Yew one uh the owners?"

"I manage the place."

"Said they was gonna pay cash. We were figurin' to have beer money by end a the day."

"You got a week's worth of work here, don't you think, before anyone cuts you a check?"

"Naw. He told us cut a hunder'-yard path."

"A hundred-yard path? Are you gentleman sure you're at the right place?"

"Whudya mean?" the ground guy asked.

The driver said, "Wayul, this here's where they tode us. Northwest corner a 6 and 80. Told us to scrape zackley hundred yards down the middle of the ranch."

"May I ask who told you?"

The driver looked back at the earth he'd moved, a little worried.

"Why oncha go get them direkshuns, Ricky."

The Okie spit a loogie out on the dirt.

Ricky slapped some dust off his jeans and walked on over to their beat-up pickup. He opened the door, leaned over, and righted himself with a piece of paper in hand.

"Sez right here. This here's whayer we 'sposed to be."

Ricky handed it to him. Andy saw the directions, a name scribbled next to it: Zero Torrentino.

"So Zero asked you guys to do this work, looks like."

Ground control sniggered. "Zero. We just got a kyik outta that name."

"That's the Italian," the driver said.

Now it was Andy's turn for a ribbing.

"Yew sure yer the farm manager?"

"Looks dubious, don't it?"

"Sure the heck duz."

"I'll let you gentleman get back to your work, then. I guess I might ask you: He say what it was for?"

They shook their heads no, then Ricky said, "Sumpn."

Something. Andy felt a little stupid, sure, like the last guy at the dance party to discover a rip in the seat of his slacks, and he was inclined to stay put till Zero arrived to settle up with the Okies, but he was scheduled to meet him out there the next day anyhow and so he let it pass. It just bothered him that they'd done it without his consultation. He imagined this wouldn't be the first time he'd have to defer to the authority of Zero. No, he supposed that no matter what the Italians said about farming it his way, he'd now and again have to step aside and let them have it their way.

THE NEXT MORNING, ZERO CAME bumbling down the road in his Cadillac an hour late, absent his sidekick. He pulled up to the barn, looking disheveled, like he been up until late, or wasn't used to getting up early.

Zero got out of the car, stretched his back. They exchanged "good morning"s and Andy said, "Why don't you and me drive around here a little and I'll give you a tour what I'm aiming to do."

Zero said okay and they both stepped up into Andy's truck. Andy doubled back toward the road and then turned left and drove the perimeter of the ranch. He made curlicues with his finger and said what he'd done so far is turn the land over, chew up the weeds, bring the good stuff up to the surface to let the soil breathe. Next he'd have to level it, spread out a nice layer of manure, and then work it all back into the dirt. Zero nodded and said if that was Andy's choice, "So be it." Andy said he appreciated the fact that he was leaving that up to him, and they turned now down the center of the ranch.

Andy told Zero how he aimed to space the rows thirty inches apart and, to facilitate a nice cross-pollination, he'd leave just about half a foot between seeds. What type of corn was another decision had to be made, but since it was field corn they were after, the decision came down to two, flint or dent, and Andy was probably going to go with flint.

Zero asked a few questions about the two corns, and asked if they grew about the same height, which Andy thought was an odd question but perfectly in keeping with how little the man knew about farming per se. Andy didn't know the answer to this question but answered it anyway, saying, "Same difference," and next he told him they could decide, Andy supposed, near about harvest time whether to leave the silage on the ground for the next year or turn it around for feed material as well. Furrows would have to be put up, especially in such mineral-rich soil, as opposed to subirrigation or border check for a good many reasons, so that's probably the way he'd go, but first, of course, he'd have to scrape the land best he could to get the furrows to carry it nice and regular, which brought him, quite literally, to his next point.

Andy had rolled up to the Okies' lane. He hit the brakes like it was a river that his truck could plummet into.

"And there's your scraper work," he said. "I came by yesterday and saw two boys doing it up. But they weren't doing it up, really. They were just doing it up for a stretch. Did you figure on this path here being some kind of test run for the whole block?"

Zero answered, "What do you think?"

"Decent work, but like I said."

Zero got out of the car, walked toward the path. "It's a landing strip."

He said it like Andy had just asked him what that squatty porcelain thing in the bathroom was used for.

"There's the last thing would've occurred to me."

"The boss wants to be able to fly in and out. Frisco, Detroit, Chicago. All over the map. And he don't go by car."

"I'll be damned. So there'll be a plane running in and out of here."

"He likes to keep his eyes on his investment."

"All that dust is gonna complicate our mite situation."

Zero started walking along the edge of the landing strip, inspecting it the way umpires inspect infields between innings. He walked half its length, paying more attention to it than anything Andy had said over the last half hour. When he saw a clod, he'd bend over and step gingerly in his pointy leather shoes to pick it up.

"If that's the case," Andy said, as though the shoe had asked a question, "I figure you need a nice big roller out here. That'll get rid of them little clods agitating you out of proportion."

"Why don't you order that up."

"Like lasagna. Hell, I'd've set the whole thing up for you, if I knew. Done it right the first time."

"We just had this here in the works before you came on board."

"Be happy to complete the job."

"It's in your hands now." He stabbed a finger at Andy.

"So, anyway. We're going to need us some equipment." Andy reached over for another clod, to show he'd do whatever it took to make things smooth.

"You get it. Like we said."

"We're talking about buying it, here? Or renting? Is that your call or mine?"

"We're going to need it more than this season, right?"

"True enough."

"There's our answer."

Zero said he'd have the money for him tomorrow, and asked how much he needed.

"I figure three, thirty-five hundred bucks should get us started."

"No problem."

"That's it."

"That's it, then."

Except for that one hitch with the landing strip, everything was proceeding so smoothly it made Andy a tad uncomfortable. He wasn't used to smooth. No, he was used to boulders and roadblocks and narrow escapes, barely squeezing through. Maybe, foreign as it felt, he thought, this is how people with money and a track record of accomplishments do it: without fuss, without hemming and hawing. They see a problem, they solve it. They see an opening, they take it.

8

AT FIRST, THE OLD LADY TRIED to court him with sweet touches and friendly calls, invited him in for *lahmajoon* or toted refreshments, lemonade, or cold mint tea out to wherever he happened to be working. Time and again he turned her down. He told her that his wife's sack lunch would do and that he only drank water when he worked (which was true) and that he had a nice cold canteen of it up on the tractor or under the elm tree.

All Andy could see was how her charms were devices for turning him into a proxy for her husband. He figured if he took the bait, next thing she'd be asking him to drive her into town for a doctor's visit, or get up on the roof to connect the TV antenna—that kind of thing. Andy suspected that part of the reason she'd rented the land to him and not someone else was because she felt he would be hers to control once he'd signed on the dotted line. It didn't work. After trying every which way to make him concede to that clause, she reversed direction and watched him like he might roll the twenty-two acres up and run away with it over the border. He wouldn't be surprised if she had a little voodoo doll of him up in her cupboards that she bound in rubber bands as a last resort. And as for the daughter, that first innocent adventure into her clandestine doll world was the last. Andy suspected that her mother had put her through the fifth degree for being friendly with him. It was just as well. God knows she might fabricate some fantasy where Andy was trying to sneak a hand up Lilit's skirt.

Days she'd sit in that old metal chair, with that dog at her heels, studying Andy's every move for a two- or three-hour stretch, like she planned to write a treatise on the subject of tomato farming, pausing only to scratch herself, or that mutt, or make notes with a finger in the dirt. He didn't know in what way Lilit was interested in him, frankly. Maybe because he was kind to her, talked to her, maybe because he was a man 'round about her age. Could be her image of him went further, deeper, into some phantasmal hole, into a fantasy doll world he didn't much care to entertain. He'd nod his head to acknowledge her presence, and that's about it.

By mid-March the plants had thrown off their jackets and stood at their most defenseless. Every day Andy would pace the field, back and forth, judging their hunger, looking for predators, but most crucially—at the time of year—mulling over the atmosphere. It had been clear-skied, absolute as a summer day, but the moisture was there in the air. Temperature was the only card left to play. March 20, he felt it ominously dip.

He walked next door to Takahashi's, where he'd seen spare rubber. Huts of mud wasps clutched to the portico ceiling. A couple of dead black widows were curled up waiting transport there for dinner. Under the eaves, he saw several dilapidated sparrows' nests. Andy couldn't decide if such neglect was a sign of mental depression, laziness, or Japanese tradition that had a man leave things in state for a certain number of years out of respect. He shook his head from disgust, just as Vince opened the door.

"Hey, Vince."

He stood, slump-shouldered, in the same ugly pair of overalls he always wore. Andy wondered whether he had a dozen pair that all looked the same or only one pair that he washed and wore time and again.

"Andy." He said his name with as much emotion as if he'd been repeating it to himself half the day.

"What are you hiding in there?"

"Nuttin'."

Vince opened the screen and stepped outside.

When the parents were alive, he'd amounted to a flunky for them. Now he was good as a hermit.

"I was wonderin', you got any spare rubber sittin' around?"

"You worried?"

"Not yet, but I'm getting ready to worry just in case. What do you think?" he asked Vince.

"I ain't worried."

"Your dad put together any machine to tackle frost? Was that trick ever up his sleeve?"

Vince grunted and walked over toward the shed.

"When's the last time these trees got hit?"

"Over theres. 'Bout six, seven years ago now." He pointed his chin at twenty, thirty young stock. "Looked same as Satan's spawn come through here. One day they were up like this," he put his arms above his head, "and the next day limp," he let them drop.

Andy reached for a pack of cigarettes in his shirt pocket and tapped one out for himself, then one for Vince. They lit their cigarettes and in silence for a spell they smoked.

"I'd never seen nothin' like it. The arms turned black as licorice."

"You're talkin' black frost."

"It wadn't no Jack Frost."

"Huh."

"I seen it comin', too. 'Dad', I says, 'You know, Chamich, Markarian, they're all movin' around gettin' ready like a hurricane's comin'."

"Setting their smudge pots up."

"But, naw, he didn't care to move."

"Instead did one of them Buddhist chants or something?"

"Went to bed normal is all."

"Just didn't believe it'd hit him?"

"Like he was playin' chicken with it. Claimed nobody could foretell when frost'd hit. There wadn't what you called no science to it. It hit you or it din't."

"I'll be damned. I'd've loved to have seen him and old man Chamichian go head to head on that philosophy."

"That's what he claimed."

"Hadn't he ever heard of dew point?"

"He was funny." Vince laughed, but not lightheartedly.

"What I hear, he was funny in a lot of ways."

Vince shook his head, like he missed the old man and at the same time was relieved he was gone.

Andy said, "Sometimes I think hiding out on a farm too long turns any man funny."

"I don't even know why he made them pots. Never used them I recollect. Got to be fifty, sixty in the shed jus' sittin' there."

The crude oil–burning lanterns were one of the only means a farmer had at his disposal to generate some heat in the field. When their smoke caught in the inversion layer it placed what amounted to a cast-iron lid over the crop.

"All you got to do is raise the temperature a smidgen. Shooting some water down the rows helps…"

"If you get it down in time."

"'If' is right."

Andy flicked the last of his cigarette to the dirt and stamped it out with his boot.

"Funny, I remember first time I saw a pot in action. I was probably six, seven. Across the street old man Schaeffer had ten acres of pomegranates. It's gotta be mid-May and I see him putting one down here, another there. No idea their purpose, I think, 'What the heck?' I remember it was cold as hell that night, and the next morning I wake to see through my bedroom window somethin' black as a witch's cowl hovering over his orchard. It scared the daylights out of me."

Andy chuckled. Vince managed a grin.

"I run looking for my mom. 'Mom,' I tell her, 'something happened to the air up there over Schaeffer's trees.' To my little imagination, I thought the devil had leveled a curse on our poor neighbor. She led me outside and showed how that very same evil hung over our vines; Dad had been burning tires since the wee hours of the morning. Now everybody was cursed!'"

"He save 'em?"

"Both men harvested that season, so must've saved them some. So how about the rubber?"

"Plenty on the south side of the shed. Go ahead."

Andy stayed out longer and longer, until night fell and then some. When he got home, first thing he'd put in a call to the airport to get a reading on the dew point and temperature. Both were regularly setting up around thirty-six.

In time, every farmer was starting to worry. Even Vince. "I don't like the smell of this weather."

Andy said, "You had no worries a couple of days ago."

"I say now it's a trend. Every six or seven years, nature don't regard its own rules."

"Nature is the rule."

"Turn them tomatoes a yers tuh toast. I wouldn't be jokin'."

"Not if I can fuckin' help it."

"Good luck."

TRUE, THERE WASN'T A HELLUVA LOT to do to protect a tomato plant if it came, but Andy wasn't about to just sit there. He went searching for even more tires. For two bucks a piece from a retread outfit in town he secured a dozen on top of the dozen he had. He tossed them on his truck bed and one by one dropped them at the top of the field. He'd already set up irrigation pipes on the rows.

Every night before he went to sleep, he put his eye to the mercury. When it got below thirty-six, he put a call into the Fresno Air Terminal to estimate how low the freezing point might go. As far as the corn went, Tom was on high alert. Short of sleeping in his car on the side of the tomato field, Andy had little option but to pop out of bed and tromp to the porch every evening at about midnight to check the temperature. On March 27, the daytime temperature was bad. Nine p.m. he called the airport. The weather guys told him it was freezing just below six thousand feet. He went to sleep, but he didn't really sleep. He got up a little before eleven. He turned on the porch light and saw it was dropping hard. Right away, he called Tom. The wife, her name was Marilyn, answered:

"He'd done left aweady for da cohn."

"Sorry to wake you."

"Das awright."

He put on his clothes quick, two layers of shirts beneath a wool jacket, checked on the kids, and headed on out.

The moon was white and bruising bright. He got in the car, rolled the window down, and turned the heat on full blast. At this critical juncture, he would stand no obstruction between himself and nature; he wanted to suffer it on his skin, know just how cold, and let his arm out there be the thermometer. The stars sparked more than sparkled. From the smell and faint flickering in the fields, he could already tell some farmers had started their pots burning. The dogs felt agitated by it all and began their preposterous howls.

What the hell—Vince was sitting in the middle of the field in his pickup with the headlights on. Not one smudge pot was burning. Probably had a thermometer on the dash, watching every tick down. Before Andy set the tires on fire, he had to get water running down the rows or else he'd choke from the smoke. He quick pulled the truck up to the standpipe. His arm was near 'bouts frozen, and his hand didn't quite grasp. It slipped off the door, landing him bad-foot-first fast onto the hard dirt, twisting his ankle. "Fuck!" he yelled. The pain made him shudder, but he had no time to baby it, and anyway, the cold air would work like an ice pack. He said fuck again, quick turned the wheel, and got the water gushing up the standpipe. He listened to it come until he could hear it churn in its concrete hull and then opened the valve and sent the water down the ditch shivering. The moon powdered the field like some incandescent silt, but it was still no daylight, and so he worked down the rows, his ankle throbbing, by a kind of instinct. He dropped to a knee, put his hand down there, felt the water pass, took the elbow-shaped pipe in his hands, put one end to his mouth, and quick sucked and gently laid it back on the berm. With the other hand, he felt for its warm flow on the other end. With his palms turned open inches from the ground he looked like a beggar showing he had nothing to his name. He'd set the pipes up every third row, but now he was beginning to think every second would've been smarter. He proceeded, sloshing forward in the frigid air, knocking down the rows he'd covered in his head because there was no other way of telling in the dark. At one point he stopped because his lungs were starting to sting from the cold. He figured the water might take a bite out of the sting—it was like sipping a hot toddy compared to the temperature of the air—and so he cupped some up from the ditch and drank. Dripping from the chin, he looked up. The moon was razor-sharp, menacing.

By the time he was done, three hours later, his knees were slick with mud, his torso steaming, his face frozen cold, one boot sopping, and his fingers might've well been kindling, to give a sense of how numb they'd become. Before he rose, his mind veered suddenly inward: the strange life of a farmer, he thought. The stupidity of battling nature, for what: tomatoes? He felt desperate and ridiculous as some widower turned to the occult. He got up off his knees and let the thought drain down the row away with the water.

Limping back down avenue, from polio and now the hell of that sprain, he grabbed the diesel can from the cab of his truck, half by sight, half by touch. He pulled on some leather gloves he'd tossed beside that can, doused with diesel a rag tied to the top of a yard-long cast-iron pipe, and lit it with a match. He carried it through the dark like a primitive lighting his way home. He swung the can over the tire and then dropped the rod down on it until it caught. The rubber threw up garish orange flames, but the rolling black smoke they shed vanished directly into the night. One by one he lit them, each tire catching and illuminating the way a little better to the next.

He shut the water valves and looked down the avenue. The tires were like twenty squatty candles set there to cleanse the land following some calamity, not to avert one. Their flames gave the field a wild luminescence. He had forgotten his watch, but he figured it coming on five o'clock. Now all he could do was keep the tires going and pray the smoke would catch in the inversion layer and flatten out over the field, trapping the air. Every now and then he'd step on the field, feel the leaves and stems. To estimate the ground temperature he'd drop to his knees and place his hands palm down on the ground, the way some Christians do on the bodies of those they hope to heal. He needed five or six degrees. It was touch and go.

He'd just finished another prayer, maybe his seventh that night, when there was a faint thinning of the dark. Within minutes, the sun came over the Sierras so that the mountains glowed like iron drawn from a blacksmith's forge. Over his field, the smoke hovered like a tar roof. Rolling balls of smoke shed off the tires, chalky and black, pools of oily dross darkening the dirt around them. Sunlight the color of maple syrup slathered the field, and now the plants came into focus. Frost could come quick and coat the plant like varnish, or hoar up. There was no evidence of the latter. He paced the field squeezing the stems and the tiny buds between his fingers, feeling for the freeze. He found none.

The vines had made it out alive. By God, they'd survived. As he grabbed a shovel to throw dirt on the tires, he spotted, between the trees, Vince's pickup. The headlights were still on. Neither the man nor the truck had moved an inch. Andy pitched dirt on the tires and thought, for all Vince's beefs against his old man, he was still testing his hypothesis. Doubt runs deep in the blood, however much men try to outrun it.

9

THE SECOND HE DROVE UP, as soon as she heard the sound of his truck, Kareen would come to the window. She'd stand there and study his exhaustion from afar, for how long he cast his head back, whether he let it fall forward onto his chest, whether he winced when he stepped out of the cab. She was fully aware that their future was directly connected to his faithful call to a mule-like existence, but she wondered too for how long he could keep it up before he had a heart attack or stroke.

All he knew was that he was a machine plowing forward fed by a hoseline manned by a nameless zealot who at any second might decide to pull it and send him body and mind into collapse. Sleep was an escape but not a restorative. He'd sometimes wake only to find that he felt worse than before he went to bed.

For two or three hours he'd struggle to find his full strength. The hectoring dust didn't help. It came from everywhere, and the best he could do was steel himself against its whirling lunacy and watch it pass, the way a city of essentially decent citizens has to wait for a raging tyrant to burn himself out. He could feel it gunk up his lungs, his nostrils. Mixed with the mucus it became a mass of blackish slag. Its effect on his body was obviously disastrous. Weirdly, it made him want to smoke even more.

He sometimes wondered if the hard work was a kind of expiation. No matter the mistakes he'd made in the past, no matter how many times he'd lied to his wife, his physical existence now was so utterly nailed shut that no possible artifice could leak in.

He'd limp up to the porch slowly and manage to find a smile for her when she opened the door.

"Hello, sweetheart."

In the laundry room, he'd pull off his dusty boots and shuck his pants caked with mud and sit there in his underwear for dinner. Bent over, his face inches from the plate, he'd spoon food into his mouth in this slow elliptical motion that reminded Kareen of the way the humble Arabs back in Egypt ate soup. His exhaustion made him dumb to her company, so she had stopped sitting with him at the table. When he was done, he would surface, take a few deep breaths, and then head directly for the shower. She would follow up after him by throwing a few extra bowls of water on the zipper of dirt that ran down the center of the tub. By eight o'clock, he was in bed and fast asleep.

WHAT HE HAD ACCOMPLISHED in those two months would have been worth bragging about if Andy was inclined or had the time or energy or anybody to brag to. (He certainly wasn't going to brag to his wife.) He had ripped the ground at Chamichian's, he had conditioned the soil and dug furrows, and plugged in, one by one and by hand, twelve inches apart down thirty eighth-of-a-mile rows, seedlings for tomatoes, and then brought them up, narrowly averting a disastrous frost. At the Italians' place, he'd leveled, nourished, furrowed, and seeded two hundred acres of dirt.

Now he could see a sliver of light come through the cracks he had made. From here to about midsummer, he'd have to make sure everything was well irrigated, especially the corn that stood about belt-high and whose thirst was damn impossible to slake. As far as the tomatoes, the main concern was pests.

The one good thing about working so many hours is Andy had shed a good fifteen pounds. The physical work had done it, but also he'd cut his drinking down to near nothing. By the end of a day, he was so punch drunk from fatigue that the need for alcohol was basically superfluous.

Still, he hadn't seen Sammy going on six, seven weeks, and he owed him a visit.

The bar was almost empty when he walked in. A few chairs in the center of the room had been pushed haphazardly around, like someone had been mopping underneath them.

The two men embraced and Sammy said, "Sit down and tell me about it. Where you been?"

Andy filled him in on the tomato deal and told him that the Italians he'd met at the bar had hired him to do some work.

Then he explained the work. Because he didn't want his creditors latching onto any income he might draw from that operation, he'd kept it all low-key, and he asked Sammy to do the same.

"One of them is this Eddie Rizzo, right?"

"Yeah," Andy said. "We all went to high school together."

"I was asking myself what you were huddling in the corner about with them guys. And then you disappear."

"Probably didn't look like a farming matter."

"To be honest with you."

"And the truth is, I owe you. We met here."

"Congratulations, Andy."

"Yeah, for the first time in a while, I feel like I can see a little down the road."

Sammy took a deep breath and let it out with a sigh.

Andy asked, "How things going with you?"

"I don't want to fill your ear."

"Business?"

"No complaints there. Naw, it's more the crowd. You know, you can't really dictate who comes in and out, and a bar is a natural magnet for 'elements.'"

"Elements? What kind of elements?"

"If you'd have been here fifteen minutes earlier, you could have seen for yourself. I had to throw two of them out just before you came."

"Is that what explains the mess over there?"

They both looked at those chairs.

"Getting too loud. When I asked them to settle it down, they laughed. I shouldn't even let these kids in the bar. Punks." Sammy shook his head. "You know, I figure, let 'em down a few beers, what the hell. Nobody slammed the door on our noses when we was that age, seventeen, eighteen."

"I wouldn't sweat it, Sammy. A few kids messed up your day. I'd leave it at that."

"Let's hope so."

"I mean, just a mental exercise, ever think about getting a bouncer in here?"

"It's like once you get a bouncer, you're announcing to your customers a different kind of atmosphere. But maybe you're right, maybe I've got to weigh the thing. Shit, if you wasn't working, I just might hire you to bounce."

"Yeah, kicking people out on their asses—my forte. I've had enough people do it to me, I've become a pro just watching them."

IT WAS GETTING ON FIVE when Andy got home. The sun was starting to recede and cut loose a breeze. The green had come back to the big sycamore trees, and the branches swayed to and fro like kids offering a piece of candy and then snatching it back. Through the picture window he could see his wife in the kitchen, laughing it up. From the cigarette smoke that clouded the room, he assumed his mother-in-law was there cutting jokes.

He opened the door, said hello, and breathed in lamb meat simmering in a bath of tomatoes, onions browning in butter.

Valentine sat with her legs crossed at the kitchen table, smoking a cigarette. "The King has come," she laughed.

Kareen leaned forward and gave the king a kiss.

"Mama and I were just talking," she said.

"About what?"

"About the time she cooked you okra."

Andy stepped into the kitchen and made a confused face, as though the episode was new to him. "When?"

Valentine slapped her knee with a hand, took a voluptuous toke, and said, "You were just dating her, you rascal. I don't know how you got through the door. I was stupid then, and I wanted to cook you a nice meal and give you a nice time, and what better than a homemade meal of okra, I thought, to oil you up. 'Here,' I said," and she made like she was placing a pot in front of him, and then she lifted its make-believe lid. "'Eat,' I said. 'Eat.'"

"And what a good boy you were," Kareen said. "You did eat."

"But for the look on your face you might as well have had a plate full of *joojus*." Valentine laughed at her choice of words.

"They damn well do look like peckers. My God, what you two put me through."

They both laughed riotously.

Little Yervant tumbled from out of the hallway into the kitchen. Andy lifted him in his arms.

Kareen said, "Oh yes, Andy, I wanted to tell you: Someone, maybe your boss, out at the ranch, he came by today."

"No kidding. Who? Zero?"

"No. This was an Eddie."

"He's one of them Italians. We went to Central together."

"I guess he was looking for you."

"You two talked, then."

"For a few minutes on the porch. He told me he was Italian, and so we spoke a little Italian. He dresses nice." She glided her hands over her body to show the shape of his suit.

"His dad was a good guy, but the kid, this Eddie, split town, got into business. I don't know about him, to be frank. All those years around his dad, a helluva farmer, I wouldn't trust the kid with a vegetable garden."

"Looks like he did just fine."

He didn't like slick and cocksure Eddie, but now he wondered if it wasn't simple jealousy.

"Sure enough. He don't need to farm. He's hiring me to do it for him."

Kareen touched his face with a hand.

"So what did you and Eddie talk about?"

"This and that. I told him you were out at the ranch. I'm surprised he didn't look for you there."

"What time was this?"

"Noon."

"Say what he wanted?"

"No. I didn't ask."

"Andy," Valentine said. "I heard something the other day. I wonder if you can tell me the truth, one way or another."

"Sure, Valentine."

"I heard that your brother's mother-in-law, she is in the hospital. Very, very sick."

"Which kind?"

"I don't know?"

"She wasn't well in the head."

"Oh, I see. Yes, you've told me. It could be."

"I think back and I wonder sometimes if my brother had a running chance surrounded by those people. I wonder did they poison him?"

"But he took the poison, my boy," Valentine said. "And for what? A spit of dirt."

"Twenty-five acres—hardly a spit."

"All the earth in the world is but a spit if you lose your brother's love."

Marky started crying from bed.

"Get up and get him," she told her daughter. "I'm having a good time."

Andy said, "I'll get him."

He brought him in like a present. They took turns kissing and gnawing on his neck.

"I'll eat you up," Valentine said and chewed on the backs of his legs. "I've had my fill. Enough." She handed him back to Andy.

"I can never get enough of him," Andy told her.

"Sit with him all day and see if you say that."

"You're probably right."

"Did I tell you the story about the golden ball?"

"Never heard that one."

"It is a very sweet story. But give me a cigarette first."

Andy obliged.

She took a deep puff and commenced:

> There was and there was not a young couple. They lived on the estate and cared for the garden and miles-long grounds of a very rich man and his wife. These rich people, they had everything. Such was their wealth and power they barely set eyes on their servants. However, each night, they would hear from the little shack that this poor couple lived in laughing and giggling and singing in voices so joyous it was impossible to ignore. This went on for a week, a month, while the rich couple sat alone at night reading each other's faces or staring into the fire. "What is going on there?" the rich husband asked. "What makes them so happy?" the woman wondered.
>
> The next day, the rich man sees his gardener. "Why do you laugh and sing so well at night?" "Oh," he said. "We have a golden ball. Every night we take it out and play with it." That night the rich man told his wife the story. The wife was jealous. "The next you see that man, tell him to come to our house and bring their golden ball with them!"
>
> The very next day he invited the poor man to his house and told him to bring along his golden ball. When the sun went down, there

was a knock at the door. The rich woman eagerly opened it. There was the poor couple. The woman was holding a basket. "Let me see," the rich wife said. She snatched the basket greedily from the poor woman and lifted the blanket. In there lay a little baby boy. "Where is your golden ball?" the rich woman wondered aloud. The man smiled, for there was no golden ball. At least, it was not made of gold and it was not a ball. He lifted his son in his arms. "This is our golden ball."

Andy said, "A very sweet story. One I bet that's old as the world." He reached for his three-year-old boy. "My golden ball," he said.

Valentine was still with that couple. "You see," she said, sadly, "these stories, though born from thin air, come from somewhere. Who is this poor couple? Survivors. They came through the desert. They are in Iran or Syria. To put food in their mouths, they will take any work. They live in a shack, of no consequence to anyone, especially this wealthy couple. Except they have something beyond riches, this golden ball. The baby was their hope, their future, their joy."

"It's time to put this one to sleep," Kareen said. Yervant had dozed off on the floor. "One up, the other down. *Babam!* Where is my rest?! Dinner is almost ready."

Andy said, "I'll take him, sweetheart. You sit."

He carried his eldest boy into the bedroom, lowered him onto the mattress, drew the blanket over his body, and then bent over and kissed him on the forehead. The window was open and he stood there for a spell listening to his son, his simple breath, his simple beating heart—I am alive, I am alive, I am alive, it was saying.

When he returned dinner was on the table: lamb shanks, pilaf glistening with butter, green beans mixed with flecks of dill, and a salad of chopped cabbage dressed in olive oil and vinegar. But they were all sitting in front of the food absently.

Andy kissed Kareen on the head.

She said, "Mama worries about them."

He looked over to see Valentine's eyes red with tears.

Andy asked, "Who are you talking about? What is it, Mom?"

"My brother and sister and her family," Kareen said.

"There is nothing left for them there," Valentine said.

On and off from the day he and Kareen had married, he'd thought about how he could help the rest of her family come to America, but each time he'd square up on the mechanics of bringing them over, he'd been thrown off-kilter by his own problems. "Nothing left for them." The sound of that choked him up. He had to do more.

Valentine said, "You see, first we had the war, and then the whole country went upside down with Nasser. When he was done, what jobs were left to us? None. This is their situation."

"It's hard to imagine, here in America, how one day you're opening the door to your store and the next day you're handing over the keys for free." On the other hand, Andy thought, that's exactly what happened to folks like the Takahashis.

Kareen said, "We should have been bitter, but how could we? The Europeans and Armenians and Jews, they owned all the land and all the factories. The poor Arab children would beg on the street while our children walked to school to learn English and French. I will tell you, sometimes I was ashamed. We were in their country, and they were our servants."

Valentine said, "And they were good people, the Arabs. Not like the Turks. The Turk was a different creature; he must be on top of you like this." She ground a downward-turned thumb into the table. "But the Arabs were gentle and deep in their faith."

Kareen recalled, "'Inshallah, it's God's will, God's way,' they would say."

Valentine bowed her head and put her palms up. "I lose my business: Inshallah. I swim across the river and drown: Inshallah."

She shook her head at the colossal faith of those Muslims.

They ate for a while and then Kareen said, "In our first house, before the war, my father had two servants, Asad and Harika. Do you remember them, Mom?"

"Of course."

"Every once in a while they would bring their youngest daughter along, a shy girl, near my age. I loved reading poetry, especially in my bedroom all alone. Some days this Harika's daughter would see me reading and look at me with wonder, like I was peering into a looking glass, into another world. One day I came home early from school—I don't know, maybe I was sick —and when I walked into my room, this little girl, she had one of my books in her hands. She turned white as a ghost. She ran up to me and threw herself at my feet: 'Please, please,' she said, 'don't tell my mother. I only wanted to know what you were reading.' The book was by Victor Hugo, *Les Miserables*, and of course, it was in French, so it was impossible that she could read it. Maybe she was looking at the pictures, or feeling the pages. I was so sad for her. I picked her up off the floor and told her, 'Don't worry. Look, it is not right for you to come into my room like this, but next time, when you come here, I will read this to you and we will look at the pictures together.' She did not believe me and ran crying out of the room. This is how it was before Nasser, so I suppose what he did was a good thing, for his own people, the Arabs. But for us, our lives there, it was finished."

Valentine shook her head, but Andy could not say if she shook it for sadness, or for her two children left behind or for the double injustice that those who had fled genocide were made to flee again. Or perhaps she shook it in wonder at being in America at last.

He rummaged around in his mind for something he could do. "You know, I was down at that foundry off of 99, some part busted on my plow a few months ago. There was a lot of action there. The owner, Peters, he's Armenian. Maybe he can help."

"Asbed is very good at making machines, any machines..." Kareen's voice was excited and pleading at the same time.

Valentine said, "You do what you can, son-in-law, and we will pray that this country opens its arms to them the way it opened its arms to us."

10

ANDY DROVE ALONGSIDE THE CORNFIELD admiring its shimmering green splendor, the stalks upright, supple but strong with their brilliant leaves sheathing the ear from harm. He was proud of what his "team" had done, but more proud for what the corn had done, the way from seed it had established roots and wiggled its way up and drove toward the heavens. Just the other day he saw the first tassels spawn and tooted a few bars of "Pomp and Circumstance" in celebration.

It had grown tall enough that a man could disappear in it, but Tom was taller than even those stalks. Standing on the floorboard of his truck, Andy looked for him over the tassel tops. There he was, forty or so yards in. Andy whistled to get his attention and listened to the rustle as he zigzagged his way out.

"How things going?" he asked warmly.

Tom batted a fly from his ear and said, "I seen dem eggs early on."

"Mites?"

Tom nodded his head.

"I knew it was sure as hell comin'. Let's go in and take a look."

Andy led the way, a little worried at what he'd find, like a father moving up the hallway to see what caused the baby to scream. They walked around in there, throwing the corn to the side and inspecting it top to bottom: a little stippling and webbing on the lower leaves, but the pests hadn't reached the ear.

"There's one." An eight-legged seed-sized thing. They were out there for sure, but not in any great numbers.

"Figure spray?"

"I don't think so, Thomas. By my guesstimation, we've got no more than a patch here and there, and even those are on the ropes. We might throw some thrips in. They'll have 'em for lunch."

"Or big-eye bugs"

"But we're just talkin'. Truth is, I think we're a little late for predators."

"Maybe a shot of poison where they be picnickin'."

"Got to keep our costs down too, my friend. No, keep an eye on it is all. Let's just make sure we're not stressing these plants. Keep them healthy and they'll do battle for themselves. And maybe get Willie to kick those damn weeds down on the margins. I don't see him today."

"He gots himself sompin' else goin'."

"Oh boy. Anyway, we got virgin soil here, more or less, so our main worry is what blows in from strangers. My bet, these mites sailed over from that damn Johnson grass across the avenue."

"Pig grass too."

"What derelict owns that piece of dirt, I wonder? Guy should be drawn and quartered."

They walked back out.

"'Notha' thing, Andy. That plane you been spectin'? Looks tuh me it done come 'round lass night."

"No shit."

They both walked to the landing strip. Andy saw no tire tracks, but Tom was right: there was a little sweeping smooth of the dirt from air pressure off what could only be an airplane's wings.

"They just pass over it?" How could that be? Just one pass? What kind of person would size up his investment with a simple pass over with a plane? Andy tried to picture the wealth, the long perspective such wealth might allow. Frankly, he couldn't picture it. "I'll be damned. What time did you leave yesterday?"

"'Bout three."

"The dust that plane is throwing up isn't going to help our mite issue any. To be honest with you, it's a knuckleheaded idea to put a landing strip in the middle of a ranch. I don't know about these people. They got an investment here, and I never see 'em."

Tom said nothing.

"Well, Mr. Jefferson, I figured I'll head out to those tomatoes."

"You go 'head."

Andy second-guessed himself. "You know, now that I'm looking at it, just spray the whole damn field. We'll pick up the cost somewhere else."

Tom nodded.

Andy scrutinized the dirt a little further. "Looks like Zero was here to meet 'em. There's tire tracks, and not off my truck."

"Looks like."

"These people confuse me. I swear…"

Andy was feeling a little left out of the equation. It was true that Zero and Eddie had hired him, and that they paid him nice and neat right on the hour, every Friday afternoon at five, and in short order came up with however much dough Andy needed to keep things rolling. But a part of Andy wanted to introduce himself to the chief, to personally give him a look at the scope and seriousness of his work. Especially if things went south, he wanted to be able to explain why to men he'd met face to face. He admitted that the vast concerns these Italians held might make them shy on time, keep them from shooting the shit over a beer, say, but it still didn't make sense that they wouldn't now and then want to sit down over a cup of coffee and properly size up their investment, and the man who oversaw it.

Zipping down the road, Andy realized he was probably scrutinizing the situation too closely. Perhaps it reflected a flaw in his character that he looked for a human connection in all that he did. Or maybe it reflected insecurity—he wanted to connect with the person who held the purse so that whoever it was might think twice before he snatched it away.

Andy was right on top of 99. The highway's roar jarred him loose of his thoughts. He took it north a few miles and then veered down the off-ramp into town toward the new foundry to meet the owner, an Armenian man who might give his brother-in-law in Egypt a job.

It was getting on a hundred degrees outside, but inside that building it must've been twenty degrees hotter. Men in gray jumpsuits with blotches of sweat on their shirts were moving here and there fetching parts, bands of steel, consulting diagrams or each other. Drill presses, welders, grinders, and saws; cyclopean fans pulling the hot air like taffy. It reminded him of the agony of certain kinds of impossible-to-escape sequences in dreams. It was like…how did that great big steelmaker put it…like hell, "like hell with the top on"—pretty much like that, Andy thought.

A big sign "OFFICE" hung over a doorway on the other end and Andy marched across the hot floor past noisy machines, spits of sparks, tang of metal shavings, and choking wafts of heat. It took exertion to move through, and he'd worked up a sweat by the time he'd walked what must've been half the length of a football field. Jesus. At least this factory's heat was generated from the sun whereas in those steel factories Back East it came from within. Andy pictured the factory at night with snow falling all around, its big smokestacks looking like upright cannons, and its windowless face cold and square. He could see Carnegie in gray gabardine go poetic from some perch, "like hell with the top on," and how after he'd offered his well-turned phrase he'd turn away to attend to his private Fort Knox.

"Andy." Through the clamor of his thoughts, the thousand machines, he could barely make out his own name; he turned searching for the source, like a smell.

"Andy," he heard again. To his right a man had pulled his goggles off and was walking his way.

"Johnny. Goddamn it, what are you doing here?" Years ago, he was the floor man at Boyajian's packing house.

They made wide swings with their arms and clasped hands in the middle.

"Whadya say?"

"Not much."

"What the hell you doing here?"

"Ah," Johnny said, "I got tired of the fruit business. Near the end there Boyajian damn near shaved my salary down to nothing. "

"This fruit deal's a bitch."

"I heard you were pulling some over the Grapevine."

"Little bit last few years. I had a nasty turn up there. That was somethin'."

"Flip?"

"Lost my brakes."

"Coming off it toward L.A.?"

"Right 'round the ridge route. For a while there it was touch-and-go. I see this cop boring down on me from behind, thought I was speeding, so I wave him ahead and lucky thing he sees my situation or I'd be chopped liver by this point. He cleared the way, to make a long story short. First and last time I ever had a kind word for a cop."

"What were you hauling, mind me asking?"

"Broccoli. Naw, God was with me all right."

They both shook their heads from the close call.

"How'd that thing turn out with your brother?"

"It didn't turn out, really. Still a mess."

"Damn shame."

"Is right. But hey, a man's got one life. No sense letting another man turn it to waste."

"But it's your brother."

"There's the rub."

"Kennedy and all. It's like one of them seasons where everything's goin' upside down."

Andy looked up and around and remarked on the size of the operation and asked Johnny if he knew whether they were hiring.

"Oh, I think so. I think they're looking for good workers. They want to turn Fresno into a major manufacturing hub for the state, that's how big I hear they want to make it. You lookin' for work yourself?"

"Naw. For my brother-in-law."

"I think he's got a shot."

"Keep our fingers crossed. Good to see you, Johnny. Damn, what a shift in work."

"At least I'm not stepping on rotten peaches anymore."

"Ain't that the truth."

INSIDE THE OFFICE was a different world. Cool, clean, and what with the air conditioner's quieting hum Andy suddenly felt his energy wane.

"A guy could take a nap in here," he told the secretary sitting behind a desk.

She wasn't amused. "May I help you?"

"I'm hoping to see Mr. Peters. Like to see the man if he's available."

She asked about what.

"Employment," he said. "If you please. Promise it'll be short."

She opened a filing cabinet, took out a piece of paper, and slid it across the counter.

"If you could fill this in, we'll see that it gets reviewed."

"I was kinda hopin' to talk to Mr. Peters himself. It's on behalf of my brother-in-law, not me. The picture's a little complicated, you see."

"Your name?"

"Andy Demerjian."

A part of him expected her to say, "Oh. You're Armenian. I'm sure he'll see you right away," but she merely asked him to wait, and not at all kindly.

When she was gone, Andy put a hand up to that refrigeration vent. Nice.

"He'll see you."

"Appreciate it."

She led him down the hallway to a door. "Leon Peters" said a brass plaque. Peters: it was Bedrossian made American. The secretary opened the door with one hand and with the other showed Andy the way in.

Behind a big desk sat a bespeckled middle-aged gentleman with a bald and narrow head. His office was absent of everything but paperwork and places to hold paperwork. No picture of the kids, the wife, the family dog. All business, Andy decided, so he got to the point right away. When he was more or less done, more or less succinctly, Peters said, "I'd like to look at this Asbed's work. I see work coming up in the near future here that requires delicate hands."

Andy was stunned by his good luck.

"That's the only reason I'm saying 'maybe.' Let's just see…" Peters said. "If the man is as good as you say he is he might be what we need."

Andy told him he'd drop by the resumé first thing tomorrow.

"That'll be fine," Peters said and turned his attention back to the stack of papers on his desk.

Andy rose and, almost as an aside, said, "Where we can help each other, why not, huh?"

Peters smiled, like he was indulging a naïf.

HER SISTER HAD ALREADY SENT Kareen a portfolio of pictures and diagrams of contraptions and widgets and metal plaques Asbed had designed and fabricated, so Andy sat down with those and put together a kind of resumé of the man's work, doctoring it up here and there, what the hell, with a few facts that would be impossible to corroborate one way or another seeing that he lived across the Atlantic.

"Don't write nothin' to your sister yet," he said. "And keep things quiet with your mom too. For the time being, sweetie. I'll take this here thing over there tomorrow."

"I won't say a word."

"I think he's qualified, from what I seen. I mean, they got this guy used to work at the packing house bending metal; from these pictures, Asbed is gonna come out some kind of wizard next to him. The guy does good work; even I can tell you that."

"How did you do it?"

"I pulled a few strings. Hey, I was born and raised here, I should have a few strings to pull, no?"

Andy turned the TV on and had only sat there a few minutes licking up his good luck when he heard, "A KMJ special, breaking news," and a newscaster appeared on the tube. "Tonight, at about five o'clock, shots were fired near the Tavern on East Belmont," he reported. "The news came to us from a neighbor of the Tavern a short while ago."

Andy froze.

"We have an onsite report by our newsman Howard Mason." There was Howard Mason standing next to Sammy.

"I'll be damned."

"What is it?" Kareen asked.

"That's Sammy there, there on the news."

"...so I heard some shots fired, and run out. I hear a bang, and a bullet comes this close to hitting me." Sammy shows how close with two fingers. "And it hits that car," he points, and the camera swings over to it: a window shattered from what had to be a bullet. "So I run inside and tell everybody to get down and stay calm." The picture bobs, then settles. "Next I call the police," he points to where they apparently stood, "and grab my gun from behind the counter and keep my eyes glued on the door. Looks like there was a shoot-out. I don't know who. Bunch of hoodlums."

"Have you noticed," Mason asked, "this kind of disturbance in the neighborhood before?"

"Never. That's what bothers me. Never."

"Guns firing. Bartenders disturbed. An increasing trend of unaccountable gun activity in this part of our city. Thank you, Mr. Hamalian."

Sammy shakes his head. Looks in bad shape.

"Some have speculated such gunfire is due to an increase in the sale of marijuana in Fresno—a turf battle between mobs who sell this marijuana. This is Police Officer Jordan." Jordan lifted his head and kind of squinted.

"Some residents suspect that marijuana is being sold in this area. And that this is a growing trend in the city at large. Do the police have a similar suspicion?"

"Hard to say. Like the barkeep said, this is a pretty isolated incident. We'll just have to wait and see."

"And we'll keep our viewers posted. This is Howard Mason reporting from North Fresno. Back to you, Steve."

"I'll be damned."

Andy put his boots back on.

"Where are you going?"

"I owe him a visit."

"Please, Andy."

"Cops are swarming around Sammy's like flies on an outhouse. Nothing else is going to happen tonight. That's the safest place you can be in town."

"Be careful, please."

"I'll be back in a half hour."

AS ANDY APPROACHED HE COULD SEE that the parking lot was all but empty. One cop, with his headlights still on, was running his engine, standing next to his trunk making notes. He took a long look at Andy as he passed. Andy nodded and rolled up to the front of the bar.

Sammy was on his haunches next to the door, smoking a cigarette, like a hitchhiker idling. When he saw Andy, he shook his head the same exact way he had on the tube.

"What, you looking to be a movie star these days?"

Sammy shifted his eyes around and ticked his head toward the door.

The bar was empty save the part-time help sweeping the floor. They took their respective places, Sammy behind the counter and Andy on a stool, except that after Sammy poured Andy his drink, he poured himself one too.

"I guess you're off duty now," Andy said.

Sammy shook his head. "It was this close, Andy."

"What the hell was all this about?"

"I think I'm gonna have to get that bouncer we talked about. The town's getting rough, Andy. Though the cops don't want to say nothin' about it right now, maybe they're staking it out. It's clear as day that dope's getting peddled, around here and everywhere."

"Marijuana?"

"Or worse."

"Back in our day, it was the blacks and the jazz crowd that puffed that stuff; now it's made its way to Main Street? I hate to see it. In Fresno. You must be worried its toll on your business. You get too much of that kind of publicity, customers'll stop coming around."

"Or a different kind of customers. You know those kids I told you about a couple of weeks ago? Those punks?"

"I remember."

"What I didn't tell you is that when I told them to shove off they laughed at me. They had the look of dope in their eyes. You know, the glassy-eyed 'who gives a shit' look. And when one of them stood up, I could smell marijuana on his body. Like piss. It reeks. There's no hiding it."

"Next time you gotta just call the cops. Now you know."

"I don't want them snooping around here, Andy. Next thing I know they might shut this place down."

"How the hell would they do that? Why?"

"They might think it's moving through here, the dope."

Andy asked, "Is it?"

"I got my suspicions."

"You're kidding me." A stippling of fear spread across his arms. "I thought they peddle that shit out in the street?"

"They peddle it everywhere."

"But why here?"

"The lights are low. The booths deep. Hell if I know."

"You have seen this kind of activity?"

"No, but again, I smelt it. In the men's bathroom. If they're not moving it, they're sure as hell smokin' it here. I can't patrol the john all day. I hate the idea, but it looks to me I got no option but a bouncer."

"It's a little early in the game to be asking, but you consider moving across town?"

Sammy didn't answer, or maybe he did answer by not answering.

"Where's this dope coming from, I wonder?"

"I don't know. Around here, out in the country, up in the foothills. Could be coming from Mexico. I hear they bootleg it here from Hawaii."

"That's a long-ass way to haul dope."

"There's big money in it, Andy. What I heard, wads of it, all rolled up, cash."

"Maybe we should get in on the action," Andy winked.

"No, we Armenians are made to work like *eshes*."

"Jackasses we are, buddy."

He tossed back the last of his bourbon and told Sammy to keep in touch, and if he needed anything to let him know.

"Maybe it'll pass. Maybe this'll all work itself out." He looked at his watch.

"It's eleven. You get home to your family. How they doin' by the way?"

"We'll save that for another conversation."

"Good enough."

When he pulled up in front of his house, he saw no lights on. From the heaviness of that evening, the atmosphere in his home felt heavier than it had just a few hours before. Moving up the hallway, he had an inexplicable sense that his kids might be in harm's way. On the bed with the sheets kicked off, a shaft of moonlight cut across his eldest son. His youngest had one hand over his head, the other flat against his chest, as though he were pledging allegiance. Andy open the window to let a little fresh air in, but from the sun's all-day pummeling nothing came, the air deadlocked out there.

He got in bed and closed his eyes to clear his head, but that one word—marijuana—and Sammy's fingers, just an inch apart, kept looping in his brain until the sheet was glued to his back and the heat sat beneath his ass like a hot-water sponge and Peters's air conditioner came to mind, its cool and luxurious strokes, its moneyed little hum. He imagined the day when he could flick a switch and dispatch the heat, when he could immerse his family in cool air like that. The secretary in Peters's office gave him a look that was meant to put him in his place, and not no refrigerated place either, but a place with another kind of air, the hot and filthy kind that the vast majority of humanity breathed. He dreamed, God be his witness, of someday having enough money to plumb all buildings with such silky air. What was the point, he thought, of building a world that spiraled to the cool heavens when people below broiled? What exactly was man after? What was the point of their billion-part machines, their billion-dollar accounts, if not to make the lot of other men run a little smoother, to make their seventy-odd years less severe? He churned over three or four other matters and shuffled back and forth between them as though he were some worker in God's great repair shop with a line of broken-down gadgets extending to infinity needing his special touch. Nasser: he had taken the jobs away from Armenians to make it better for all those Arabs, and now Andy was trying to get his brother-in-law a job on the other side of the earth because his was taken away to right some national wrong. What made Andy think the whole of the human race could bask at the equator? Why did he continue to dream of a world that was shaped of fair play? Maybe because he, maybe because man in general, needed to have something outside of this lopsided ball to look forward to, a God to petition, a God in whose eyes the world was but a bead, a marble in his galactic game. Maybe this explained why the prophets of old shouting from a hilltop or from the bottom of a hole always envisioned the day when this miserable little orb was wiped off the board.

On and on he laundered until it seemed every last sheet in the cosmos was flung in. Back to Nasser, how Andy would never have known his wife if it weren't for him, how if his big national plan hadn't included pushing her family out of Egypt she never would've landed in his bed. Amazing, amazing how humanity, whatever godforsaken place it is dropped, manages to figure a future. What an industrious breed of animal, cobbling together from the refuse a home, a place from which soon enough smells of breakfast and the sound of kids rise, how the daily rhythms eventually drown out the grief, the sounds of guns and bombs, like little birds setting up among the cinders their nests, chirping and twittering, as though to say, "To hell with the past; this is what our bodies were given to us to do, this is what our brains were engineered for, this—look—this is what our souls were spun to enjoy."

AFTER ALL THAT COMMOTION in his brain the night before, he didn't really feel like walking back into the foundry, but he needed to get that resumé off his hands and into Peters's.

"Just want to drop something off." The secretary looked at him again like he was a beggar after a meal ticket.

"You can leave it with me."

"If you don't mind."

She swung open the half-door and started quickly down the hall ahead of him, with one hand holding him back like a mom trying to keep her kid from getting too excited. She knocked on her boss's door, poked her head in, and told Peters, "The man who was here the other day looking for work for his brother-in-law is here to see you," and then opened the door wide for that man. Peters looked up from his work. Andy winked, like they'd downed a few beers together way back when. "Just thought I'd drop off this Asbed's resumé."

Peters nodded and motioned with a finger for Andy to put it on his desk.

Andy put it there, politely. "Not that I'm pushing or anything," Andy said, "but you think you might have an answer for me sooner rather than later?"

The work he anticipated getting, Peters claimed, was still two months away, and so if the man fit the bill he just might be able to let him know in short order.

"I think he's already ahead on his papers. If he gets a job, I think he's ready to hop on the next boat."

"I'll let you know."

"Thanks for considering it, again. By the way, how did your folks get here, if you don't mind me asking, Mr. Peters?"

"I don't talk about that," he said.

Andy was taken aback but not so far aback that he forgot to thank the man before he stepped out the door. He was halfway to his car when those words hit him again: "I don't talk about that"? "That" was the genocide, no two ways about it. "That" referred to their people's cataclysmic gash. He wondered if Peters meant "not now" or "not ever" or "not to you" or "not even to my loved ones." Or maybe "not even to myself." Andy was embarrassed to have asked, and the embarrassment brought into focus a supposition he had made: that the stories Armenians told, especially where their suffering was concerned, were from a single book that each member of his tribe had the birthright to read. Your story is my story, he had assumed, but Peters had told him something different: my story is my own—and I don't tell it.

Andy wondered whether there wasn't something to Peters's approach. A picture began to assemble in his head: the big industry all around Peters, the mess of movement, the attention to the second hand of the clock, the relentless press to get things done and on their way might just depend on not talking about "that." Maybe the past sits in front of a man, not in back of him, like a forest, Andy thought, and only a man who can fell these trees can get a clear-eyed view into the future.

Speaking of forests, there was also the petrified kind, where any number of old-timers had found a quiet place to sit and chew on the cud of loss till their teeth dropped out. That was no way to live. It made him nervous, though he was even more nervous with Peters's approach—even if that was what it took to be a successful businessman. To claim his stake in the future the man felt the need to fell his own name. What kind of Armenian name is Peters?

Not that Andy could blame him. The Armenians hardly arrived there like ambassadors on a Rose Bowl float. No, they flooded out of the dank hulls of ships, long-faced and long-nosed, in search of a place to seed, and in general were greeted with as much goodwill as Johnson grass. The Germans and Swedes would cringe from the effulgence of smells—sumac and cumin and Aleppo pepper—that wafted off the hirsute bodies of these darkies, and they made sure to add clauses that stipulated "No Armenians Allowed" in original deeds of tract after tract of homes. And in case you thought to wiggle your way in by changing your name, the developers made sure to add "no former inhabitants of current-day Turkey or the former Ottoman Empire."

Shunted from the fashionable parts of town, they gathered down-town, where they set up their *lavosh* and bulgur and shish kebob shops. In no time they threw up a house of worship: a seven-hundred-seat brick structure inspired by the apostolic churches of old, with a floor plan the shape of an Armenian crucifix. It dwarfed the Protestant churches around town, and even gave the Catholic one down the road a run for its money. Far from earning them respect, the white folk viewed it as a kind of financial recklessness, if not an assault on Christian humility, to throw up a structure so large so early in the going.

Every Sunday they would shed their farm clothes and dress to the nines. He remembered watching his father walk up the steps of the church. The snugness of his tie, the luster of his shoes, the sureness of the hat on his head, they all seemed to illustrate his dignity as much as his humility before the redeemer, as though here he were saying, "I may be your servant, but I will never be your slave."

Soon, the priests with long beards and dark eyes and black cone-shaped hoods were circling up there in robes that swept the marble floor. Deacons on either side of them, two steps back, caped blue and white, precisely like bluebirds, jerking their censers. Incense drifted like fog. Clamped between his parents, in the straightjacket of his wool suit, it amounted to a kind of torture. He remembered sitting and rising and sitting and rising: this holy calisthenics the only thing that broke the ungodly monotony.

Occasionally, after church they'd head to the river or Kearney Park or the fairgrounds for picnics that reunited the townsfolk from Van and Bitlis and Kharpet and Zeytoun. He remembered old men strolling side by side with their hands behind their backs, and other men on the cement dance floor forming a circle, a hand-clasping human pack, and his father, the finest dancer among them, at the head, starting it up with a towel in his hand. The men danced like a great chain, whipping forward and back, and soon Yervant would cut loose, strut to the middle, frame his head with his arms, and slide it along his shoulders, this way and that, until the audience roared and someone made the peacocks call, and then he'd drop to his haunches, kicking, his arms folded at his chest, then pop up, then down again, making Andy think the man was built of springs.

He remembered, too, when the song ended, his shirt matted to his chest, the strong odor of tobacco and onion and beer in his sweat. He remembered looking up at his dad with an unspoken question, and his dad unspoken answering: "Yes, you are my son, but see, I am more than your father," or "Yes, I am in America now, but the blood running through my veins will always be Armenian."

It made him think of Harry Berberian and Sons out in Sanger. The label for their Ararat Brand fruit box featured a white-bearded Noah, shovel over his shoulder, strolling down a path from Ararat. For generations the Armenians cultivated their crops and grazed their sheep on land that stretched from that Biblical mountain. That mountain was a symbol for what they were and where they were, the two things, three thousand years intertwined, now shredded. In the picture, two doves fly around a red ark that rests at the mountain's summit. On the path in front of Noah there is a bounty of apricots and a vine heavy with grapes, and behind Mount Ararat rolls a lush valley, the San Joaquin. It stops at the edge of what is unmistakably the Sierra Nevada. "Produce U.S.A." is boldly stamped on the label.

That was an image of life that a man could live with, a kind of poetry that allowed one to neither deny where he came from nor be afraid of giving thanks for where he had arrived. It allowed him to say he'd survived where others had perished but also allowed that a future was out there that the dead had no claim on. In its homespun way, that label aimed to tell the story of the refugees from front to back, Andy thought. The Armenians were a kind of Noah: they arrived here on a boat, barely surviving the deluge of the massacres. They stepped off and began putting together their world again: one in Albany, another in Racine, and yet another in Watertown. Those that came as far west as the Central Valley became farmers. All worked hard to raise from the ashes of the past a new world, a place where, when they came home, they could say, "I am home."

I I

MID-JULY, THE STONE FRUIT was ready to explode: peaches and plums and nectarines—so many varieties and covering such a vast tract of land that it took several armies of men to get them off.

At the stop sign on the corner of Manning and Central, it looked to Andy like some nocturnal demolition derby. Cars banged up and barely bandaged lurched and jerked, jockeying for position on the road and off of it. In the headlights' yellow glow, Andy made out a mess of nationalities: Japanese, Filipinos, Mexicans, Volga Germans, a foursome of towheaded Swedes. All were hoping to beat the heat, even though by any normal definition it had already beaten every one of them to the punch. It was a little after five and the temperature was pushing eighty degrees.

This would be the last deep drink the tomato vines would get before he cut them off for a spell. He had nourished, turned, and worked the soil for just this moment when the roots penetrated three, four feet deep. Now he would force them even deeper.

The vines rose in their beds, their fuzzy trunks thick as a thumb. A smothering and fulsome green smell infused the field. He waded through it, checking the integrity of the trellises and beds with his shovel, adjusting and buttressing here and there. He could hear insects hum, could almost feel the fruit elbowing for room to size.

As he made toward the corner nearest the house, he caught a whiff of piano music: ragtime, Joplin probably. The girl had any number of songs in her odd repertoire; everything from Cole Porter to Prokofiev flew rowdily out of the house. He wanted to bat each down like a mosquito. "Give it a little oxygen," he wanted to tell her. "Let it, for God's sake, breathe!" For all her virtuosity, she might well have been tapping out some legal form on a typewriter.

He was at the back end of the field. Irrigation water was inching up the rows. He remembered lying alone in his dorm bed with his trumpet to his lips reaching for what laid mostly beyond his reach. He wanted her to know the joy of hitting a stretch of notes with just the right feeling. He wanted her to know the rectitude of even a single note, how if played just right it gave more pleasure than all of the hullabaloo she threw up.

He made his way back down the dirt drive toward the road. Halfway there, the dog rushed up, out of nowhere, and stopped on a dime about twenty feet from Andy.

He let his hand slip down the shovel's long shaft to better get a grip and then let its heart-shaped head bob at the end. With his own heart-shaped head tilted to the right, the dog seemed to be weighing his options. "Go ahead now," Andy said, thinning those options to one. The dog made to charge, then stood his ground again. It was playing a game of chicken. Andy was raised around mongrels that trundled into a household late in the game and he was plenty aware of the bad manners they picked up roaming the countryside in packs. He thought of them, generally, as stupid, but this dog, its brainpower seemed as big as its big head. Andy turned his eyes away and made toward the road slowly, his ears wide open to a sudden scrabbling of feet, any indication of an attack he was half hoping that mutt might try just so he'd have an excuse to swing that shovel around and split the motherfucker's face in half.

When he got to the end of the road, he relaxed his grip. The old lady must've been watching it all go down because she stepped onto the front porch and came scurrying down the steps.

"That dog of yours, someday somebody's going to do it some damage."

She leveled her eyes down the road. The dog hadn't moved a yard. With a hand she made to shoo him away.

"Don't think that'll do it."

"He's a little absent in the head," she said.

"Oh, I wouldn't put nothin' past that dog."

"What can I say? Lilit loves him. They sleep together at night, you know. I was wondering when you are going to pick those tomatoes?"

It was Monday. She'd asked him the same question Friday.

"I'm giving them a short drink today and will be back Friday or Saturday to check. So don't expect me around much this week."

"Where are you going?" There was panic in her voice. "I'm worried."

"'Bout what?"

"About everything."

"All that mental activity won't do nothin' for them tomatoes."

"I see Lilit has been talking to you. I wonder what she tells you. She says nothing to me."

"Just chatting."

"What is there to chat about?"

"Plenty. Life. Weather."

She spat at their insignificance.

"Let me ask you somethin': She ever get out of the house, a picnic or something? She obviously likes music."

"Not the kind they play at those picnics. It plays with her nerves."

"A dance or something?"

"A dance, what's that?"

"You know, the kind they have down at the Rainbow Ballroom."

"With boys and girls toe to toe? Never."

"How you expect her to meet anybody, then?"

"Don't you worry. She will meet somebody, but not like that, not in such a shameful place."

"She don't go to church, so where else?"

"God will take care of it."

"Let's hope he does. Well, anyway. I'll keep you posted."

"Why do you always have somewhere to go? Come in and have some *choreg*."

HE'D LEARNED FROM EXPERIENCE that when a farmer got too close to his crop, too close to the harvest, he'd start making himself believe that the fruit was ready to harvest before it actually was. But now he began to think he'd gone a little overboard by staying away for nearly a week to tend to the corn. The tomatoes, the way they do sometimes, seemed to have broken overnight. Green fruit had turned red without even bothering to pass through pink. It was Friday and he planned on getting in there with a short crew come middle of that next week, but now it was becoming obvious that he better shove some men in there and in serious numbers Sunday, if not tomorrow.

His contractor was Jose Gonzales, but Jose had stayed with Andy's brother, Abe, or rather, he stayed with the farm, which made Andy feel complicit in a betrayal. Still, rather than getting on with it, each time he'd go to think about labor, Jose was the only one he could consider, as though there were only one contractor for the entire valley, but that since his brother used him everybody else was out of luck. Now the harvest was right on top of him and he had to find pickers quick. Standing in the middle of the tomato patch he made a panicked calculation whether he and Tom and Willie might be able to knock off the first pick all on their own.

After he'd flicked that ridiculous idea aside, he ambled over to Vince's. He saw no sign of the man on the tractor and so he went ahead down the dirt driveway and knocked on his front door.

Vince opened the door with a blank expression, as though he'd been saying no to Hoover salesmen all day.

"Hey, Vince."

Vince grunted.

"You know, I was gonna ask you, think you can spare a few braceros for my tomatoes?"

"First it's tires and then it's hands. What's next?"

"Your wife?"

"Wondering when you were going to pick."

"I've been keeping my eye on them."

"That right."

"Truth is, they came up on me like gangbusters. So you think your contractor, what his name, Felipe can spare a few?"

"Doubt it. Startin' to get a little agitated?"

It was natural enough that Vince wouldn't want to short his crew. He may not be picking today, but only God knew what next week might bring.

"Where you at with your plums?"

"We're pickin'."

"This weekend?" Andy looked for any opening.

"We'll see," Vince wasn't gonna give him one.

"What, you on your second crop?" Andy pressed.

"'Bout there."

"Jesus, Vince. You got some personality, you know that? How 'bout that Herrera, Hilario Herrera? He's got hands around these parts, don't he?"

"Should."

"Got his number?"

Vince turned around and headed back into his house. Except for that nasty stay in the camps, the damn guy had barely strayed beyond the four corners of his farm since he was born. What right did he have to so peremptorily size up the world? Andy wanted to knock the living crap out of him just to give him a legitimate reason. Vince opened the screen door and handed Andy a scrap of paper.

"'Preciate it, Vince."

Andy was going to ask to borrow his phone, but he was afraid of what he'd find if he stepped inside that house. He decided to make the call back at the old lady's.

She was sitting in her chair watching TV. The drone of people talking in straight English told him so. He knocked and she opened the door and before she could say hello Andy said, "Pardon me for disturbing, but could I borrow your phone?"

"Of course, of course, honey, come on in. We missed you."

Andy smiled. "Thanks. Missed you too." He paused in front of the tube, as though the anonymous couple radiating from its oval world were guests come round for morning tea. It was a soap opera.

"They have no shame, these Americans. The things that come out of their mouths, the secrets they tell." She shook a finger and said, *"Ahs cakoorenk uh,"* this good-for-nothing piece of shit, "he makes trouble for everyone. This poor girl has nobody. Why does he molest her?" She turned her attention back to the TV, careful not to miss a beat.

"I'm just going to use the phone."

"What's ours is yours," she said. "In the kitchen."

On the stove green beans simmered in a tomato sauce. As he dialed the number, he regarded how the ten a.m. light bleached out the yellow linoleum table where a leather-covered Bible lay. The little finger tabs—Gen, Eze, Matt, Rev—were worn. Andy waited what must've been ten, twelve rings. A woman, short-breathed, answered: *"Hola."* In his sloppy Spanish Andy asked if Herrera was home.

"El no está aquí," she said.

He explained he needed a crew by Monday at the latest, possibly tomorrow, out at old man Chamichian's.

"Sí, sí, Luna, Luna, está bien."

"At Chamichian's," he said again.

"Sí, sí," she said, but Andy knew that "yes" coming from someone speaking Spanish amounted to not helluva lot more than "I heard you" and could just as well mean the opposite.

"Bueno. Gracias. Make sure you tell that Hilario," he said.

Andy hung up feeling like he'd slid all of his chips in front of a bad hand and it was too late to take it back. He stopped at the door just long enough to say goodbye to the old lady.

She looked up. *"As the World Turns,* they call it." She laughed derisively. "What do they know about the world? What do they know about how this world turns?"

ANDY GOT OUT TO THE FARM by five Monday morning. He pulled the tractor out of the barn and hitched the trailer and laid down the length of it twelve lugs, two rows wide and six deep, and then drove it down the middle transport row that cut the field in two and then killed the engine.

Andy figured it fifty-fifty whether this Hilario would show up, but come ten till six the odds seem to be plummeting. Then he heard a diesel engine, way off in the distance. The sound got big and bigger and soon he could hear tires scrabble and next headlights make the side of the road glow. A bus—it stood, brooding at the intersection. As Andy waited, he felt just like a schoolgirl on the sideline of a sock hop hoping that boy she had a crush on would turn her way. Then it did, slowly, turned the corner, and pulled off onto the dirt avenue half a mile down.

The two hands of his wristwatch were straight up and down as a candlestick. In the first blush of sunlight, Andy saw a Mexican in a big cowboy hat jump off—must be Hilario. One by one the pickers stepped of the bus, stretching the sleep from their limbs and dusting their jeans down, like it was the end not the start of the day. The way their bandanas hung from their back pockets, they looked to be one and all braceros.

Andy punched the truck forward. In his headlights, he could see all eyes turn toward him, and then between the men a quick exchange of words.

He stepped out of the truck and nodded to the workers, kindly. They nodded kindly back. Hilario came forward. Fair-skinned, tall, thin-hipped, and with a big belt buckle that held up a belly shaped like a kangaroo's from too much beer, except for his black goatee and handlebar moustache he looked like a gringo, a Texan maybe.

"Thanks for coming. Right on time. Hope you make it a habit."

"*De nada,*" Hilario said. For a few minutes, they sized each other up. Who Hilario had picked for, where he was from, how long he'd been doing such work, shit like that until Andy rounded back to the business at hand. "Today it's going to be all about color."

"Beefsteaks," Hilario said, taking a few steps toward the plants.

"All Brandywines."

"They bruise easy."

"Like a baby's arse. But nothin' tastes better."

"When did they break?"

"Friday, maybe Thursday. Round about twenty men, looks like."

"*Veintidós.*"

"That'll do. Let's put two to swamp between picking. I don't want anybody sitting on their asses. You have a tractor driver—or you gonna do it?"

"No," he said and chuckled as though long ago he'd put such work behind him. "But I got," he whistled and called, "Manuel."

Manuel ran up to Hilario, holding up his pants with one hand.

"My tractor man. He's easy on the clutch; that's why he's good."

"That's what I'm looking for."

Andy noticed two men sharpening their knives on flat stones they held in their palms.

"They know they're here for tomatoes, I hope. It's obvious we ain't standing next to no vineyard."

"Don't worry," Hilario said.

They had started paring their nails.

The sun hung delicately on the knife-edge of the Sierras.

"Market good, I hear," Hilario said as they waited.

Not a single tomato had been picked and already the man was snooping around for a raise. "One day to the next you don't know whether you should be picking or plowing them under," Andy said.

Hilario tilted his head to the side and nodded.

"Main thing, we gotta stay on top of the color today."

The contractor put a hand out. "I hear it's good, the market, though."

Andy had had enough. "Anyway, let's break the buckets out."

Hilario whistled and sent instructions flying this way and that.

"We can go hourly today, just to break the guys in, but starting tomorrow it's gotta be piecework."

"The boys want nine."

"As long as we're cleaning up by three—we've got to leave enough time to get the last run to the packing house."

"*Está bien.*" With buckets strapped around their necks, the pickers were eager to go in.

"Bear with me today. We need a liiiittle more light. First pick, the packing house is gonna watch them like hawks."

"*Sperate, por favor,*" Hilario told his crew.

They nodded. To the beat of two men playing their buckets like drums, another man sang a song, what sounded like a ranchera.

"Nice," Andy said.

"Jimènez," Hilario told him.

"Huh." Andy turned his focus to the field. He weighed the light as carefully as would any painter—Turner, say—and when ruby turned to gold and gold softened into yellow and thinned, he turned to Hilario and said, "Let's start this end." He marched over to the corner closest the house, where he believed he saw the best color.

"I don't want to spread this deal out so much I can't keep a tab on their work. Let's put four men to a row to start out."

Hilario divided them up with finger-pointing and whistles. Into the rows they strode wearing long-sleeved shirts buttoned up to their necks and pants with legs that tucked into the sides of their boots, broad straw hats, or bandanas wrapped 'round their heads and tied beneath their necks. To an innocent observer, they might as well have bundled up for a trek into the mountain cold. The men adjusted the pails at their sides, stooped, and started twisting the fruits from the stems and laying them in.

Andy moved up and down and across the field making sure that they went easy on the vines ("watcha la vina"), didn't manhandle the fruit ("cuidado, no son baseballs, amigo"), got color from the side hidden from the sun ("poco un más rojo, por favor"), pressing them to do it the way he wanted and at the same time allow for the natural judgment of their hands. When the buckets were full the pickers walked rapidly to the end of the row and gently ("como un bebé") dumped the fruit into the lugs on the trailer. Andy believed he'd seen good size on the vines all along, but he also knew how there was no telling for sure until a critical mass was laid out bare-assed in the sun. He gently scrutinized their bottoms, checking for growth cracks, zippering, cat-facing, sunscald, soft spots, bruising. "Nice," he said to Hilario, "and so far, nice job." He picked up a tomato and turned it in his hand. "Pretty, huh?" Then he put it down, picked up a second, and buffed it on his shirt until it shone. "Wait till they see these beauties at the packing house. They'll want them for their Christmas tree."

It was nearing eight when the first haul of tomatoes left the field. The swampers hopped on the back of the trailer and it waddled up the avenue and pulled up to the shady side of the shed. Andy was ahead of them on foot.

"*Mira,*" he said to Hilario. "Stack 'em five high," and he showed them how. "I don't want them laid out like dominoes, see," and he wagged a finger parallel the ground. "Let them get shade from each other. Put that burlap on the topmost boxes."

"Of course."

"And just to get ahead ourselves, Hilario, when the sun moves over there," he pointed west, "a little after noon, say, we unload the fruit on the other side of the shed. Shade, shade, shade. I mean, this is common sense, except out here I've learned that common sense is sometimes the first thing to skip a contractor's mind."

Hilario smiled and put it all in Spanish to the men.

"Let's get this wired early in the going so we don't have no troubles later on." He figured four loads, tops, was what he could carry on his flatbed over the course of the day, and now estimated that he'd be able to take the first load to the packing house around ten.

The men stacked up the balance of the lugs.

"Enough monkeying around. Let's go get that fruit." They loaded some empties, stepped on the hitch end of the trailer, and rambled back to the field.

Now, all alone with his tomatoes, Andy grabbed two blindly from the top box and took them over to a table near the shed and set them down. From the side pocket of his overalls, he lifted a pocketknife and opened it, deftly slicing the tomato into four parts. He admired its insides glittering with juice, the intricate networking of the wall, the proportion of the pulp, the way the big fat placenta marbled it like a prime cut of beef. He poked it with a thumb to get a sense how dense and sturdy was the flesh, and squeezed it until the juice ran down his fingers. Then he brought it up to his nose. He got a whiff of the acid, the sugar, the barely perceptible green, like fox fire in a log, still burning in there. Flicking the mess from his hand, he picked up a fresh quarter and plugged it in his mouth. Lord. Delicious. Damn good tomatoes. He pictured cutting one up and layering it over fresh *peda* bread and drizzling olive oil all over it. Add a pinch of salt, pepper, and he'd have himself some lunch. He went over to the hose and washed his hands. From the corner of his eye, he saw that dog take a quick step down the back porch. Andy asked it, "What's your intention?" He turned the spigot off. Then he noticed what he hadn't: Lilit was a step behind him.

"Good morning," he said. "We got our first run here. Would you like to take some in and give to your mom?"

She shook her head no. The way that dog stared him down made Andy furious and fearful at the same time. He turned and started back toward the field with a hand flipping open the knife in his pocket.

It's only a dog; ain't got no agenda, Andy told himself. On the other hand, an animal didn't have to be evil to act evil. Just like humans. In every human society there exist such dogs and, evil or no, society smartly keeps them on a leash. Then there's times when the whole society becomes a pack of evil-doing dogs, and there's no one left to leash them up...

The pickers were lollygagging. When Andy sized up the meager pick in the lugs, his blood pressure rose yet another tick. Damn these Mexicans. He spotted Hilario and gave him a whistle. The contractor came gingerly through the beds and nodded.

Andy took off his hat and wiped the sweat from his forehead with a sleeve.

"Hilario, I don't mean to give you grief so early in the going, but I'm not paying these people to do no fiesta."

Hilario cocked his head back and to the side, then nodded pensively.

"Don't give me any shit about them slowing down for color. There's plenty of fruit out there ready for market."

"You told us go easy, *Patrón*." He slowly put his hands up. "But if you want..." He opened those same hands to show that the world was Andy's should he desire it.

"Point is, at this rate, the packing house has got to dole me out three bucks a tomato to break even. That's my situation here."

"I understand your siduajian." He pronounced it like it was an Armenian surname. "I'll talk to the boys."

"Appreciate it."

"*De nada, Patrón*. The boys, they work good. Good crew, no?"

Andy hated when someone fished for a compliment on the heels of a complaint. He just hated it.

"Just put a match under their ass. But keep off those green-shoulders!"

Hilario smiled, turned around, and shouted "*¡Pendejos!*" All the workers stood upright from their crouched positions, mortified, like they'd heard gunshot over their shoulders. *"¡Usted se mueve como lagartos!"*

Lizards? Andy cringed. The workers nodded obsequiously.

"Si uno de ustedes falla, todos ustedes consigues el fuego. ¿Me entiende usted?" Except for the crude curse words, the guy used a high-class Spanish, which he sang more than spoke in a deafening baritone. Now Andy started to get a picture of the situation: This white Mexican was Spanish to the bone. Not too long ago he and his kind whipped their Indian slaves with the same sharp tongue, and when they said, "You'll all get the fire," they meant it. Andy rubbed his face from embarrassment, but also frustration with the contractor, whose job, after all, was to cool down the farmer's coals, not take a bellows to them.

That was how the roles were normally played; but this Hilario, he obviously played it his own way. "You push me, I'll push them," Hilario was telling him, "but it ain't gonna be pretty. And maybe, *Patrón,* you push my crew too much tomorrow and you'll be looking for another one." The pickers got back to work. Sweat stained their shirts, streaks of green stained their knees and sleeves. He watched them plunge their hands into the vines and quick twist the fruit off and drop it into their side-baskets. Bent over, turning this way and that at their hips, they moved as though hinged like a swinging dentist tray. The sun was falling down like hot plates. Andy moved out of the way under the elm tree but it only amounted to a different kind of torment, like choosing between getting cooked in an oven or under a broiler.

Andy dropped to his haunches, stood, paced into the field, paced out, leaned against the tree. One, two, three hours passed. In the stubborn air, the green from the fruit hung pungent and musty. Now and again a picker would send up a Mexican song, a kind of yelp, to release for a moment his spirits from the boiler room of his body. Now and then another would stop and make the sign of the cross, or pour water from an army surplus canteen over his head.

BUD KAPRELIAN HAD ANDY SET half a dozen lugs on the ground before he took a single box in.

"Hey, it's your fruit to manage from here on out; I don't blame you," Andy said.

Bud looked over the lot.

"Pretty good color this early in the going, huh, Bud?"

Bud moved his head right and left.

"Little green, but hey, you don't want no tomato sauce either."

"Okay," he told Andy, "let's get it off that truck. What do we have here?" he said. "Forty lugs?"

"Forty," Andy agreed.

In the office, they went over the method for packing out the fruit. Kaprelian explained he was looking at between two and two and a half boxes per lug after culling, and that bruised fruit would end up wherever, and fetch whatever it could, which sounded to Andy like another way of saying don't expect nothin'.

"Just let's make sure the rubies sell at a decent price, Bud. Do that for me, please, and you can have the culls for lunch money."

Bud briefly went over the debt issue. For Andy the bottom line was how fast his debt would get met, which brought him to how much the tomatoes presently fetched. He asked Bud. The packer reached for a piece of paper off to the side, like the number wasn't already flashing loud as a neon sign against his skull. "Let's see here," he said and brought the paper into focus through his spectacles. "Not bad."

No shit, Andy thought. "Would you say that's the same as 'pretty good'?"

"We're looking at about four bucks a box. But that was yesterday."

Andy thought, And from what I hear, today's a little higher.

"Decent," Andy said.

"But I wouldn't start lickin' my chops."

And don't lick yours or this fruit might end up down the road, he thought. "I don't see it dropping that fast, do you, Bud?"

"There's a lot of green-shoulders coming through right now. Could scare 'em off."

"Why don't you just tell these damn farmers to hold off a week?"

"Do they listen? Every year, they just keep pushing the envelope on color. One of these days the buyers are going to throw up their hands and say, 'No more!' I keep telling 'em."

Yeah, and folks'll start using apples for spaghetti sauce. "You're giving me a pretty good scare here," Andy said.

"Keep picking what you're picking. My only fear is we'll go from four to two bucks a box. That's my fear. Overnight."

"Son of a bitch." Both the price and the jackass who was trying to scare him.

"Is right."

On the way out, Andy tramped through the packing shed to get a look for himself. The girls were letting color pass more than even the packer let on, and he suspected that Kaprelian was pushing the envelope as much as or even more so than the farmer.

FOR TWO WEEKS HE COULDN'T HARVEST fast enough. "Hey, Andy, *paregam*, friend," Kaprelian sang, all of a sudden chummy, as he damn well should have been seeing as cash was pouring into his kitty like he was on a once-in-a-lifetime run at the slots. The pickers pocketed in eight hours what they usually did in twelve. Everyone was slaphappy.

Except the farmer. Packers settled accounts with farmers thirty days after the fruit was sold, but to finance the pick a farmer was forced to borrow money up front from that same packer. In Andy's case, a cut of the profit was already set aside for the old lady along with another fat cut to pay down his debt to Kaprelian. After all that cutting there wasn't much left but a stump. Kaprelian, of course, was no idiot: he knew you had to pay to get the fruit off the vine and into his shed, and he gave Andy what he "figured" Andy needed. But to move the fruit through at breakneck speed, Kaprelian's advance came up short. In turn, Andy shorted the Italians cash from their operation to his: a temporary Ponzi scheme.

He kept a little ledger in the glove compartment in his car marked "R" for "real costs" and "P" for "phony." The difference between those two letters came to a little over one hundred and fifty bucks a week. In conversation with the Italians, he introduced a few atmospherics ("Hell, I didn't see the cost of seed coming in so high," or "I'll be damned if cow shit ain't diamonds these days"), but since the Italians were hands-off cash operators and in no hurry for the receipts ("Hold onto them until the deal's settled," Zero told him) not even those fibs were necessary. By the end of the season, he'd settle up the accounts. Painless. No harm, no foul, all the way around.

1 2

SEPTEMBER SEVEN, ANDY STEPPED ONTO his front porch and felt a disturbing pressure, a kind of unsettling stillness in the atmosphere. He looked up. No stars, but they might have been hidden behind the shroud of dust that rose from a thousand farms the day before. No water marks on the dusty windshield of his pickup and neither did he see any rain stains on the road, but still...the feel, it was weird.

He was just past Selma when the sun shot over the mountains and splashed against the bottom of what very well might be rain clouds, long and flattish. Their undersides suddenly grew radiant pink and as the light continued to spread it revealed a thick gray crust extending to the Coast Range, or beyond. They were blowing in from the ocean, but with what danger and depth he could only guess.

It's possible they had already dumped rain somewhere out there, and as he cut off of the highway he looked for signs on either side of the road.

At Chamichian's the air was stagnant as a mausoleum. Even the birds had stopped cheeping. In the muddy light, the vines seemed sleepy, defenseless, on some kind of tranquilizer. He paid more attention than he ever had to the canopy, their natural cover for rain. Vince punched his pickup out of his yard, rolled up the avenue, and stopped.

Andy walked out of the field shaking his head.

"Ain't this something," he said.

Rain was not supposed to happen this time of year. Even though every six or seven years it did, nature let the memory die and so each time it came it was met with the same fresh dread.

They both looked up.

"First we had that frost, and now this."

"Sliding in from the west something wicked," Vince said.

"'Fore they explode. Anyway, those plums of yours should be okay. But these tomatoes," he said, "don't mix with rain for nothing. Situation's volatile as gasoline. If the sun comes out afterward too powerful, if the ground is wet they'll stew on the vine."

"Less than half an inch, you're out of the woods."

"If we get help from wind afterward."

Vince said, "Lose your blush is all."

"Don't knock that blush: keeps 'em from frying."

"Rounded second base on the pick?"

"'Bout. With this market, though, every stride is money in the bank."

"Nice breeze to blow 'em dry is what you'll need."

"Here we're sittin' talkin' like nature's considerin' our conversation."

"Naw, it's notorious for not listenin'. A bitch is what it is."

Andy said, "I don't think it's got no agendas one way or another."

"Ends up doin' jus' the opposite to spite ya."

Vince rolled up a loogie at the back of his throat. Andy took a step sideways to let him get rid of it.

"Jus' before it comes, I always get all stuffed up."

Vince struggled to get the clutch in and then lurched forward and up the road, just as the crew came around the corner.

The bus rolled up to Andy, its transmission gurgling, and stopped.

Hilario stepped out.

"*Patrón*."

"Grinding something terrible, that tranny."

"Maybe I'll have time today to fix it."

"Don't look so good, do it?" Up there, the storm clouds were now thick as a chest full of phlegm. "Hate to get your boys out of bed for nothin'."

"Whatever you decide, *Patrón*."

"See if this thing clears up."

"Whatever you decide."

"Why don't you just let the boys sit for a while. I hate to lose a day's pick."

"They make no money sitting at home."

"That's true enough."

Then he saw it, eye-level on the horizon: a hairline crack of light, then thunder, a hundred bowling balls all striking at once. He scanned the foothills—one, then two, three slivers more.

The thunder was now falling in chunks. The old lady stepped out into the yard and covered her head with two hands. Behind the wall of black was a field of light. The wall cracked and then closed suddenly up. He said a quick prayer that it stay and do whatever havoc it would up there, but then it hit him on the brim of his hat, a demoralizing drop.

God might as well have just spit on him.

Hilario, who'd stepped back in the bus, stepped out again.

"Let's call it a day," Andy told him.

Hilario nodded.

"We'll talk tomorrow."

"Andale," he said.

The raindrops, big and fleshy, began *puh-puh-puh*ing the parched dirt, making little explosions of dust. Clouds now totally cloaked the Sierras. In the distance he could see silver rain falling in feathery strokes. To the west the dark clouds were drifting in shreds. He scratched his brow and considered giving the tomatoes hats to wear, all however many thousands were out there, even though the futility of it at this point was plain.

He had nurtured those tomatoes, given them his best, he'd taken

Mother Nature into his confidence, patiently consulted her, and arrived, he believed, at an amicable compact. Now she seemed to be yawning in cruel indifference. He stood there like an outcast turned inward.

The corn would hold its own against the rain. It stood up high off the ground and each ear had its own slicker. To think of the mess they'd be in had he cut it down to dry on the ground...There he had lucked out, but here was a different story. The tomatoes lay low and in naked clusters. He could hear the leaves chattering as the kernel-sized drops struck and pooled at the stem and gathered in tears at their plump bottoms. He could almost feel them panicking from the wet on their skins, the sound of rain puddling beneath them in the beds. He looked back toward the house. The old lady had gone inside, but the dog had taken her place. He nipped at the raindrops like they were bees. Andy put his hand out and caught a swarm himself.

As the ground started to wet and cool down, an ashy smell rose as though the earth were venting some ancient grief. He could almost smell the old leftover spores pullulate to life. With each passing hour, the fruit would lose its will to fight and blister and pus and slip its skin.

Andy got into the car, lit a cigarette, rolled the window up all but an inch, and watched the raindrops hit the windshield. He didn't want to leave the tomatoes, as though he might any second be asked to petition on their behalf before nature's docket. Up against the Sierras the clouds were stacked shades of gray, deep, monotonous, and motionless. Here and there lightning, snippets of wire, flashed agonizingly white. Thunder made the car windows shake. Between the booms the *tick, tick, tick* of rain was oddly calming, like being in a store that sold grandfather clocks. Everything depended on how long and how strong the rain came, how many waves of it were out there, and he looked again to see if he could tell. The western horizon was a slate-gray plate with a whitish middle that had the appearance of clotted milk. Beyond those two, he thought he saw a wafer-thin layer of blue.

And then all at once it stopped. He looked out the window. Up above, the clouds were breaking up, barely, the sun darkening their migrating margins the way watercolors bleed to the paper's edge. For five minutes or so he watched them up there lightheaded, and then the rain started in again.

After about an hour of this kind of back-and-forth, he left the field. Four months of sun and dust had bleached the color out of most everything, but now the rain had brought that color back. The barns and old water towers stood slick and dramatically blackened against the hard gray horizon. He really had nowhere to go, as though he'd been booted out of a motel room squarely between cities. His wife would be at home and he simply couldn't face another round of questions and worry, so he drove toward town.

Andy pulled off 99, drove down Clovis, and then right-turned onto Kings Canyon Boulevard. He'd be in the rain, and then out, and then two miles down the road it was smearing the windshield again. On either side of the wide road tall and stately palm trees rose now dark as molasses. Between the palms, stands of oleanders had gotten a bath, their musk impregnating the air.

Around three o'clock the western clouds began to uncouple and spread for longer periods before coupling again. The sun shot through the rends in dramatic slabs, silver-plating the road, and toward the mountains a vast rainbow materialized against the whitening gray. When the wind began to blow nice and steady Andy relaxed his hands on the wheel and made back toward the field.

Steam rose from the tomato field the way it does from a man who steps out of a sauna. The air was profuse with sulphur and ash and countless minerals. The wind gently bumped the plants. Across the field the leaves flashed like aluminum foil. Andy walked between the beds and parted the vines. Andy could tell that the vines were already starting to sponge the water up. From one plant to the next, he walked all the way to the end of the row and was about to turn and go down another when he spotted the old lady standing on the avenue at the back of the house. She lifted her skirt and waddled a few steps toward him and then stopped and waited.

He supposed he was obliged to settle down her nerves. He came out of the field with a half-hearted smile on his face.

He asked, "How you doing?"

"What do you mean 'How am I doing?'"

"I wouldn't worry about it."

"What do you mean? Won't this rain hurt the tomatoes?"

"Naw. They needed a drink anyhow."

"Are you playing with me?"

"Seriously, there's nothing to worry about," he said, letting his eyes retire over her shoulder. "Whatever it is, we'll handle it."

"You know, if I had a son like you, I'd be proud."

"But since I ain't your son, you're suspicious."

"I don't trust anybody anymore. Not after what these people did."

"We got one life here on this earth; no use making it harder on ourselves by entertaining ancient feuds." He sliced it right down the middle.

"It's easy for people to say."

"Oh," he said, "I've had my share of betrayal."

"With your brother?" she asked, curious in a gossipy way.

"You know, if I were to make a pass over the whole of my life, I'd say I had it tough—and from pretty early in the going." He didn't want to get into it, but he was keen to put her in her place, so he said, "My parents died too, when I was young." He patted the bad leg with a hand and said, "I mean, it's kind of obvious, I got this here polio." Then all at once he was silenced by the tastelessness of parading around his woe.

"*Zavali,*" she said; it was Turkish or Armenian, which he didn't know, for "sadly poor," if not "pathetic." She had a companion now, someone with whom she could warm her ass at the campfire of misery, and he resented himself for joining her there, however briefly. Going at her from the opposite direction now, he said, "On the other hand, I'm one lucky dude. I got air to breathe, plenty of it, and a wife and kids and food on my table."

"Every day you are sounding more and more like a philosophe," she said.

"If I ain't already, a rain like this will sure as hell make me one."

13

"*PAISANO.* HOW YOU BEEN?" It was Zero. Andy assumed the call had to do with the rain.

"Good. Damn you guys, where the hell you been? Shit, we've turned the corner on September. Ready to harvest next week."

"Oh, we've been out there—don't you worry about that."

Andy said, "How's it look to you? Pretty crop, huh?"

"Look, Eddie and me wanted to talk."

"You tell me when."

"How 'bout I tell you right about now."

"Well, I'm finishin' dinner here. Where are you guys?"

"At the bar. You know, Sammy's."

"Don't you guys ever meet at your place of business—out at the ranch?"

"We consider this our office, let's say."

"Give me half an hour."

"Take your time. We'll have a scotch waiting for you."

LAST THING HE WANTED was to kick the shit with a couple of drunk Italians, but he supposed they had a right to know how their investment had fared through the rain, and so he gave the kids a kiss, told the wife he'd see her in an hour, no longer, and hopped in the car.

Andy pulled into the parking lot and was surprised to find it was practically full. A dozen or so motorbikes were parked at angles just in front of the door.

When he opened that door, sitting there on a stool was this gorilla of a man, close-cropped hair, a cigarette in the crook of his ear, and a chest so large the T-shirt he wore seemed in jeopardy. Andy paused—precisely what such a monster was put there to get him to do. The bouncer ticked his head to allow him in. "Thanks," Andy said.

The music—it was loud. Too loud. So were several guys in tight leather jackets at the end of the bar closest to the door. He'd put in a couple of calls to Sammy since the commotion outside his bar and missed him both times. He'd felt guilty for not visiting in two months, but now he wondered if his guilt wasn't misplaced: the joint was hopping like it never had before. Down its entire length the bar was nearly three patrons deep. He noticed that on the far side of the room where there used to be a cozy lounge a bunch of men were playing pool. He wended his way toward the booths, repeating to himself, "What the hell?"

The Italians stood and nodded their heads.

"How you guys doing?"

Andy put out a hand. There wasn't much to bank on in the shake.

"What are you drinking, Andy?" Zero asked.

"Sit," Eddie said.

"Scotch'll be fine. You guys seen Sammy?"

"He's around."

"Shit, for a second I thought maybe he'd flipped the place to a new owner without me even knowing. It's a different crowd than usual."

Andy sat down.

Zero lifted a hand up to get one of the new waitresses' attention. She made a beeline toward them. She was damn pretty but also looked barely old enough to be serving soda pop.

"Sweetheart, Andy'll take a scotch."

She smiled at Andy. Andy smiled back.

"Another round, you gents?" she asked.

"Just the scotch."

"To be honest with you, I'm kind of surprised at what I'm seeing. It's a whole different crowd than regular in just a couple of months. A whole different vibe, as the kids say. Including that waitress. She's damn young to be tending tables."

"I think Sammy got wise," Zero said. "He saw the way he was going wasn't headed to nowhere. You either join in or jump off."

"He must've dumped a shitload of cash into the place."

"Whatever it is, it's working. Bottom line."

"Yeah. Bottom line," Andy nodded. "Don't get me wrong. I'm glad for ol' Sammy. But this crowd…"

"So, Andy. We wanted to go over a few things."

What kind of a few things? Had they deduced he was skimming the kitty on the side? "I don't blame you there." He did a detour. "I don't think the rain did much. I wouldn't worry about it."

"Oh, we got no worries on that end."

Two, three beats passed in silence.

"You got yourself a coon out there."

"That's right. Thomas. You met him."

"We saw him."

"Been with me for just about the whole time." Andy was relieved but, in another way, insulted.

"Never caught our eye."

"Big tall black man edge of a cornfield ain't easy to miss."

"Anyway, now we know."

"On the other hand, you haven't seen much of me either."

"We usually meet the boss out there late. Four or five."

"We cut off around three. Tom sometimes earlier. Days Tom and Willie don't come out at all. So, okay, maybe there's your explanation."

"Two coons you got out there?"

"Brothers. That Willie's got the damnedest eye: roves around like it's dazed." Andy formed a claw with his hand and moved it sideways, up and down.

"What the hell we care about his eye?"

"Just weird is all." About as weird as the conversation. Andy thought that was the end of it—he was praying that was the end of it—and shifted the topic back to the crop. But they weren't done with Tom.

"We don't know about this situation, coons working out there," Eddie said to Zero.

"Them so-called coons is my right hand and left hand. I wouldn't knock either man. Especially if it's on account of them being colored."

"Don't get us wrong," Zero said.

"Those folks, they picked the cotton made the drawers we wore on our butts before machines came around and tossed them on *their* butts."

Eddie explained, "It's just that you never said nothing about it. We like to be up to speed, see?"

The conversation was starting to give him a headache. The waitress came back with the drink. Frankly, it hadn't occurred to Andy to mention Tom and Willie from the start; maybe that was a mistake.

"Put it on my tab," Zero told her.

She nodded and winked. She was too young to be winking.

Then it occurred to Andy: "Maybe I see where you guys are coming from. His wages is coming out of *my* pocket. He's *my* burden, if that's your concern."

"That was one of our concerns," Zero said.

"It's just too much for one man. Maybe I should've told you guys that up front. For that, I'm sorry. But the aim is to get the job done right, whatever it takes. If I needed three men out there, I'd hire them tomorrow. It's like anything else. I appreciate that you guys hold the kitty, but I'm the farmer."

Zero flicked a hand across the table, like he was clearing it of crumbs, and said, "It's you we got the relationship with, Andy, see? We don't want any of what you call 'interference.'"

He didn't know where to go with that comment, he really didn't. Neither did the Italians. It was all over their faces, though: they were in some pickle. For Andy, the bottom line was he'd rather drop the whole fucking job if firing Thomas was one of their mandates.

"We'll let you know on this coon, Andy."

Andy hadn't gotten two sips down of his drink, and he certainly didn't feel like sitting there and making buddy-buddy after a conversation like that, so he shook their hands, told them, "Let me know," and without even pausing to check in with Sammy he walked right past the gorilla and on out the door. As he turned from the parking lot, he thought, "That's what you get for going on the payroll of jackasses who never so much as handled a hoe." They sit counting gnats while buzzards are wheeling overhead.

FOR THE MOST PART ANDY'S FRUIT shook off the rain. Instead of boils and blisters on his tomatoes, all that showed up was a little growth crack here and there. He credited himself some—he had well-nourished the plants and let their roots go deep—but the weather that followed didn't hurt either. The sun came out like it was sorry it had ever left, and the consoling wind a step behind kept the weaker fruit from weeping.

Several spots where his competitors had unluckily planted, the rain had hit with merciless fury and four times as long. The poor bastards tried to shove the fruit through before the cracks showed up, but Kaprelian was no fool and put a bung on it. One, two, three days passed, a kind of quarantine, and when Kaprelian finally whistled, "Let 'em through," everybody jumped at once, pushing one hundred men in a twenty-acre field to salvage what they could.

The sorting line was like some medical triage following a large-scale natural disaster. The cull boxes beneath the stations were brimming with fruit in thirty minutes' time. Every spare hand was put to lugging the uglies to the cull bins and God knows how many forklifts were set in motion to dump these bins into the gondola trucks—in any single hour stacked no less than four deep in the yard—headed for the ketchup factory. To keep from swallowing the clouds of gnats, the sorters, all girls, tied scarves over their mouths. The few lonesome fruit that made it to the end of the packing line was better than if none had made it at all—but barely.

After two days of this kind of grueling culling, the sorters' hands began to flag from exhaustion, and there was serious talk of a walkout. Just to keep them on board, Kaprelian had to up their wages two bits. The farmer was already paying what they called a "surcharge" for the heavy cost of sorting, but now Kaprelian was charging a surcharge on top of the surcharge. With that news, a dozen or so farmers called it a season and put the pitiless disc to work. Probably what Kaprelian was praying for: he didn't want to burn his goodwill with the growers by denying a pack-out, but he also wasn't about to burn his packing house to the ground with putrid fruit.

The fresh market buyers did what they always do: panic. What are we going to put on our hamburgers, salads? With wedges of what will we garnish our cottage cheese? Tomatoes were no potatoes or leafy green for which there was a ready substitute, no. They were in a class all their own, one of the reasons Andy planted them in the first place. Andy hated to see it happen—terrible—but he'd had his share of bad luck and wasn't beyond counting his blessings when the good stuff came his way. He saw a quarter-cent leap per the first day, twice that the second. Kaprelian, already glad to have his business, start greeting him like some debutante at a produce ball.

He kept picking like hell, six days a week. If left to Hilario, seven.

"They're just going to sit on their butts—better be out here."

"But the packing house is closed on Sunday, Hilario."

"That's all right. We'll put them in shade and shove them in on Monday."

"I don't think so."

Predictably, after five weeks of running the field like locusts, the pickers were finding it harder and harder to find good fruit, and so to keep the momentum going, they started to push color. The first sign of it showed up late Friday. Andy pulled into the yard after just delivering a load and saw forty-some-odd lugs ready to go, and the swampers unloading another trailer onto the ground.

He came to a stop and watched them finish up from the cab. The blush was rubbed off. They were not only pushing color but packing way too many tomatoes into the lugs. They were throwing them in. He'd already half-decided to let the color pass—Kaprelian was the beggar who dared not be choosy—but bruised fruit was no excuse. He got out of the cab and put his complaint to the swampers, who nodded toward the field—"Your complaint, *Patrón*, is out there." He looked at his watch. Getting on nine.

Andy had made enough money to pay down nearly all of his debts and meet his obligation to the old lady. In any normal situation he'd been looking at gravy, but as it stood he looked to pocket not a whole helluva lot—two Gs, maybe a little more.

Hilario was stationed on the avenue, feet spread and arms folded on his chest, chewing on a thin stick. He reminded Andy of a captain on the deck of a large ship making a measure of the sea.

Hilario doffed his hat. "*Patrón.*"

"These swampers are going to kill my ass. They're flinging them around like potatoes."

Hilario spit the stick out. He flicked his tongue against his teeth and shook his head in grave disappointment.

"I mean, don't pistol-whip them, just give them a reminder. *Por favor.*"

"I'll remind them, don't worry."

"I'm going to take this load in, but if when I come back that third run looks the same, I won't be too happy."

"Don't worry."

"I'll let you do the worrying, how's that?"

Andy walked back to the house cursing. As he stepped out of the last row, he saw Lilit standing next to the lugs, that dog at her side.

"Pari louyce," good morning, Andy said, but his heart wasn't in it.

The girl put up a hand and grabbed at the air. It took a second for Andy to establish she was mimicking the blinking of the sun.

He nodded.

The dog growled, rounded back toward the porch, and then stood still. It came back and rounded once again. Andy didn't like the look of it.

Andy bent over and picked up a v-board to secure the load. From the corner of his eye, he saw the dog do one more roundabout, then sprint toward him, *at* him! Son of a bitch. Andy swung the board instinctively like a baseball bat and *bam* sent the dog flying, like they do in cartoons. Otherwise, it was no joke, his heart was in his throat, and the girl was screaming, *"che, che,"* no, no, rushing between them with her arms flailing "stop." The dog lunged at the girl—clasping her at the soft part in her arm. The girl sent up a banshee's cry. Andy dropped the corner board and grabbed the first short-handled thing he saw—a galvanized pipe—and stepped forward and came down hard on the dog's back. The dog stopped a tick and then proceeded to drag Lilit down as though his aim were to make her prostrate. *"Che, che,"* no, no, she screamed again, shaking her head, shuffling hideously forward with that arm like it was a stick the dog was playing fetch with. She wanted Andy to stop; it only occurred to him just as he wheeled the pipe down with monumental force on the dog's thick neck. The jaw snapped back. Lilit let out a terrific howl. The dog dropped to the ground like a sack of flour. The mother was now on the patio, wailing too. Blood, thick as pomegranate syrup, was splattered on the dirt, leaking obscenely from her arm.

"It was the dog," he told her. The mom rushed forward and threw herself on her daughter, hysterical. Andy composed himself and reached for one of his tie-downs, looped it above the girl's elbow, and cinched it up good. "We got to get some stitches in her." It was a command.

The old woman picked her daughter up off the ground. Andy's truck was on its last drop of diesel. He had no time to tie down the flatbed. He more or less shoved them both into the cab.

AS THEY WERE WAITING for the surgeon to stitch the girl up, the mother sat next to him repeating *"Agh,"* an abstract cry but at the same time the Armenian word, Andy couldn't help noticing, for "salt." He wondered if somewhere in the past folks screamed these words when salt was poured in the wound and how maybe after a time the word itself was left behind to express any kind of unbearable pain. His mind ricocheted between this kind of philological speculation and images of the girl, himself, the dog, and the sound of those lugs on the back of his flatbed blasted into bits on the road.

The girl came down the hall, led by a nurse. Her arm was bandaged up and she appeared calm. The nurse explained that the doctor had given her a sedative. Her mother took Lilit's head in her arms and caressed it, repeating "salt."

They got back to the farm a little past noon. Andy stopped in front of the house and escorted mother and daughter quietly inside, then pulled the flatbed into the back of the yard. The dog was laying there, eyes glassy, thin gruel leaking from its mouth and from its ass. Its lips were pulled back so its teeth and gums were visible—the god-ugliest smile he'd ever seen. On the back of its neck, his pipe had left a nasty welt. What with the scalding heat, it was already starting to stink.

A good sixty bins were all stacked up and waiting to be hauled to the packing plant. He'd put a call in to Kaprelian while at the hospital to hold the door open until he arrived. Kindly, Bud agreed, but Andy still had no time to bury that dog, and anyway, maybe the girl would want to do that herself. He took a tarp and draped it over the body, then proceeded to stack the balance of the lugs on the flatbed.

As he pulled out, he saw Vince on the far end of the field, helping himself to a few tomatoes. He rolled up to Vince and stopped.

"Take all you want. I figure, maybe, we got one more pick."

Vince grunted.

"I mean, hell, just because you didn't offer me no peaches this summer don't mean I'm keeping tabs."

Vince went around it. "What happened to that dog? I seen it lying there when I drove by."

Andy explained what had happened.

"That bitch had it comin'."

"That dog turn on you ever?"

"Naw. I'd've been dead already if it did."

"I don't know what the girl saw in that dog."

"She wuddn't hittin' on all cylinders to begin with. She ain't what you call normal."

"She always been like that, huh?"

"I don't know."

"I mean, you grew up next to her."

"That don't mean nothin'. Like I says, she ain't what you call normal."

"Anyway, I gotta get this fruit in before they put a padlock on the plant. What a helluva day."

HE PULLED UP TO HIS HOME DIZZY with exhaustion. His wife was waiting for him on the porch as he started out of the car.

"I have some news, honey. Peters called. From the foundry."

It had been nearly two months since Andy had dropped off Asbed's resumé at his office. "Okay."

"He said to come by and see him." With hope in her voice, she asked, "You think this is about hiring Asbed?"

"He's got no other reason to call, so I suppose it is. But let's just keep our fingers crossed."

"Mama is so excited."

"Let's just wait and see, sweetie."

"You don't look good, honey. What happened?"

"Ah, nothing," he said. He didn't want to break her spirit. "Just a long day."

"You sure?"

"I need a beer."

"I will put together dinner."

Marky was on the carpet rolling over a scatter of building blocks, seeming to enjoy the bumpy pain. Andy watched him and wondered if the movement of grown men wasn't similar, a larger variation of testing themselves. Inconsequential play. Marky saw his dad and ran up to him, wrapping his arm around Andy's leg. "Daddy, Daddy, Daddy," he said. Andy lifted him up and brought him to his chest. This is the only thing of real consequence, Andy told himself, this little body, this little breath. Andy carried him into the kitchen, opened the icebox, and grabbed for a beer. Marky put his hands around the stem and they played tug-of-war for half a minute before Andy peeled the tiny fingers away and emptied nearly half the bottle down his throat.

Kareen had set the table for him. Lamb shank cooked up in a tomato stew next to steaming-hot pilaf glistening with butter. He wanted to talk about the dog, that incident, but everything—the kids, the food, his own exhaustion, very near to nausea—conspired against it. By the time they'd put the kids to bed it was getting on nine o'clock.

"I'm hitting the hay," he told his wife and fell into bed without even bothering to take a bath.

APPARENTLY, WHO KNOWS, possibly in the middle of the night, by the bright of the moon, she had buried the dog, because when he got there it was gone.

The swampers were loading the last of the fruit on the trailer when Andy pulled up the middle avenue.

They said *buenos días* all around. Andy picked up a tomato and the two men followed suit. They all three studied the fruit's firmness and hue. The meat was getting hard, barely starting to pucker, and the color was pushing dirty pink. Andy had to make a decision. With hardly any decent fruit left to pick, should he pull the crew and call it a season? Or should he leave them in there and let them sweat it out? Most crews would have made that decision for him—when it no longer penciled out, said *adiós*—but not this one. This crew was faithful to Hilario. They wouldn't move five feet one way or another without the contractor's consent, and neither would Hilario move without Andy's consent. The economic choice was all of a sudden becoming a moral choice. Everyone was waiting for Andy to make the call. He wasn't ready to make it.

They hadn't mentioned anything about the dog, the patches of blood staining the earth not ten feet from where they loaded the fruit. In Spanish, Andy asked them if they had noticed.

They nodded.

"He came at the girl," he explained, and grabbed his arm where the dog had grabbed her.

They shook their heads. The tractor driver pointed a finger at Andy and with the other finger sliced a line across his throat.

"With a pipe," Andy said, and struck the back of his neck with the sharp side of his hand.

"It had a big neck," the driver said in Spanish. "The blow must have been even bigger."

From up a row, Hilario was striding toward them. The men

stood at attention. Andy brought Hilario up to speed and Hilario remarked that he'd observed an uncanny intimacy between that dog and the girl.

"It's true," Andy agreed. "They had some sort of weird thing going."

"Some people are very close to animals," Hilario said. "The old Mexicans, they have a story for this."

"Is that right?"

"They say that when we are born our soul is like a great plain where many animals live. There is also the animal 'man,' but his station at this time is not so high, and he is forced to work alongside all the other animals."

The swampers were listening, but their English comprehension was poor, so Hilario paused to explain it to them in their own tongue.

"*Sí,*" the tractor driver said.

"If a baby is buried in an earthquake, he will slow his heartbeat to hibernate. He can remain in this state for weeks, like a bear cub. If you put a finger in an infant's hand, it will close like the claw of a crab. Have you ever thrown a young child into a pool? He will rise to the surface like a fish without ever having been taught."

They all smiled.

Hilario smiled too and continued: "But it brings him confusion, because the animals inside of him are constantly at war. So, being the smartest of the kingdom, the human one by one kills them thinking this way he will bring harmony to himself. It will make him the God of his own life. By the time he is a young boy, they are nearly all dead inside of him. Except for one or maybe two."

"You're one helluva storyteller, Hilario. I didn't figure it was in you."

"These stories are not mine. I heard these stories when I was young, in Ciudad Juárez."

"Just across the border from El Paso."

"Those animals that live by our side, what you call…" he searched for the word.

"Domestication."

"Yes—the dog, the cat, the horse, the cow. Because these are the animals that are the least violent they are the ones we let live."

They paused to shoo fleas away from their faces, to wipe the sweat from their brows.

"Why did we start this story?"

"It was about that girl."

"Oh yes. Well. Now, there are some people who, instead of killing the animals, befriend them. These people are only half-suited for the human world. But they have special powers: some can talk to horses, others can read the coming and going of ants. Sometimes their sexual desire is so overwhelming only the behavior of rabbits can explain it."

The swamper recalled a retarded cousin of his who now and then would hump a tree, positioned on it like a bull.

"You see," Hilario said.

All four men laughed uneasily.

"So what you're saying is that humans start out like some wild kingdom. One by one they knock these animals off in a kind of warfare within. Some people, like this girl, do the opposite. They make peace with the animals. They're still roaming around in her, so to speak. As a result, the rest of the human world doesn't look kindly upon these folks."

"Yes. The Wolf Girl of Devil Creek—do you know her story?"

"Let's hear it."

"Here is what they say: A man and a woman were having a baby, but the labor was difficult, and then very dangerous. On a horse, the husband left to find help, but a great storm rose and he was struck down by lightning. The friends came upon the body and rushed to his home. There they found the woman and the baby gone, coarse hair and a trickle blood on the floor. These two, they decided, sadly, were taken away and devoured by wolves. They searched for the bodies and found nothing, and so with nothing to bury, they put three crosses over the body of the father, lit a candle for them all, and left it at that.

"Years later, a young farm boy walking a ridge above his field saw in the distance two wolves attacking a goat. With them was a girl. When he called out, the girl began to run away on all fours. In no time, a posse was put together to track her down. They found her—the girl, of course, that everyone believed was dead. They dragged her kicking and screaming to a ranch home, hidden deep in a valley. At night she would howl, crazy, crazy, and wolves all around would answer her mad cries. Then one night a pack of them gathered and attacked the ranch animals. With shotguns, the hands start shooting to scare them off. The girl escaped. She had lived so long with these animals that the human world was like a curse."

"I'll be darned. When did this supposedly happen?"

"I heard this when I was a child, but who knows when."

"Anyway, listen. I think we lay off for a few days. What do you think, Hilario?"

"That's up to you, *Patrón*."

"I hate to miss any fruit that's ripe, but also we just might be spinning our wheels at this point."

Andy picked up a tomato that was a little green in the shoulders.

"See what I mean here? A little too much of this shit. I mean, I don't blame the men: if they're on piecework, they gotta pick something even if that something ain't ready to pick, no?"

"What you say."

"I'd say three, four days, we'll take another look. Just promise me you're not going to take on no big job. I'm going to need 'em back, and they know the field. I don't want to start from scratch."

"Don't worry, *Patrón*."

"*Está bien. Adiós*," he'd told them: God go with you to your next destination. And God go with you too, Andy said to himself.

AS HE MADE A PASS toward the house, he saw the old lady sitting on the front porch and decided to see how the girl was doing.

"Ishte," she said, meaning "as well as can be expected."

"Is she in pain?"

"She is not bothered by that sort of thing. She cuts herself and stares at the blood pouring out of the wound. Sometimes I feel she will be on the verge of death and I will not know it."

"I see you buried the dog."

"Out there, in the garden. Every time she shoved the shovel into the earth, it was like she was shoving it into my heart. She has her mother's love, her sister's concern, her drawings, her piano to pass the time. But that dog was her friend."

"I was thinking this morning: maybe we can get her another one. This time, maybe, one that's a little better behaved. I mean, that dog had to be put down one way or another. It wasn't bred for human society."

"Half the human world is not bred for society. They are worse than that animal."

"And many of them are put down too."

"And even more survive. They conquer and they write their story of goodness and bravery on the graves of the dead. She believed that dog would protect her."

"But it's all up in here," he said, tapping his head with a finger.

She cocked her head back, as though a bad smell were in the air. "What do you know about what's up here and what's down there?"

"She's got to learn how to protect herself. I mean, the girl's scared of most everything." And you most of all, Andy thought.

"Most everything!" She rolled her eyes and wagged her head at his farm-boy stupidity. It's true, he hadn't been through what she'd been through—he was young, sure, but he'd struggled plenty. She wasn't going to take that away from him, not that easy.

"I mean, that dog wasn't going to protect her from life itself. Neither are you."

"Not most everything," she said. "That boy, that Takahashi boy."

"Vince? She's scared of Vince?"

"Vince. Mince." Her jaw trembled. "Let's not talk about it. It's over now."

"Vince did something to her?"

Dread spread across his back in anticipation of what she might say next.

"As you say, 'most everything.'"

They both noticed the girl was stirring in the kitchen. Had she been listening in?

"Go now," she said. "What's done is done." She lifted her chin twice, to push him back.

He stood his ground. "What do you mean 'What's done is done'?" He was whispering, but whispering emphatically.

"Not even her father knew. And I should tell you?"

But she had already told Andy—she had told him everything and nothing at all.

"Now you know my grievance with that boy." She dusted her hands and turned back inside the house.

Andy walked back to his truck. He got in the cab and sat, frozen with confusion, keys in hand. "Most everything." What did she mean? Had Vince raped her? Had he beat her? Was it a one-time thing? When they were kids? When he came back from the camps? How deep did the violation go? For some Armenian mothers "most everything" might mean little more than some guy tried to sneak a hand up her daughter's blouse. Did this explain Lilit's turned-in self? Those paintings she showed him. A ceramic girl, an oriental girl! holding a box in her hands. He felt sick to his stomach. A box! Was she trying to tell him, take him into her confidence? He shook his head to clear it, started the engine, and punched the truck forward. "What's done is done." It was the other side of the coin to "Enough is enough." She had waved a hand at the air when she said it. That wave meant "Long ago," it meant "Leave it be," it meant "There is no longer anything that anyone can do about it." Or did it mean that any attempt to repair the past would only aggravate the wound?

14

THE FOUNDRY WORKERS HAD GATHERED into small packs, talking like they were on lunch break though it was only nine o'clock; those still at their stations seemed to be moving conspicuously slow. He wondered if they had all just been told the foundry was cutting their wages when he saw up ahead two janitors in blue jumpsuits pushing mops over the cement floor. As he passed he saw a smear of blood on the floor. One of the workers had just been injured, and pretty bad from what he could gather.

He walked into the office and removed his hat, still a little dazed from the spillage of human blood.

"I'm here to see Mr. Peters," he told the secretary. "He called on me this time."

She led him back to his office.

Peters put out a hand. "Sit down."

"Thank you, sir."

He brought a stack of manila folders close to his chest and thumbed through them. He pulled one out, opened it, reviewed whatever was of import, and said, "I think we can use your brother-in-law. His resumé looks sound. You see, we're expanding our foundry to include a machining operation."

"You mean stuff that isn't cast. You'll need him to work on those kinds of projects?"

"Mostly designing parts and making prototypes. His draftsmanship is at a very high level."

"Looked to me that way as well. We appreciate it. This is gonna make my wife awful happy. Damn, this is great news. This is gonna change the man's life." It was like a blessing from on high.

"There will be a probation period. Six months."

Andy hadn't heard of it outside of an alternative to jail time.

"Just like it sounds. He puts out the work, he stays. If he doesn't we let him go."

"A six-month test, then."

"Yes."

"The man'll have to pass. What's his option?"

"I've already drawn up the papers. A work visa."

"You have?"

"We'd like to get him here sooner rather than later."

"Sounds beautiful."

"If everything goes as expected, you should have him here in three to four months."

"That's just around the corner."

Andy was chary to move out of that chair, as though to do so might jinx the good news. On the other hand, he thought, I better get the hell out of here before he changes his mind.

He stood. "Well, shit, I thank you—from the bottom of my heart."

"We will be in touch."

"Good enough. Hey, mind me asking: Looks like there was something happened here this morning. Someone get hurt?"

"One of the men caught his hand in a lathe."

"Ah, shit. I figured something like that."

Peters warned Andy, "It's dangerous work."

"Plenty dangerous, I bet."

"Especially if you don't watch your liquor."

"What dumbass would be drinking early in the morning like that?"

"Just as bad to be hungover."

"Is he gonna be all right?"

"We'll see."

"I mean, did he lose it, his hand?"

"We'll see."

"What's he gonna do, poor guy?"

The answer was no answer, obviously. Did he have some job that a one-handed man could do? He was this close to asking before Peters stuck out one of his own hands to end the discussion.

All the workers had now dispersed to their assigned stations. A little worried that his friend might've been the one maimed, "Johnny around here?" he asked a guy on a drill press.

"Somewheres," he answered.

"That's all right," he said. "What happened here today?"

The man left his goggles on, looked around, and then said, "One of our men, his hand." He made a lateral slicing motion across his fingers.

"Yeah. Peters told me."

"He did?"

"Maybe the guy was a little hungover, you think?"

"Is that what he said?"

"I was just thinking."

"You're thinking wrong, pal. There's something screwy with that lathe is what it is."

"What makes you think?"

"Two other men injured same way. In one year. I don't think bourbon explains it."

"That right?"

"I'd work down in the furnace with a crucible all day before I'd take a slot with that machine. So would everyone else here. But that ain't gonna stop him from finding a rookie don't know his head from his arse happy to jump right on it. And what are we supposed to do? If we tell him, jobs will be on the line."

"It's not your deal. You all gotta complain to Peters. He's gotta fix it."

"They come in and look it over, replace a couple of bolts, and then proclaim the problem has been solved—back to business, back to losing fingers."

"That's not right."

"It's some kind of newfangled lathe. Cuts finishing time by half, so they say."

"And eats up half the hands you have. Does it take some kind of special training to operate? Is that it?"

"It's a lathe, for criminy. Speeds up with the press of a button but takes your hand along with it. But you're right: it's like everybody's looking out for their own ass."

"I don't know how to fix that."

When Andy stepped outside, the heat was immense. He could feel it on the side of his face like a hot water bottle was pressed there.

Back onto the 99, he could see the big gray factory shimmy in the heat like some apparition. He had half a mind to turn around and tell Peters to shove it. He would never put his body in the employ of a man like that, and then it occurred to him, as though it weren't hard-as-steel obvious, that he'd just agreed to put his brother-in-law in the employ of a man like that. Though he wouldn't have to worry about Asbed working with that lathe, he couldn't help worrying for the man who next would, that nameless rookie, with two hands and two kids.

WHEN ANDY TOLD HIS WIFE the "good" news, she screamed. Then she proceeded to dance around the house and then she picked up the three-year-old and danced around with him. After a few minutes of this, she handed him over and called her sister in Oakland, and then her mom two blocks away.

As she came through the door, Valentine wagged her head like a woman adoring her statuesque son. She took Andy's face in her hands, kissed him on both cheeks. "Prince," she called him, and then, "Our prince."

They wanted to celebrate with a feast, so off they went to the butcher's. They asked Andy if he wanted anything, and he imagined just then he could've asked for the moon, but he settled for a six-pack of Olympia.

Now he stood in his small backyard stoking the fire with the side of a cardboard box, swilling a bottle of that beer. Sparrows were jumping from tree to tree, whose branches were thick with rusty leaves. With a poker he moved the coals around and watched the sparks jump and die.

His wife came out toting a card table and with a small cloth over her shoulder.

"Let me help," he said and put the poker down.

"No, no, it's nothing," she said.

From holding the kids, her arms had grown strong. He watched her throw the legs of the table out, lift it upright. She unfolded the tablecloth, swung it out, and let it drape over the table. Though she was plenty aware of the way men focused their eyes on her, and though she held her shoulders back and her head up high, in an almost dramatically enhanced way, the woman was almost totally innocent of conceit.

He hadn't intended on drinking more than a couple of beers, but he was feeling a bodily need. In the kitchen he could smell vermicelli browning in butter at the bottom of a pan, bunches of parsley chopped up for *taboule*. Valentine pulled from a tub the last of the lamb cubes all smothered in onions and drew them down a long skewer.

"Take them out with you," she said. "I'm done." She threw up her fat-slicked hands. "Let me finish this pilaf and then I will join you."

In one hand he carried the skewers and in another his cold can of beer. He put the beer on the ground and lowered the skewers one by one carefully over the white-hot coals. As he stood there, the irony hit him that Valentine and Kareen yearned for family half a world away while Andy was in exile from a brother who lived just around the bend. Why couldn't he just hop in the car, career down the road, pull up to the house, knock on the door, and put his hand out and say, "Abe, this is crazy. Something went wrong here. We got to fix it."

He sometimes felt they were stage actors pitted against one another in a play. Everyday, come rain or shine, they turned up for a director they could not name to enact their roles with unflinching commitment. The audience—their sisters and cousins and friends— watched the play develop, scene to scene, with incredulity until not even the principals, Abe and Andy, could believe where it was taking them. Andy had done a semester of drama in college and he remembered learning that the best plays are unpredictable and yet possess an arc of inevitability. That pretty well described it. But on the other hand, Andy could glimpse twenty years hence shaking his head at how shopworn it read. Title: "Two Brothers Struggle over a Single Piece of Land." He'd see the day that he'd say, "How the hell did we allow ourselves to get swallowed up in that?! Hadn't everyone already seen that play a thousand times before?!"

If it had been written, it could have unfolded an entirely other way. It would've taken the both of them, true. It would've taken ingenuity, sacrifice, the kind of commitment that he had no reason to believe they weren't up to.

They had a chance after Abe ended up in that mental ward. Andy believed that the pummeling Abe suffered would have softened up his spirit. His visit with Abe gave him a jolt of hope. But what is malleable in one hand is malleable in another, and the hand that Abe had fallen into, perhaps the most skillful of them all, was his wife's.

The sun was setting over the fruit trees now. Sparrows flashed in the branches. He watched them frolic for a spell, in a kind of spell, and then came back to the fire and turned the meat.

Did Abe wrestle with his conscience once he got back home? Did he at least hem and haw when his wife, Zabel, said, "It's time to get on with our life. That's the past now. What's happened has happened"? He pictured Abe finally nodding his consent: "Difficult as it might be, I can live with it—betraying my brother." He could also picture him deciding, as men sometimes do decide, to evacuate the object of his torment from his mind. To henceforth live as though Andy had never lived.

That picture tore into Andy's spirit the deepest, made him hate Zabel the most. To have succeeded in that—succeeded, Andy admitted, in the time-honored way that the weak time and again succeed—through insinuations, suggestion, patiently arranging whatever tiny facts are at hand…In the end, he would not be surprised if she rendered herself the victim. The villain staring into the mirror and beholding a martyred saint. Behind her, with a petition in his hand, the enemy, Andy, whose only sin would be to continue to accuse them of a sin. Who continued to curse them by insisting they were guilty.

Kareen threw open the door with her hip, a steaming plate of pilaf in her hands. Behind her was Valentine carrying a bowl of salad and a platter for the kebobs. The meat was rust-colored, blistered, and bleeding just right, the fringes of the vegetables blackened.

They set it all there on the table, along with the napkins and forks and knives. *"Are,"* take, Valentine said, handing him the platter.

He lifted a shish like a conductor lifts a baton. With a fork he nudged a chunk off. Holding it there, he cut it down the center with a knife. The pink middle ran clear with fatty juice.

"Voila," he said.

"Our magician," Valentine said.

Now they all sat down. Andy got himself a fresh bottle of Olympia, and when he returned he found his plate piled with pilaf and five chunks of kebob, but he was in no hurry to eat.

He took Marky from his grandma's lap and said, "Go ahead, I'm just gonna sit here and enjoy this boy and this beer."

As he held the ball of joy, he paused to take in as best he could the paradise they'd fashioned beneath that tree behind that modest house. The sun cast its lengthy light against the wall and on the cement walk. The leaves were turning gold, as if reflecting some otherworldly riches.

His mother-in-law asked him how it was going with the tomatoes, as though she didn't know the upshot front to back from her daughter.

Marky squirmed out of Andy's arms and joined his brother for a game of chasing the cat.

Andy said, "Thank God, well."

She remarked on their flavor this year.

"Vintage year," he said.

They all laughed.

He told them that the price of corn was strong and that in a week or so they'd be bringing that in too.

"How is the lady, Mrs. Chamichian?"

"Fine."

"It must be hard living out in the country alone that way," Valentine said. "I like the country, its air, but I cannot see myself everyday rising in the morning with only the rooster to greet me. When she walks down the street, she might walk half a mile before she has anyone to say hello to. No, I like cities; even this one is too small for my taste. But thank God we are here."

"She has a daughter that lives with her, you know?"

Valentine said, "I hear she is crippled in the head?"

"Not really retarded."

"What is she, then?"

"She is very very shy. If you try to make a conversation, she closes in on herself like a roly-poly."

"What does she look like?" Kareen asked.

"I wouldn't say ugly. It's hard to know, the way she hunches over like an old woman. Her hair comes down in front of her face like a drape. Through it she peeks at you like this." Andy tilted his head and squinted.

Valentine put a hand up to her ear and shook it, as though to indicate that something in there must be loose, and then said, *"Khent eh,"* she is crazy.

Andy said, "It's hard to know," but was he was thinking more "It's hard to know exactly why." He wanted to tell them about Vince, what old lady Chamichian had told him, but it would be violating a secret—"not even her father knew." It was the kind of secret that no person had the right to ever divulge.

He downed the last of his beer and set the bottle down. "Something happened out there a few days ago amounts to an example," Andy said. He went on to describe the incident with the dog, told them of how Lilit had implored him to stop striking the dog while it was making mincemeat of her arm. Kareen's jaw dropped. Valentine held a hand over her mouth.

Andy said, "Ain't that something," and shook his head.

Kareen tried to make sense of it. "Maybe she was saying no to the dog."

"Uh-uh," he said. "No. She wanted *me* to stop. No two ways."

"It was like a mother protecting her baby," Valentine speculated.

"Sure enough, but that baby—it might've killed her." And he had unwittingly killed the only thing that she believed protected her from Vince. "I didn't see no option. I had no time to weigh anything. It was like a reflex."

"Of course, you did the right thing," Valentine assured him.

"Still. It wasn't easy. It really wasn't. Seeing how upset the girl was."

The women rose from their seats and made toward the kitchen. Only a dribble of light remained, and in it he saw her, the girl and her imploring face: *Che, che.* She did not want to be maimed, but neither could she allow the dog—her protector—to die without protest. Her heart was being torn in two, and she was saying two things at once: "Don't" and "Do what you must do; I will not hold it against you."

"Here, a coffee for you, our prince!"

Valentine placed on the table a tray with three demitasses of Turkish coffee and a small plate of quarter-moon-shaped cookies. They lit the candles on the table and sat back to enjoy the coffee, thick and aromatic, some heavenly mud. Andy finished his quickly and then turned his cup over.

They let the dregs rest, crust, and then Valentine asked if she might read the cup.

Through his sadness for that girl, he said, "I was hoping."

He took his two boys on his lap and then brought them close to his chest. Valentine studied the cup, tilting it this way and that in the light of a candle.

"You are a lucky man, Andy. You have moved very slowly down a bumpy road until you've traveled to the foot of a mountain, a mountain so tall it seems to touch the sky."

"Hear that, boys?"

Yervant looked up at his father. Andy nodded as though they had reached an agreement.

"But you have crossed over it safely," Valentine continued, "and at the bottom, in a valley, there is a pool, a pool of riches waiting for you."

Andy knew it was just a story, Andy knew that the reading of cups was something people in the old country did, a leftover from Armenians and their pagan past, but just then he believed it.

"Ain't that something?" he said, patting his two boys on their shoulders.

Even after, or maybe especially because of all the hell he had been through, he believed it just might be true.

15

IT WAS WINDY OUT THERE, enough so that a good-sized dust devil, actually something closer to a miniature twister, had sprung to life adjacent to the cornfield. It was shaped like a lazy Y and its bottom arm looked to be doodling. Fascinating, Andy thought, that from such random particulars a thing of such lovely force and form is born. Made a man entertain the possibility that the human species evolved from dust too, like all we were was some kind of dust devil that popped up on a timeline a billion years long and would just as suddenly peter out. But not before it had done a world of hurt, Andy had to admit as he caught a fine drift of the stuff across his windshield.

As he approached the field, he saw the stalks whip around like dervishes. A cloud of debris hung over the backside of the ranch where the machine was knocking down the corn. Andy drove the pickup along the side road, careful not to throw up any more dust, though at this point the gesture was obviously meaningless, and then he made a right turn and pulled up a way. It was the first day of harvest, but he decided that he'd let Tom and Willie get up to speed on their own, as a sign of his respect, to acknowledge their competence.

Watching them throw down the corn, he felt proud for having stuck up for those men. After making such a stink about it, the Italians had quietly let their complaint about the men die. They were probably just looking for a reason to make themselves feel in charge. He felt proud, even blessed, to have Tom and Willie on his team. The quiet seriousness with which they went at their work was more than he could ask for: it was a gift.

The combine was squarely lined up on four rows, slowly mowing down the stalks almost exactly like the four-pronged electric gadgets the barber uses to bald a sailor's head. From a short distance, the sound *dun-dun-dun-dun-dun* was like some ear infection, like some kid striking at a drum. Scissors cut and sucked the heads of corn off from the stalks and stripped the kernels from the head and then spewed the kernels out a long spout into a truck pulled alongside it that Willie was driving.

Andy had bought the combine secondhand, negotiating the deal same as he would if the money were coming out of his own bank, but now he wondered if, what with the gobs of chaff it threw up, the machine was up to speed. Tom pulled the combine out, made a neat turn, inched up to the top of the next drive, and cut the engine. The men left their machines and waited for Andy. The dust settled against their skin like confectioners' sugar.

"Look here: We gotta watch for overheating on these bearings and belts. I'm not so sure about this machine."

"Naw," Tom said, "it runs pretty."

"Especially here—near the manifold. Gets too hot it'll catch your ass and this field on fire."

The image gave Tom pause.

"The thing about machines, they don't sweat. It's no joke. I wouldn't even be smoking up there, to be honest with you," he said, and then eased up on Tom, a chain-smoker. "Just watch where you're throwing your matches."

Tom patted the square pack he had in his shirt pocket.

Willie nodded. The way that one eye jumped from side to side was something to behold. Andy had wanted to ask what was its problem for some time. Now he did.

"It don't work."

"You mean like you're blind there?"

"Uh-huh. Come undone some point."

"Anyways, it don't trouble your driving habits."

"One's plenty. With it, I thread a needle need be."

"It's amazing the things we can do without, ain't it," Andy said.

The two shook their heads as though they could provide plenty of examples.

Andy recalled a friend of his in college who had stubs for hands. The kid played offensive guard on the football team and even taught himself to stroke a guitar.

"Damnedest thing," Andy said. "I mean, he wasn't no virtuoso, but still."

Andy turned his attention back to the machine: "So, main thing is, you feel you're pulling too hard or things ain't movin' smooth the way you see they should, just kill the machine—quick clean it out. You got somethin' in that truck to handle that?"

"We wearin' gloves."

"Naw. I'd don't want nobody burning themselves. I'll go fetch a rake."

"Alrighty."

When Andy got back to the barn, he saw a car coming down the main drive throwing out a god-awful commotion of dust. The Italians rolled up on him and stopped in front of the barn.

"*Paisano.*" Zero stepped out and extended his arms to Andy like he meant to bear-hug him.

Eddie was right behind. Both of them wore suits and shiny shoes.

"Good to see you guys. There's your first crop comin' in."

"How's it look?"

"We're not talking no Michelangelo, but for corn…"

"Heh," Zero went.

"Why don't you guys hop into my limo and I'll drive you out there—that is unless you guys came out here to study my pretty face."

"Naw, naw, naw. Let's go," Zero said. "Let's go look at our corn."

As they bobbed toward the far end of the ranch, the Italians wanted to know why they'd started where they'd started, and Andy told them it was no science but that in general you try to work from one end to the other and that he liked to start from the end farthest the exit road, otherwise the back and forth of the trucks would throw dust over what hadn't been picked.

Eddie said, "You got a problem with dust, don't you?"

"Dust like this ain't something you wipe off with a rag. It clogs your nose, for one." He stuck a finger up his nose and loosened a clinker in crude illustration. "See?"

He flicked it out the window and told them all the other reasons dust was a menace and, while he was at it, he lectured them on slowing down whenever they chanced drive in. Anyways, the ranch was more or less a rectangle formed of half-mile rows, and they aimed to move from east to west cutting down as many as they could in a day without overheating the harvester. Andy had rented two trucks and the idea was to fill them both, deliver them to the granary in Corcoran, and then round back and finish up the day. If they had a silo they could dry and store it there in one shot—not a bad idea if they intended to keep the operation going into the future.

"Silo sounds good," Zero said.

"Just something to keep in mind."

"How much are we talking?"

"Never thrown one up, so I can't say."

Andy told them he figured that at the pace they were going they'd be finished in about twelve days.

The harvester was halfway done with its second run. They watched it hammer forward.

"Those are my men," he said. "You've already met Tom. The one driving the truck is his brother, Willie."

Zero nodded and tapped out a cigarette. "Andy?" he offered.

Andy appreciated the gesture but declined all the same. "Ever seen a combine in action?"

Neither man had.

He explained that long ago, when the whole operation was done by hand, they'd found ways to use every component of corn—even the waste—and that the stuff flying out at the back was fertilizer for the next planting.

"People are amazed at the belts and levers, but actually, the most amazing thing about any machine is how many thousands of drafts of experience it took to get it to work the way it works. It's like the physical embodiment of know-how. Like experience in motion. Anyways," Andy said, "they're finishing up this run, so let's go look at the corn." They drove toward the end, got out of the car, all three, and stood waiting. The sound was so intense that Eddie plugged his ears with his fingers as it came. When Tom hit the top of the row, Andy caught his eye and cut his throat with a finger.

In their shiny shoes the Italians stepped over the ground cover like they were stepping over so many piles of shit. They got up on the backboard of the truck and looked down. Andy scooped up a handful of the stuff.

"Enough corn there to make yourself...what's that stuff you Italians make? That corn mush..."

"Polenta."

"That's it. Enough polenta here to feed the Italian army, huh?"

Andy hopped off and fetched the rake and long bar.

"Here you go," he told Willie, opening the passenger-side door. "I'll just set it here." He laid the equipment on the seat.

Willie looked nervous. Maybe he thought they were undercover cops come to check on his parole.

"They're the guys who bankroll the operation," he said. "No worries. I'll be on the combine in a little bit."

Back at the barn, Andy told the men, "I should have some numbers for you by tomorrow if you want to stop by. Or you can call."

"Whatever it is, Andy."

"Last I checked, we were looking at a little over a dollar a bushel. That's damn good money."

"And we were figuring how many bushels per acre?"

"Maybe a hundred, maybe more. Counting my chickens before they hatch...off this two hundred, we're looking 'round twenty Gs."

"That's decent dough."

"I'd like to shoot the breeze with you guys but I gotta give Tom a breather." He glanced at his watch and shook his head. "We're barely getting on nine and we're ninety degrees or better."

"We'll talk tomorrow then, huh, Andy?"

"I'll be around."

Through his rearview mirror he saw the two men walk up to the curtain of corn, part the stalks, and step inside. He'd beaten back the mites as best he could, but he now worried they'd spot a section or two still infested. He hated to be evaluated late in the game, when it was impossible or too late to change direction, but he had to admit they were well within their rights.

He drove the truck over the dross and pulled up to the harvester.

Tom idled the roaring machine.

"I think you might need a small break," he yelled.

Tom shook his head no.

"That's all right. I want to get a feel for this rig anyhow."

Andy settled into the seat and pushed the combine forward, the vibration and din and debris flying around him awesome. Corn spilled out of the mouth of the pipe in lavish, endless lots. After about an hour up there the all-out assault on his senses made him numb from head to toe and so he finished that drive and handed it back.

"That's some machine," he said, stepping off it.

"Beat you silly, don't it?"

"Sure does. Never been on a combine before."

"It be like ridin' a tornado."

Andy stayed out there, watching the corn get moved until late in the afternoon. By the time he got back to the tomatoes, the last run had already gone to the packing house. Someone was on the north back end that they'd finished up with the day before; maybe a picker figured he'd earned himself some leftovers. Andy puttered down the avenue, intending to tell him "Take as much as you want, friend," when a pair of blue overalls came into focus: Vince. When he heard Andy, he stood from his crouched picking position and headed out of the row. Andy pulled up and cut the engine.

"Helping yourself to some fruit?" he asked Vince. It was a question, accusation, and fact all wrapped up in one.

Vince had no answer.

"I don't think you're welcome on this field anymore, Vince."

Vince cocked his head back. "How's that?"

"I figure you've taken enough."

"Where you figuring that?" He didn't wait for an answer. "Shit, I came in here once is all."

He started mumbling something about the rubber when Andy said, "Just take the shitty little pailfull you got there and leave."

"I mean, if that's the way you see it, the hell..." Vince paused, "Where you..."

"Now that I think about it, leave the tomatoes stay."

Andy stepped out of his truck and pulled a shovel out from the cab.

"Where you come off like that?"

He leaned against the shovel. "The other day we were talkin' about that dog, its dying and all. You said something stuck in my craw: you said, "That bitch had it comin'.""

Vince shrugged.

"It occurred to me, Vince, that that dog, pair of balls and all, wasn't no bitch by a long shot. Naw, the bitch you were referrin' to was that girl. Wasn't it?"

"I never said nothin' like that."

"Like hell you didn't. And now that you claim you never said it, I reason you meant it the way I suspected you meant it, too."

"I don't recollect," he stammered.

"And you did it..." Andy said.

The man froze, as though it was clear as day that he had violated that girl and that Andy had seen him doing it.

Andy laid the shovel over his shoulder and marched to the boundary between the dead men's lands. Vince followed to his left and a step or two back, like some schoolkid on the way to the principal's. He couldn't look Andy in the eye. He couldn't look him in the eye because the man was surely guileless as he was guilty, transparent as he was a pervert—it was all in the way he stammered and froze like a popsicle.

Andy stepped up to the last end post and said what he believed he had to say: "Your land ends here."

He pointed at the ground. He shoved a shovel where he had pointed. He squared up on Vince so that the man should not misinterpret him an iota. "If you should trespass again, I'll have your hide."

"You threatenin' me?"

"From this point on, you touch this dirt, you'll be treated as a trespasser."

"This ain't your dirt." There was no gumption left in his voice.

"Neither is it yours."

Andy could almost see Vince weighing it all in his head. He lowered the pail of tomatoes to the ground, then walked past Andy and toward his trees.

Andy got back in his truck, shifted into first, and started out of the field. He felt his heart twist up in rage. He wanted to turn around and run the motherfucker over. Through his rearview mirror, Andy watched him skulk, slump-shouldered, into his orchard. Did he feel shame for what he had done or shame for being caught? Pathetic. Just pathetic. He couldn't fathom a man forfeiting all the wonder of romance for such a decrepit approach. Who knows—maybe that horrible stay in the camps had deformed the sex aspect of his brain. Maybe he'd come out of there full of quiet rage, full of smoldering shame, so that the best he could figure for his folded-in self was forcing love his way by force. Still, he had no right. He had no fucking right to lay a hand on that girl. Pathetic bastard, pathetic just like his brother was pathetic. Pathetic Abe. Poor Abe. Poor Abe when he started to put the screws to Andy. Through the shock, anguish, and hate, through the fog and with that gun leveled at him—Poor Abe. Maybe that's why Andy couldn't muster a fight. Yes, it was true the law offered him no recourse. Yes, it was true that he was ashamed. But even deeper down, even more of a secret, was that Andy felt pity for his brother. Just as surely as Vince and Abe had grown to normal size, they were shrunken and deformed. From the small of their turned-in world they waged their selfish campaigns. Dangerous in measure to how small and turned in they were.

They had reduced existence into a single dark facet and then tried to magnify that facet so it was all there was to see. Had Abe sat for an hour to turn the jewel of existence in his hands, there might've been a chance. But he never did. "Can't you see what I'm saying here, where I'm coming from?" he'd asked his brother. Abe gave him a blank expression. He was looking at it, yes, but at the angle from which nothing came back.

"I want to die," he had said. He'd gotten his wish and dragged the world down with him. That farm was now his graveyard. Andy would never step back onto it. He didn't want to anymore.

By the time Andy got home, he was so worn out he paused in front of those three porch steps as if they amounted to a triathlon. He made it up eventually, opened the front door, and through the thick of his thoughts forced a smile.

Kareen was sitting on the floor in front of the TV, folding laundry.

The boys ran to him and he picked them up and gave each a big kiss on the cheek.

"Wait," she said.

On the tube, a woman was supposed to guess whether there was a dud or a sofa behind a curtain. Before heading to the laundry room,

Andy paused to watch which it would be. The curtain parted. She had chosen the dud, a donkey.

"Too bad," Kareen said, and then asked him how his day was, and he told her beautiful, that the corn was coming off nice and thick. "It's gonna be a sweet windfall."

"By the way, this morning, this Eddie person came by again."

"I don't see any reason they're coming by here. I really don't. What did he want this time?"

"He just came by to say hello."

"Did you two mix it up in Italian again?"

"No, I was too busy. I left him at the door."

"Did you slam it on him?"

"What are you talking about? He's your business partner, right?"

"That's what they claim."

16

ANDY DOUBTED HE'D EVER WORKED so hard. If someone took a shovel to his head it would've taken a second or two to notice, that's how dumb he was from exhaustion. It was like football's "double days": weighted down with pads, drill for four hours, take a little break, drill four hours more. But whereas that situation lasted only four weeks, this one was going on four months. There were times he'd pause to measure his exhaustion, just to get some perspective, heave it up on some kind of scale, but before he was halfway up with it he'd set it down, stare at it, stupid.

With a break in the tomatoes, and the corn in good hands, he decided for a little self-indulgence—not much, a shish kebob sandwich lunch and a cold beer or two at the Asabarez Club in town.

It had been a good four years since he'd stepped into that hole, and it looked like it hadn't been touched up in that many years or more. Faded prints of Ararat, the Catholicos, and the Armenian alphabet hung on the tobacco-stained walls. There was Arto Jibilian, the dentist; and there was the jeweler, Agop Yeralian. Topalian the shoe repair man. This is where they came now that their shops were closed. Battling it out in backgammon, reading Armenian-language weeklies, weighing their pinochle hands or their fate—this is how they spent it.

Andy went to the counter and ordered.

His generation was looking to play a new game, by the rules of America, at clubs called the Rainbow, the Flamingo, and the Melody Inn. He noticed that the ceiling lamps were thick with the ashes of moths and that the swamp cooler howled so he could barely hear the plucking of an *oud* on the record player.

"Hey, Andy."

He looked to his right. In the far corner someone was waving him over. It was the tailor, Yeralian. The man used to cut his father's suits.

Andy thought it as good a place as any to lunch.

A very old man was next to him, a pair playing backgammon a little farther down.

"Where have you been, boy?"

"Ah, just around, Agop."

He sat across from the old man, who seemed to be half-asleep. Still, Andy smiled and said hello.

The man lifted his head and nodded.

"What are you doing these days? Farming with your brother?" asked Yeralian.

"Naw, I've got my own place now."

"Good. Baron Shishmanian," he tapped the old man's shoulder. "You knew this boy's father. Yervant."

The man turned his head, barely. "Heh?"

"Demerjian. Yervant Demerjian. This is his son. Andy."

"Ohhh. Demerjian." He looked up.

Andy smiled kindly, put out a hand, and the old man took it into both of his own.

"You're Yervant's son." His hands trembled in such a way there was no telling whether he was shaking Andy's hand or just shaking. "Ahh. I knew your father," he said in Armenian.

"Is that right?"

"Sure! I am from Bursa." He spoke as though everyone in the world should already know. "We knew each other as boys."

"No kidding?"

His skin was calming—smooth and cool as soap.

"Oh yes," he said. "He was fearless. He used to bring you in here when you were a boy. I remember now."

He now reached over to touch Andy's face.

"But you don't look like your father."

"They say I got my mother's looks."

"What we went through," he said.

"I imagine much."

"Much. Very much."

There was commotion at the backgammon board. *"Shesh besh,"* the player kissed the dice and flung them on the board. They watched the outcome: one die settled on six—there was his *shesh*—and the other spun, wobbled…five.

"Besh!"

Slap, slap. Game over. The loser held his head.

"Cold, cold…bring it cold," the winner demanded.

"Like your heart." The loser threw a hand at his bad luck and shuffled off to get the beers.

"Who's this?" the winner asked Yeralian, who seemed happy enough to entertain just about anyone.

Yeralian introduced them. Topalian—meaning "the lame one's son"—was the man's name.

"Demerjian?"

He asked Andy if he was related to another Demerjian, but since Andy's father had changed his name when he came to this country, and Andy had only one full sister, who hadn't been a Demerjian since her marriage six years ago, he was the only one in the family left holding that name.

"Baron Shishmanian knew him." He looked to the old man to add something to the conversation.

"I knew your grandfather too," the old man said, waving a hand at far ago. "He was a very intelligent man—French, English, he had many tongues. European-trained, an *Agha*."

"Do you know what that is?" Topalian asked Andy.

"Not really. Kind of. I know he was an attorney."

"These men were the highest you could go in Armenian society. Just below the Turks."

"That ain't so high," Andy said in jest.

The men laughed.

Shishmanian said, "My father, he owned a spice shop. One day I was there with him when your grandfather came by…"

Andy's order was called. He excused himself and headed up the aisle. About his grandfather, he had a few facts at hand. He knew the man was an attorney who worked as a liaison between Armenians and Turks. He knew the Turks had killed him and that his son, Yervant— Andy's father—had years later assassinated the two assassins. When word got out that he was going to be arrested, he fled on a moment's notice, leaving his wife and two children behind. He promised to send for them, and soon, but not soon enough. Within months, the Turks had rounded up the citizens of Bursa and herded them into the desert. All he knew was that his wife and two children had died en route and that he, a murderer, by the strangest turn of fate, had survived.

Andy returned with his plate. The losing player came in behind him holding four bottles of beer by the necks. He passed them around. Even the old man got one.

"I would have brought one more."

"I'm fine, thank you." Andy showed him his own was still half full.

"Go ahead, Baron," Yeralian said. "We all want to hear this story."

"It is the past anyway. What are we going to do about it?"

"Please, Baron."

"Very well. Where was I?"

"With your father in the spice shop, with the cumin and anise."

"Yes, he owned a spice shop, you are right."

"And you were with him one day…when Jonig *Agha*, Andy's grandfather, came by?"

"I would help my father on occasion, after school, you know, and I remember one day this *Agha*, Jonig *Agha* they called him, came looking for some spice. My father was a welcoming shopkeeper, but I remember him dropping everything to attend to this *Agha* in such a way that left no doubt he was a man of great importance. After he left, my father explained to me that he was indeed an important man. Therefore, the next time he came into the shop I studied him, to see how important men behaved. I noticed he was precise in the way he moved, he talked little but was not rude. When he paid money, he put out a hand to show the change was unnecessary."

"You have a good memory, Baron."

"As you get older, your flesh is swallowed up in shadows, but your memory is still bright. I don't know why…So, I had, in my own way, come to know him."

"Did you know his son, Andy's father, at this time?"

"No. We became friends or, better, we came to know each other many years later. Anyway, one day after school I went to the shop. My father was very glum. I asked him, 'What has happened, Father?' He explained that this *Agha* had been killed. This was your grandfather," the old man said.

Andy had been listening carefully but was still chewing on that sandwich. Now he put it down.

"They tricked him, you see!" said the man who had earlier lost the game. "'We have some business,' they told him. He went to a meeting with the Turks and never came back. The bastards had set a trap!"

Andy did not even know this man's name.

"I am Dikran Samuelian. Your father and I played pinochle right here. He told me these stories. I know them all." He spoke it like a boast.

"Yes," the old man said. "They tricked him. My father took me to the funeral. Everybody was there. The whole town. It was an event. People lined the streets," he said and wagged a hand repeatedly to show the distance they covered. "I remember watching your father.

He was in a black suit. Two or three other children were with him—all girls, his sister's, no doubt—and they along with the mother, your grandmother, shook the earth with their cries as they followed the cortege. I tell you this to tell you something else: you see, your father, he must have been ten years old, no older…his eyes—I remember like it was yesterday—his eyes were dry as dust. I remember marveling at his courage." With his thumb the old man made as though plucking something out of his eye. "They took out his eyes and in their place he set stones."

"Eventually," Samuelian said, "he assassinated the Turks that butchered his father."

The old man nodded.

"He had planned it for years, his revenge," Samuelian continued. "By the time he executed his plans he was in his early twenties, with a wife and two children. His father's death was like a sack of rocks that he carried."

"Of course," Yeralian said.

"But it was the way that the Jonig *Agha* died, too." Samuelian's voice was charged with anger. "In a bag they stuck his body and threw it at the foot of the door."

It sucked the air out of Andy. It must've been all over his face that it had.

"Did I tell you something you didn't know, Andy?"

"I'd heard something. But to be honest, I wasn't sure whether it was just some story. My dad never talked about it himself."

"Some story!" Samuelian roared. "They cut him up in pieces, like a chicken."

The old man clicked his tongue against his teeth and put a hand up, "stop." It amounted to stanching a severed artery.

"I will tell it," Samuelian said evenly. He patted the air with a hand. "Sit, my son, sit."

But Andy was already sitting. In fact, he was locked to his chair.

"This is what happened: He had been gone for three days, your grandfather. The adults knew, of course, that something terrible must have happened, but the children were led to believe that their father would soon return. It must have been Sunday, for the entire family was home—one can only imagine they'd been to church, praying— when there was a knock at their door. Yervant ran to the door, hoping for his father. When he opened it, he found that sack of parts. It lay at his feet. And they ask us why we cannot forget."

"What's that?" Andy said.

"They tell us, 'Let it go.' We will never let it go. For ten million years, after time itself has ended—we will remember. Not if they were to return it all, not if they were to deliver to us our homes, our olive groves, our rugs, our churches, our books, not if they were to raise, like Jesus, the dead."

Andy felt his body chill, his stomach shrivel up. There was no way he was going to finish that sandwich, so he stood, thanked them for being frank, and shook hands with each man. He got in his truck and started down the road, his thoughts frozen and liquid at the same time, a kind of nauseating sleet. Suddenly, hatred rose up through it, hatred of Samuelian. For having indulged a reasonable doubt, that bastard had wanted to punish Andy with the most delicious, the most sadistic details—"like a chicken…" That was the reason the old man had put a hand up, "stop." That's why Andy had avoided that place for so many years. That's why his friends no longer went to those clubs, no longer gave the time of day to Samuelian and his ilk. He wanted to pass the burden to Andy, to his entire generation, to make life heavier, to alleviate their own pain by elevating that of others, by forming a pack with the next generation, an unbroken chain of pain, like clouds need each other, need to gather for a storm. "Not in ten million years!" He'd gone there for shish kebob and beer and he'd stepped into a world of lurid memories, a dark and bloody mud.

Maybe it wasn't true. Maybe they had cobbled the story together from bits and pieces, or caught drift of the same myth that circulated around Andy when he was a boy? If his father hadn't told *him*, what were the chances that he had told these men? After fifty years, who was to say the difference between what was and what might have been and what should have been. Their lives had been busted to bits and they came to the future trying to piece it back together. But too many bits were missing or worn or didn't fit, and anyway, they used what they had, traded pieces, and even fashioned a few bits out of thin air, until their memories became a composite—a kind of masterpiece, a still life to gaze at, to show their children, to certify before the world, to cry over, to light candles before, and to protect.

Then his own gaze fell back on one image at the heart of his own family masterpiece: a blood-soaked burlap sack. He saw his father opening that door, he saw his bewilderment, his shock, and he saw him pacing behind that cortege, his eyes turning to stone. He felt sorrow for that boy, warped, cut off from his youth, suddenly old, his mirror image in full-grown form shattered, and he felt for him no less than if that boy were his own. He cried for him, cried thinking now about Kennedy, about his boy, John Jr., standing in his little suit as the cortege passed, saluting the passing of his childhood, saluting one last time the man whom he had loved so enormously, like only a son can love, like only a son can salute.

THE NEXT MORNING, ANDY WAS SITTING at the kitchen table, staring into the dark of his coffee mug, when it occurred to him that the question for his generation was less "To be or not to be" than "To forget or not to forget."

The phone rang.

Tom was on the line. Andy wondered where the hell he was even before why he'd called.

"Gas station down 'round 23 and 12. Look, Andy, might you come out here? There's something here ya oughta look at."

"Like what?"

"Well, we donst know. Donst want to toy with it case it's somethin'."

"Something what? Is someone hurt?"

"Nothin' like dat. We come cross somethin' is all. Maybe jus' wait till tomorrow."

Andy could see he wasn't going to get anywhere, so he put on his hat and headed out.

It must not have been anything that important, or at least not important enough to stall the work because Andy could see that the men were still harvesting.

He came on top of them, slowed, and let the dust pass. Both men stopped their machines, stepped off, and shuffled his way, patting chaff off their jeans.

"What the hell, Thomas?" They met up a few paces short of the rig.

"I was taking down that there row, and that tip hit, throwing it front of Willie on da truck."

"Okay." Andy thought it might've been some rare animal they'd hit until Tom said, "It's in the cab."

They stepped up to the cab, opened the door.

There was a bale-shaped package, about half the size of a cotton one, wrapped in brown canvas, and all around the canvas crisscrossed green packing tape. Looked like something the army might've lost.

"What the hell is it?"

Together, the men shook their heads.

"Well, hell, anybody got a knife?"

Tom reached into his back pocket and handed it to Andy.

Andy cut the twine and then slit it open down the middle and along the edges and peeled the canvas back.

Hot dog bun–shaped packages, wrapped in green cellophane. Andy picked one up and unwrapped it.

"Huh?" It was some leaves, one wound 'round another—like a rough-hewn cigar.

"Cigar?"

Tom shook his head.

Willie took it out of Andy's hand and put it up to his nose.

"That's weed."

"Huh. How do you know?"

Andy studied it closer now.

"Got a match?"

Andy handed him his lighter.

Willie took a leaf, flipped the hood of his lighter back, and held the flame beneath it until it smoked, slowly, luxuriously, emitting an odor, a stench, really, new to Andy's nose.

"Thas fer sure grass."

"Shit stinks. What the hell would marijuana be doing here, in the middle of this field?"

"Kids—they bank it here aimin' to pick it up later, cash it in."

"I'll be damned. I wonder if there's any more out here." He wrapped it back up and gingerly tucked it into the lot like it just might be combustible on its own.

"Could be."

"Well, shit, what're we going to do with this stuff?"

"Awful lotsa lettuce here."

"Think so?"

Willie took the package, weighed it in his hands.

"That be pennies from heaven."

"How much is that?"

"Half G. Maybe more."

"You're shitting me. Well, let's fuckin' sell it!"

Willie lifted his eyebrows, like he might just know where.

"I'm bullshitting. Gotta turn this shit over to the cops."

Willie and Tom both said, "Wooaahh."

They must know something Andy didn't know.

"That be a baaaad idea, Andy."

"Like they might think we grew it?"

"Nothin' like that, 'cept they might aks a few questions."

"So, what do I have to hide? I don't like this shit. It 'bout ruined a friend of mine's business. I suppose I better let the Lasagnas know." He picked up the package. "Let's just keep harvesting. If you find another one, I say just run it over. So we mix a little junk in with it...Make for good cornbread."

"They be back fer it, Andy. Thas fer sure."

"Well, let 'em. They won't find nothing here. Fuck 'em."

Tom shook his head like he was wary to say what Andy should've known long ago.

"Andy," he gritted his teeth. "They come lookin' fer it. Fer sure. They might come lookin' fer you, or me, or Willie."

Andy let his voice get big. "Well, what the fuck are we supposed to do? Put it out on the road with a sign says 'Merry Christmas, we found your present'?"

They dropped their heads.

"Fuck them!"

Andy took off with the package under his arm. Fuck them, he kept muttering, dropping their shit on my fucking field. Let them kiss my fucking ass.

Not an hour had passed since his lunch at the Asbarez that he hadn't thought of his dad. Not an hour passed when he wasn't thrust back into his childhood world, imagining his pain, up close and far, speculating by what means he coped, so this new anger did him good; it seemed to hose down his brain of those images and thoughts of his father. He hosed it more, kept the volume flowing against the bastards. Who the fuck are they? He pictured these smartass beatniks or dipshits or shitnicks, whatever they're called, good-for-nothings, never put a hard day of work in their lives, trying to use his corn for cover, they could kiss his ass, dropping their shit into his field, wise guys probably never figured on the shit hitting a combine. Andy laughed. He wondered if they hadn't dropped it off in the middle of the night...dumbfucks. He could see them panicking when they'd come to pick it up. "Where the hell is it?!" Chumps deserve as much. God be his witness, he'd take a shovel to their collective fucking heads if they showed up on his watch, that's what he'd do. He'd love to get a dog out there, some badass mongrel, like that big-headed evil he had killed, so that in the middle of the night when they came back to fetch their little present, this dog would bound in and tear into their skinny limbs. Punks. He never liked people like that. He never liked people tried to bypass hard work. Get ahead on the cheap. Lazy dicks. That's what most bothered him. How dare they drop it…Drop it? From a goddamn fucking plane!

THIS PUT A WHOLE NEW PERSPECTIVE on his operation. That's exactly what it did, by golly. A whole new perspective on everything. How could he have been so stupid? What was he? An outhouse? Did he wear a sign on his forehead that said "Be my guest, shit here"?! Here he was cock-a-doodle-doing, here he was letting his mind entertain matters far and wide, about what makes the world turn, all sorts of philosophical abstractions, while inches above his head people were lining up to take a big fat shit. Was he a criminal by association? If the cops found out, would he be facing jail time too? How could he not have known? Wasn't he there every day? He could see himself tongue-tied in front of a judge. No one would believe he'd been so stupid. He could barely believe he'd been so stupid. His only option was to go to the cops, head it off at the pass. But if he ratted on them, there would be consequences. Oh, shit! They had eyes everywhere, these people. That's who this Eddie was, this bastard who'd left his father's homemade winery for Chicago. He was their eyes, the man who'd get the call if or when Andy turned to the cops. He thought they were idiots, but they weren't idiots, they were pros, pros at playing a game Andy hadn't even imagined existed. Andy was the idiot. These people are the fucking mafia. He was farming for the fucking mob. They'd just as soon put a bullet in your head as take a stroll down the street. Jesus.

But they must've already been spotted, by someone, an air-traffic controller. How could they land that plane without it dropping off the radar, and if it dropped off the radar wouldn't the cops come out there to see why? They weren't that stupid. Maybe Andy was imagining things. There was only one explanation, and when Andy studied it closely, it actually amounted to a pretty damn good one: they never landed that plane; they just swooped down, dumped the load, and swooped back up. That's why they didn't want Tom out there. Jesus. Everything was fitting together like a kinder-school puzzle.

Maybe he should turn that little package he had over to the Italians with a wink? "Hey, whatever you guys do on your property is your business. I see no evil, I speak no evil. Done."

The Italians—big surprise!—had stopped coming by for their daily "inspections." Whether they decided Andy or his crew had stumbled upon the package, swept it into the combine, or passed recklessly by it, who knew? Half of him wanted to track them down and see what was in their eyes, the other half of him wanted to avoid them like the plague.

He hadn't been to church in over a month, but that Sunday he joined his wife and the kids, leading them with his hands folded in front of him to the very first pew. He'd stopped thinking about Jesus in spectacular terms long ago, but just then he needed some spectacular intervention.

THE NEXT DAY AROUND ELEVEN A.M. Andy rolled into Sammy's parking lot. There were only two cars parked there and neither was a vehicle he'd known the Italians to own.

Sammy was leaning against the bar, taking in a Giants game on a TV perched in the corner.

He turned around and saw his friend.

"Andy, *paregam*, friend. Where you been?"

"Hey, hey, *paregam*. Busy. Busy."

"Sit down."

They shook hands.

"Shit, I was here a few weeks ago, but the place was so busy I couldn't find you."

"You dumbass, why the hell didn't you look? I've been spending more time behind the desk in the office. Scotch?"

"It's early, but why not."

As he poured it, Andy wondered now what he'd come to say, or rather how, exactly, he aimed to say it.

"Anyways," Andy said, looking around at the new digs, "I noticed you changed the décor a little."

"I decided, you know, if I'm going to stay here, I might as well jump in with two feet."

"Different crowd, from what I saw."

"Younger crowd."

"And you finally got that bouncer."

"Remember, we'd been talking about that."

"Guy reminds me of King Kong."

Sammy laughed.

"Yeah, there's days I wonder whether he'll let *me* through the door."

"Anyways," Andy said. "Who's throwing?"

"This Marichal. He's got one helluva arm. Up 3-1, bottom of the seventh."

"That kid's got a future. What's he in, his second year?"

"Third."

A terrific cheer went up from the TV. When they looked up, Mays was rounding first, headed toward second.

"Go...go..."

A solid double. Two men in.

Andy had watched, all the while massaging the rim of his glass. Now he let out a big sigh, not quite intending to but then again happy he did to spur himself into some sort of action. Finally, "So whatever happened with that shit that was floating around here? Anything come of that?"

"Naw. It was no big shakes. The cops got me covered."

"Well, that's good."

"Yeah."

Sammy didn't seem in the mood to talk about it. Not that Andy could blame him. A man who is thinking into the future doesn't have the time to ruminate on the past. Except, of course, if that man's past is his friend's present.

"It's a son of a bitch, Sammy, but believe this or not, something happened to me same."

Sammy had been cleaning glasses with a towel, but now he put the towel aside and leaned over and laid his hands flat on the counter.

"You know, I've got this corn deal out near Corcoran. Two hundred acres of it."

"You must be harvesting around now, or just finished."

"Yeah. Yeah. Well, that's kind of where the boat got rocked. We were in there the other day with the combine and came upon this package."

"A package?"

"Yeah, about yea big." He showed its size between his hands. "It was out there in the field."

"No kidding?"

"You ain't heard nothin' yet. Turns out it was marijuana."

"You're shitting me."

"And the thing is, I think I know how it got there, who put it there. You know these two, Eddie we went to school with, and that other Italian, Zero."

"Sure."

"The bottom line is, I think they…" he dropped his voice to a whisper. "I think they are dumping dope in that field. I don't see no other way it got there."

Andy explained to him about the so-called landing strip, about the plane that came like a phantom—all the details that made the picture firm up in his skull. Sammy stood listening, his hands glued to the counter.

"Now, I ask myself, what the hell am I supposed to do?"

Sammy shook his head and cocked his jaw to one side so that his lower lip bugged out at the corner—the facial equivalent of "Friend, you're fucked." His response took Andy by surprise, and he waited a moment for that face to change, for Sammy to give him a crumb of sympathy.

"Well, you'll be done with the harvest soon enough. I wouldn't pay no attention to it." He grabbed a glass, the towel, and picked up where he left off polishing. "Just finish up and call it a day."

"Yeah," Andy said.

"I'd just leeeave it rest. I wish I could give you some other advice, but take it from me, the way things operate in this city, my advice: Just let it go."

17

HE STRUGGLED FOR A RESOLUTION. He'd come to a point, but no sooner did he come to it than he'd drop it. So he'd pick up another resolution. Go a few steps. Drop that one, pick up yet another, juggle a little more, but then reach down to pick up the one he'd just dropped and put it in the mix again. After a while, he was juggling several resolutions at once. It was pathetic. It was getting him dizzy.

Hilario asked: "Do you want us to go slow over the whole field one more shot, *Patrón*, or go over it once quick and round back?"

Andy answered: "Huh?"

Kaprelian: "What do you think you got left out there, Andy?"

Andy: "Say that again?"

Kareen: "Do you want a beer, honey?"

Andy: "What's that? Do I want honey?"

He drove by the police station—five, six times.

He worked out a conversation, actually several conversations, with the Italians—elaborate, down to the last handshake, "See you later, then." Why had the Italians not called? One minute the reason was no reason, the next it was because they were deciding where and how exactly to take care of him. Bing bang boom. That's how easy it would be. He was afraid to leave the house. Saturday night, when he usually unwound with a couple of drinks, became an occasion to get smashed.

He woke Sunday morning so hungover it was as though a bartender had used his head to mix martinis. The consequences of having no consequences seemed worse than the worst of consequences—it was getting that bad. Andy was this close to doing something neither here nor there, just to get on with it.

All of a sudden, his tomatoes seemed like the devoted relatives he'd stupidly neglected for some high-rolling pack of friends. Every day he'd drive out there to see how they were doing, though they didn't have much to show. The vines, God bless them, were on the home stretch. As he walked down the row now, he doubted it was worth the trouble. He must've lifted the skirt of a hundred plants to find a few plum tomatoes to take home to the wife.

When he got home, it was around two p.m., the time of day when Kareen and the kids all napped. He snuck through the back door, put the tomatoes on the kitchen table, and walked down the backyard path to the garage.

It was dark in there but for the sun that came in like sheets of glass through the gaps in the old wooden slats. He passed through them over to where he'd stacked four leather trunks. The top two contained junk he'd salvaged from the house after the fallout with his brother: a letterman's jacket, a green blanket with Cal Poly Mustangs stitched in gold. His trumpet, tarnished, and here and there a few trophies he'd earned along the way, a football signed by every member of his senior year team down to third string. Yearbooks from back to junior high, letters from friends, scalloped-edged black-and-whites: Andy sitting on a short stone wall, Half Dome rising behind him; Andy and his college cabal—young men in jeans and T-shirts, broad-shouldered and smooth-skinned, holding bottles of beer by their necks, unlit cigarettes angled from their suave jaws. Objects that tell a person, "I was here, there; I did this, that was done to me." He hadn't looked at them in years, but there they were, as though they all on their own decided to stay around, just in case Andy needed some help down the road remembering. As though someday these physical testaments might vouchsafe he'd actually lived and not merely appeared to live.

There was a third trunk, the one he now opened, that belonged to a different era, where another kind of story was told, the negative of what he'd done, what he hadn't done and didn't care to think about, one that testified to his failure in that particularly American way—through bills not paid, checks returned, vaguely and outright threatening letters. He thought back now on the year after his brother had turned on him. He thought on how he would receive a bill and look at it and place it in that trunk. Dozens he never bothered to open. Punch drunk from the blows his brother delivered, he was numb to wave after wave of bills breaking over his head until the gas was shut off, the electricity was cut, and the phone line went dead.

If he were alone then, he probably would have lived that way, a closed-up hermit, bundled up against the elements in a cave, cooking things he caught with his hands on a stick over a fire. What did he care what people would say? How derelict he looked, how badly he stank. Did they care enough to help him up when he was down? Why should he pretend to be part of a society that had no use for him? You get pushed back enough in a corner and you get a clear view of who's with and who's not with you. But he wasn't alone. He had kids, and a wife. They kept intruding. Thank God they did.

There, in the bottom trunk, he'd stashed the dope. He lifted the bundle onto his lap, untied it, and then shred a couple of leaves into bits and laid these bits on cigarette paper, licked and rolled. He'd smoked for years, in other words he was no rookie there, but this shit went down like acid. He coughed, studying its harsh and heavy smell. He flicked another match and kept it under the tip until it glowed orange and then inhaled more cautiously. This time it went down well. He didn't know what to expect, so he sat back and waited, his mind drifting into the bars of sun where the smoke turned and turned.

He took another suck. He was beginning to think the stuff was a farce, one of them things kids do to tell themselves they're hip or flip or whatever it is, but that don't amount to jackshit in the end.

Bored, he stood and reached into one of his old trunks and pulled out a baseball glove. It was tight, but not so tight that he couldn't squeeze it on. He punched a fist into it. I'll be damned, he said to himself, surprised it still worked. He chuckled at that good old catcher's glove—what a beauty—creased and wrinkled and right there in the pocket—bruised, smooth and cool to his touch, he put his nose to the pocket and smelled—smelled good—leather and sweat and grease, the perfect human perfume. Interesting, that smoke, the way it turned in the light as though turning on a lathe: like the mind at work spinning a dream. That glove was a big ear. A baby elephant's ear. He'd always loved elephants, their proud, quiet, and mighty way. He drew it up to his mouth and whispered, "You're a good boy," and then two words from nowhere leapt into his head: "You're high."

"Wow," he said, and now he tried to study its effects, but no sooner did he commit to that than he was deep into the effects themselves— how the light ridiculously wobbled on the wall, how the sparrows outside fanatically chirped—relax, my friends—how the old garage creaked like it was in pain. Poor guy.

Time had passed (when doesn't it?) but how much? Enough that the wife was going to wake up any minute—now! If she came looking for him he'd be in deep shit. Smoking dope in the vicinity of her home, much less by someone named Andy, her husband, was a bad idea. He made his way outside, closed the doors, oops, forgot to pack the stuff up, went back inside, the dirt floor smelled all of a sudden gorgeous, a bar of baker's chocolate. The smoke, still turning in those slats of light—what marble probably looked like when God first conjured it up. The pot—he packed it up, went back outside, forgot to close the door, closed the door, it was like every stupid thing vied for his attention, refused to sit back and enjoy the company of others. It wasn't all that hot out but the truck was so hot to his touch that he believed he'd burnt his hand, and when he got into the cab the dashboard was a jumble of gadgets, way too many for a four-wheel thing that rolled down the road, almost comically too many, like it wanted to be some jet plane. He laughed, and the laughter seemed to have an alien source, like that alien was using his body to express itself—wow. Kind of scary.

He started the engine but then it occurred to him that he was in no shape to drive, and so he punched the truck into the shade of their big sycamore tree, closed the engine, and lay down lengthwise on the seat. A blue jay looked down on him, head cocked to one side. He never did like blue jays. The way they kamikaze-like plunged at their prey. They were mean, deep down, and now that bird was eyeing him with malicious thoughts in its small head. He wondered about his eyeballs, their vulnerability, getting pecked out, say, and hurriedly rolled the window up a tad to bar its chance of slipping through. The light shook down from the tree. He caught a few flecks on his shirt, watched them wobble. It was like there were five, six, a hundred realities all going on at once, each linked to the other by a thread. From out of nowhere, his mind would shoot from one reality to another, like a spider on a web, and an entirely different perspective would commence spinning. The mind was a great knitting factory, with countless workers on his pattern, each with his own spool of thread. Who knows, Andy thought, maybe the factory is God's factory. Sleep was coming on him, thick, and from every direction, a kind of lava. Just a few minutes, he told himself, just a few minutes.

He had no idea how he ended up in his own bed. The first thing his wife said to him was she thought he was dead. Kareen explained to him that he'd slept the whole afternoon and through the night. The sun was out. It lit up the blinds weirdly. You must have been so tired you fell asleep in the car, she said. Poor thing. Yeah, he said, I think I was just catching up from pushing so hard.

He sat down and ate more for breakfast than he'd probably eaten since college. Three eggs, half a pound of bacon, God only knows, maybe a half a loaf of buttered toast. On his way out the door, he grabbed two *choreg* in a napkin. His lungs ached a little, he felt a little shaky in the brain, and he noticed his speech stumbled behind his thoughts, but other than that he didn't feel too bad.

He got in the car and headed out, out of town, into the country, because that's where he'd been going for the last five months, absentmindedly, or maybe not. He passed a sign that said "PUPPIES" and did a U-turn, stopping in front of a house.

The owner was a grumbling Okie. He'd stuffed a dozen pups in a cardboard box, and on that box he'd written "$2," though he'd let three go for five if Andy was inclined.

"Got tuh gyit rid of 'em."

Andy dropped to a knee and looked them over. He had no doubt that in two, three days the Okie was going to grab what remained like a bunch of carrots and drop them in a hole. Three of his own kids, in their underwear, tumbled out of his torn-up house. "Which do you like?" Andy asked one of them.

The boy pointed to a sad-looking one in the corner. Andy picked it up and looked to see its sex.

"A girl," he said. "You got good taste."

He gave the Okie five bucks, put the puppy there next to his seat, and pulled out.

The puppy stood, at first flummoxed by what was happening under her feet. But after a few minutes, she curled up and fell asleep.

She was still sleeping when Andy pulled up to Chamichian's. He grabbed the pup under his arm, walked up the porch, and rang the doorbell. If she didn't want her, he'd take it home for the family— what the hell. The old lady answered. He told her he had brought a little present for Lilit. The lady looked at the dog and opened the door.

"This?" she said.

"I thought she might like another dog. It might not be much of a watchdog," Andy said, "but I think it'll be a good friend."

"It's up to her," she said.

"Well. Is she around?"

"I will get her."

She yelled, "Lilit, come here, sweetheart! The Demerjian boy, he is here to give you something."

Andy was nervous. He heard the floorboards creak and then go quiet.

"Come, sweetheart. It's the Demerjian boy."

She poked her head out to see what for.

"I have something for you," he said.

She saw it was a dog.

He went to a knee and put the puppy on the carpet. It stood, wagging its tail, scampered up to the old lady and licked her foot.

"Puch," she went.

"I've been looking for a dog that I thought you might like. Maybe you can just give her a try. See how it goes."

"Inchoo?" she said. "Why?"

"She needs a home."

"We all need homes…" the mother said, meaning Who the hell went out of his way to give me one in my time of need?

"Would you just hold on here a second?" he asked her.

She sat on the piano bench.

"Out in the country is where dogs are meant to live. That's first. Second, it takes a way with dogs to make them happy. It's obvious you're a natural at it. You'd be the perfect person to give this dog a little happiness."

"Do you want it?" her mother asked.

Lilit nodded her head yes.

Andy picked it up and took it over to her.

"A peace offering," he said.

She smiled quietly and nodded.

"Agheg," she said, "very good," and nodded again.

"You know I'll be around. Let's say that till this dog grows up to protect you, you've got a friend in me. As far as you and your mom are concerned, this place is good as a fortress."

The old lady reached for his wrist and squeezed it.

"Good as a damn fortress. Imagine a wall from one corner of this acreage to the next. Nothing can climb over it. Okay?"

"Agheg," she said. "Okay."

They had reached an agreement. It felt as big an agreement as two humans had ever reached. He handed her the pup. She cradled it in her arms, its little body shivering from excitement.

"We thank you," the mother said. "We thank you for the dog and we thank you for your promise."

"It's not much."

"Sometimes 'not much' is all we need."

"Ain't it the truth."

EARLY THE NEXT MORNING Sammy called. He told Andy to meet him at Central High, 'round four-thirty, behind the old backstop. He said he'd been thinking of Andy and that he might have a little information about his "situation."

Andy drove by at three-thirty, as though he had traveled there from some great distance and arrived much earlier than expected. He sat in his truck and took in the old schoolhouse, the cafeteria, and the football field. At four he got out of the car, squeezed through the school gate, and walked over to the baseball diamond. He loved the game of baseball. He had a great arm, he could hit the ball. The coordination, the eye, the peripheral sense of where you are on the field, it was all there, but because of his polio he couldn't run the bases fast enough. So he focused on football, eventually making all-league center.

From years of walking on crutches as a young boy, his shoulders and chest had been buffed to cement hardness and heft before he'd even reached puberty. He remembered the first time he walked into a weight room: he was fifteen years old, just starting high school, and athletes in shorts, wrestlers and football players and a few would-be bodybuilders were grunting, puffing, and sweating like factory workers in the bowels of some industry whose purpose was superfluous. Over at the bench press, a stand of guys was encouraging one of their trembling brethren beneath a bar. Presently the guy rasped for help, and quickly they lifted the bar back up on the rack. "That's a lot of weight," one of the spotters said. "How much?" Andy asked. "Two hundred," someone answered. "Go ahead." The guy sat up and with a sweep of his hand invited Andy to have a try.

Though he had no idea how heavy two hundred pounds was in that lengthwise configuration—he was more accustomed to lugs of grapes or bales of feed—he slid up under it and took it in his hands. He remembered how, when he lifted it an inch above the slots, his muscles understood what they were asked to carry and the way they surprisingly answered yes when he lowered the bar and let it barely touch his chest and then, with all the power of his upper body, heaved it back on the rack. "Wow," everyone said. He sat up, a little embarrassed, and a little shocked himself. Andy had no idea why this memory came to mind. Maybe it was a kind of consolation—a small consolation: the body strong and whole and full of promise at this juncture, a bridge, when he felt so weak.

Sammy came up from the opposite side of the field and made his way toward Andy with worried steps. So many years had passed, but they were still like two kids.

"Andy," Sammy said, and he looked around nervously, like he was in a rush. "Let's go over here."

"Here" was behind the backstop. Sammy dropped to one knee. Andy dropped to a knee. They looked about to say their prayers. Sammy started marking the dirt with a finger, drawing a line this way and then a line that way, and then he drew a circle around them both. It was just a nervous gesture, but Andy fancied it a marking that held a clue to unlocking some age-old mystery.

"I've been thinking—'bout your situation. I felt terrible after you left. Terrible. Okay, I gotta tell you something."

"Go ahead, Sammy. Tell away."

"Okay. This dope stuff. The Italians—you're right about them. They're right up there, moving it."

Andy saw the ugly consequences, all at once, for both of them.

"But I had no idea how they were getting it in here, up until you sat down that day and told me. I should've known, okay. I mean, it only makes sense. Sorry, Andy, I should've said something right there…"

"Take it easy, Sammy. Hey, you're telling me now."

"They shook me down, Andy. I had no option, see."

"What do you mean 'shook you down'?"

"They told me either I play the game or fold."

"Your business."

"Or more. They run the stuff through my bar."

"You're not selling it?"

"No, no, no, no. I don't even see it. All they wanted is for me to hush up and don't make no trouble."

"You're shitting me, Sammy. Go to the cops. I mean, this is some kind of criminal activity. This is some kind of extortion."

"I did. I did go to the cops. They said they'd look into it, said they'd handle it. But nothing happened. Then, there was that gunshot, that night. Scared the shit out of me. The next day, Zero and Eddie, they came back to me, nice, nice, you know. 'Don't worry, Sammy. That commotion, it was just one of our guys,' they told me. 'He got a little out of hand.' Right there, basically announcing they were behind it. Somehow they got word I went to the cops. I thought they were going to put a bullet through my head right there and then. And here I was thinking, hey, these guys sure like their martinis."

"Martinis," Andy said.

"Anyways, they tell me, 'Don't worry, Sammy, we told our boys to settle down.' I told them, 'Hey, I'm just trying to make a living here, just run a good operation.' They says they were 'all for me, see.' They liked my operation. They said they'd take care of it. They told me they just didn't want any trouble, and they'd make sure there wasn't any. But they expected something in return."

"I can't believe this. This is how they operate."

"They even made some suggestions, you know, how to doll the place up. That bouncer, they hired him. Keep out the riffraff. You saw the changes. It's like I got this noose around my neck, this fucking noose. Maybe I should've closed down the joint. Maybe I should have."

"But you're in with the mob."

"Same as you, pal. We both are."

"I don't like this, Sammy. People telling you you gotta play or pay. That's messing with fire is what it is. I ain't gonna get on a soapbox. What do I got to lose? A few months' work? But you got everything wrapped up in that bar. That's your livelihood. No, my worry is for you, handing these guys the hammer to either build up or demolish your business. That, I consider dangerous. Looks flush now, but how about tomorrow? I don't like the way it smells—for me or for you."

"I know, Andy. I tell myself the same thing, every day, but, to be truthful, the way business is going, in a couple of years I can just walk away from all of this. Pick up and start me some other business."

"Until the cops catch up with you. Until then, maybe."

Sammy paused to think about something. He lowered his head, made a few more scribbles in the dirt. "The truth is, Andy, the cops are in on it too."

"That's some heavy accusation."

"Believe me when I say this. There's no other way to put it together. The sheriff, he's taking his cut. If he ain't, he's looking the other way for a reason."

"You got evidence?"

"No, but I can put two and two together. The way everybody sees it, it's no big shakes, dope. Maybe ten years ago, yeah, but these days… Hey, times change. It's like prohibition, you know, wink between the bootleggers, the speakeasies, and the law. I don't much like it, but that's the way it's going down."

"Shit, this is a whole new world."

"I don't know what the hell to do."

A couple of schoolkids had stepped through the gate and were now running toward the open field. One kid, the one with the football, stopped, and the other sprinted up the grass. The quarterback waved him farther, farther, until it seemed an impossible distance, and then he took a half-step back, cocked his arm, and threw. The ball spiraled through the air and kept climbing. The receiver looked over his shoulder, extended his arms, and the ball landed in his hands.

It was one helluva throw and one helluva catch. Andy felt that he should clap. Instead, he patted Sammy on the back. "We'll just have to see," he said. They were two men playing on a different kind of field, in a new game with a new set of rules.

18

"GENTLEMEN," ANDY SAID, "I figure that wraps it up." The land was bushed. A gentle wind drummed against their faces, and Tom and Willie seemed to be at a loss. They trod in their dirty boots over what was once a tall-as-a-man crop. Here and there the wind shaped exotic figures from the chaff. Andy stopped at a spot in the field and shook his head, as though finally accepting the futility of going into it any deeper. They stood there like three stalks saved from the reaping. Andy pulled two envelopes from out of his back pocket. One read "Tom," the other "Willie."

"This is just a little bonus for your good work."

They took the money, politely, and stuck the envelopes into their back pockets.

"You figure on shoving in another crop?" Willie asked. "If you be, we be there to help."

"I will, but probably not here, Willie. To be truthful, I kinda doubt it."

"Well, I wouldn't let that little package worry you none. It probably nuttin'."

"It ain't got nothing to do with that. I think I just come to the recognition I don't have what it takes to be a farm manager."

"You plenty good, Andy."

"I appreciate that, Willie. And the truth is I couldn't have done it without your help. Funny how things work out. Here I was expecting to do this job front to back all by myself, and you two show up."

"We just doin' our job."

"More than that, my friend. I appreciate it. No, we're gonna do us some business again, I got a feelin'. Mark my word, we're gonna find ourselves another piece of dirt to work."

"I hope so, Andy."

As he drove away, he felt a deep kinship with those two men. He was thankful for them, he was thankful for the quiet and selfless way they had soldiered together. He rolled his window down and let the wind plane against his face. A tear came, from that wind or the depth of his feeling he could not say. The valley stretched out in front of him in every direction, the Sierras a great and jagged expanse rising beyond.

THE MEN WERE SITTING in their regular booth—like they owned it, like next they were going to screw a plaque above their noggins in honor of their regular contribution to the bar's bottom line. Sammy was behind the bar, and Andy went straight up to him and put out a hand.

"How are you doing, brother?"

Sammy had a vexed look on his face

Andy winked, "Good, Sammy, good."

They had much more to say, but neither of them said it, or rather both of them realized it was hopeless trying to cut in on reality with a few syllables, so Andy just patted him on the back of the hand and then made through the center of the room over to the back booths.

The Italians watched him approach, smiling, nodding, like "Hey, there's our man," which told Andy just like that that they had no inkling he'd discovered the dope. His worry about that had been for nothing.

"Have a seat, Andy." Zero winked.

"Thank you."

Eddie said, "You look good, Andy. Looks like them coons rub off on you, though, huh?"

Zero chuckled.

"End-of-the-season tan. You know, there's some Armenians, like some Italians, dark as coffee. Others blizzard white. Just goes to show you."

"Sure, sure. What's it show *you*?"

"That we're mongrels, one and all. A lot of blood mixed up from where we come."

"You saying I got nigger blood running?"

Andy scrutinized the color of his skin.

"Could be."

Eddie blew some air through his lips.

"Come to think of it, in no time America will be a country of nothing but mongrels. Something to think about, anyway."

"So, Andy, we like the way it turned out. Real nice. We want to let you know that."

"'Preciate it."

"We wanted to talk to you, you know, about what comes next out there. But how about a drink? Scotch?"

"I'm fine, thanks."

"What—you on the wagon?"

"Maybe we should settle up this account."

"If you want."

"I'd like to do it that way. I like to put one thing behind me before I head in to another."

"You got your own ways, don't you, Andy?"

Andy opened the manila envelope and pulled out a bunch of receipts and weight tags. "These are for you guys; there's no use me hanging on to them anymore. File 'em away with your bookkeeper. And here's a breakdown of what we got." He slid a piece of paper their way.

"There's the bushels," he put his finger next to the number, "and there's the price. And that's where we sit at the end of the day."

Zero pulled it close. The two men looked it over.

"Looks good."

"I had the granary cut two checks, according to our agreement. Here's your lion's share." He reached into his pocket and pulled it out. The money he'd skimmed on the side, he had also—hard as it was—tucked back in. "Don't spend it all in one place."

"Heh."

"My share comes to twenty-three hundred bucks."

He took out another check.

"Good money, huh? Happy about that, Andy?"

"Got no complaints. Be honest, it's a good chunk of change for corn. On the price, we caught a handsome headwind."

"Good. We're glad you got no complaints. We like to keep everybody well greased. So the machine runs smooth, see."

"It's a good philosophy: that way nobody feels jacked around in the end."

"That's our philosophy. Give everybody a piece of the action, huh?"

"Piece of the pie," Eddie agreed.

Andy looked around the bar. A couple was dancing to Sinatra's "Come Fly with Me." Andy loved ol' blue eyes, a crooner that made you happy for what you had but wondering at the same what romance might lie ahead. Andy pursed his lips as though he were an old man hearing some song from his younger days.

"It's the damnedest world, ain't it?" he said.

"Oh yeah," Zero agreed.

"What is it that Honest Abe said? 'Four score and twenty...'"

"We wanted to talk to you about what's next, Andy. What's coming up."

"But I wasn't through talkin'."

Eddie chuckled, "We don't know what the hell you're talking about."

"Well. Let's keep it simple then: You see this check?" Andy slid it over to them. "I left it blank. I thought about this long and hard, but the upshot is I don't want this money."

The two men looked at one another.

"I don't like to be taken for a fool, see." The tone of his voice was indignant but not angry. "It's about you, but it ain't about you—so, in a way, I wouldn't take it too personal. It's just something about me. I don't like being taken for a fool. It rubs me the wrong way."

Zero said, "How did we do that, Andy? Make you look a fool?" The two Italians were genuinely perplexed.

"Is it about them coons?" Zero wondered. "We saw you was upset about it. Hey, no harm, no foul, huh? We never said another word about it."

"I appreciate that. Those two men got a lot of class. They work to get the job done right; they run into a problem and they do whatever it takes to fix it. To me, that's class." He paused and said it again, "That is high-class. So I'm glad you had a change of heart there."

"Hey, we got nothin' but heart. We got heart to spare, huh?"

"Nope, it's about that dope you've been dropping off in the field."

They'd had their glasses up to their mouths, but now, in tandem, they eased them back on the table.

"I ran into one of your packages."

There was a long pause.

"What package?" Eddie said.

Zero fast threw up a hand, "stop!"

"What did you do with that, Andy?" he asked.

"I was out there walking the field, see, 'bout where you were inspecting the corn for a week. First, I figured a couple of punks dropped it there. Kids, you know, hustlers aiming to hide it from the law. So I just burned it. It had one helluva smell, that much dope going up in smoke. Good thing I was way out to hell and back in the country."

"You burned it?"

"Like wood left for dead."

"What, you think we dropped off the banana boat? What the fuck did you do with it?" Eddie said.

"Then I put two and two together. Shit, I thought, them Italians are dropping it off that plane." He made his hand glide over the table and then released the contents from his fingers.

"You burned it?"

"Hey," Eddie said it so that the "ey" quivered.

"I could have never brought it up. Let the whole things slide. If you're worried about me going to cops with it, I got no interest in that. I been fooled enough and don't care to be fooled again. That's the bottom line. And to show you I mean what I'm saying, you see this here check—blank. It's there for you to write your name."

Eddie picked it up.

"It's a lot of money, for me and my family. But I just don't want no part of it." Andy stood. "I just can't cash it."

"Andy's a big shot now, Zero. He don't want no part of it."

"Andy, sit down," Zero said.

Andy sat down, but at the edge of the U-shaped seat.

"Look, I see where you're coming from. You figure they track that check back to you, it's gonna look like you got some piece in the activity. Like you played ball with us on these runs. You're worried, hey, if the cops start blowing the house down..." He turned to Eddie, to explain it better: "See, Eddie, it's one thing for us to pay him some chicken-feed salary for farming that corn the way we been doin' it, and 'nother thing to take a piece of the nut."

Zero's way of analyzing the situation impressed Andy, so much so that he nodded his head.

"Look, Andy. I mean, what you're telling me is you burned the package before you knew it was ours. I can't blame you for that—you're no mindreader."

"That I'm not, not by no long shot."

"You give us this check, we'll slip it back to you off the table, cash. Clean. Huh, Andy? We got your back."

"Any which way, I don't want the loot."

"It's just a bad idea, Andy," Zero explained. "See, we vouched for you to the capo. I told him you were a friend of mine."

With a hand Eddie made a gesture over the table like he was shooing a fly away and said, "I don't want you turning into a problem. Don't make us look too good either, like *cafones*."

"I'm too old to improve my looks. Everybody at some point has gotta make peace with the mirror, Eddie."

"What is this?" Eddie said. "Heyyyyy."

Zero said, "You think about it, Andy. I'll hold this check for you, huh? See if in a couple of days things look different in your mirror."

He felt sick and afraid, but also strangely sad over the fact that he and Eddie, two boys raised under the same patch of sky and whose bare feet knew the same dusty patch of earth, should be inches from maiming each other over a few measly marijuana leaves. He thought of Noninnis and Pagagnis and Lamanuzzis, all those old Italians who have shoved off from the old country with a few lira in their pockets and a few words of English in their vocabulary. He saw them sitting beneath a tall vineyard trellis sipping their homemade wines.

"You know my old man, Yervant? Yervant was his name..."

"You mean the Melon King?" Eddie said.

"Yeah. The Melon King, Eddie."

Eddie let out a puff of disgust.

"You know, when I look at your face, Eddie, I see something I've seen plenty of in my day. You ain't nothing special."

Eddie tilted his head to the side, as though to give Andy a different look.

"What I see is what you call 'getting there on the cheap.' Never did trust and never did like that look."

Eddie sat back in the booth and crossed his arms, nonchalant, as though he'd already determined his next step and was just relaxing a beat before he took it.

It made Andy's brain, at least the part the family engineer had fashioned, scramble for the nearest exit. But the other part—a part he believed had all but disappeared—refused to budge an inch. Indeed, against all common sense—his wife, his kids, his own person!—it was hunkering down.

"It gets you to thinking about Satan. How he just carried a bag of tricks, like some snake-oil salesman. 'Here,' he says, 'take this potion and in no time you'll be whole. Paradise,' he proclaimed, 'is just a swig away.'"

"Only you gotta sell your soul, right?" Eddie said. "To get it—that paradise."

"I don't know. Maybe your soul just stays a kind of dwarf."

"Andy," Zero said, "that hole you're digging—it keeps getting deeper."

Andy saw himself in it, knee deep, but he just kept going down. "The bottom line is," Andy said, "if I take this money, I say to you, 'That's just fine with me.' All that hard work—it's what I did because nobody ever offered me the oil yet. I don't care to turn on myself, and I don't care to turn on my old man that way." For a fraction of a second, he saw his father trodding behind that cortege. The image brought him calm, as though it was impossible to suffer beyond a point, the point his dad had reached, and by mysterious extension, so had he. "Yep, those folks—those old Italians and Basques and Volgas—those folks, including yours, Eddie—they struggled through a world of hurt to make something for themselves here, in America."

Eddie grimaced.

Andy took a deep breath. "I just don't care to do it is all. Not at this point in my life."

He stood and said *adiós*.

"Hey," Eddie went again.

Andy made toward the door and beelined up the aisle, Eddie's "hey" hanging in the air and turning vaguely droll, like he might've had in mind what horses eat. Still, there might very well be a knife or bullet in the next draw of the cards, and so mixed in with the comic element was a coiling sense of dread. As Andy approached the door he saw the bouncer quickly assume a kind of offensive position, and for a tick, just a tick, Andy thought maybe it wasn't such a good idea to retire the Italians that way. Just then the bouncer nodded, in the very direction Andy had come from, and he knew right away that there was going to be a complication.

He came up slowly, and the grunt took a step between him and the door. Andy stood, waiting, not exactly for instructions.

"The boys want to see you."

"I think I saw 'nough of them tonight."

"Looks like they want to see you again."

Andy chuckled, kind of.

"I don't take marching orders, friend."

The bouncer made an arc with his hand, like he was showing how to lob a ball.

"You're lookin' to keep me here against my will?"

The bouncer's eyes said he was uncertain about that.

From the margin of Andy's tunneled vision, some swift movement sliced the air. Quickly, he turned. Sammy—in his hand a bat.

"Get the fuck out of here."

It was no mean weapon in the grip of any man, least of all one who hit .333 in the minors.

"But these…" the grunt mumbled. "They…This guy…"

Sammy wasn't long on words either: "This is my bar," he sneered. "And this is my friend. So leave it."

The bouncer looked around like a bully surprised at his sudden need for some shoring up, and then said, "Up to you, Sammy."

"And I'll be dead in hell when it ain't," Sammy said.

The bouncer grabbed his jacket off the back of his chair and went out the door.

Half a dozen patrons around a table next to the door followed him. Andy glanced back over at the Italians. Eddie was going big with his arms, like he was miming an explosion, and Zero was nodding, as if to acknowledge its terrible consequences.

Andy and Sammy stepped outside. The weather had turned chilly enough so that their breath scummed the air in front of them.

Andy fetched a cigarette. Sammy wasn't a smoker but he asked for one all the same. Andy held it in front of Sammy's mouth like he was offering the man communion.

Sammy took a deep drag. Andy lit his own. For a couple of minutes the men sat there smoking.

A guy and girl came out, scurrying toward their car. They watched them go, like two men just forced off a train in a foreign land looking for any small clue on where to go, what step to take next.

19

THE SUN HAD FALLEN BACK, the trees had given us their leaves, and the shoulders of the vines were slumped in exhaustion. It was late afternoon and the light was amber and glassy on Kearney Boulevard.

In those early days when his brother booted him out, Andy found solace driving that marvelous road. Flanked on either side by columns of palm trees, gently wending for miles on end, it was a stately passage to nowhere. He drove it when his life had no direction, and it received him like the outstretched arms of a mother. It received him the way a library receives a threadbare man into its reading room.

Oddly, maybe something of the life—the man, Kearney—also gave him solace. He had written a thirty-page paper on him in college, for a class called Local Agricultural History. He'd learned that they had called him the Raisin King of California, a dubious title for a boy born in Liverpool, England, and with the common Irish name Carney. He was twelve years old when his parents had immigrated. The father worked as a clerk for a trunk manufacturer just outside of Boston and slowly moved up the ladder until he was the manager of the whole shebang. The boy had seen the ugly lot of his kinsman in Boston, potato famine refugees, sleeping side by side in tenement housing and laboring in putrid factories by day. In the shadows of these downtrodden, he decided to better himself. He studied French, German, the arts and sciences, even learned how to ballroom dance toward the goal of becoming a gentleman.

238

He became one and, at the age of twenty-seven, headed west, leaving forever behind Boston and his Irish brogue. His aim was to promote and sell land in California's Central Valley. Before long, he had in hand one thousand acres of his own.

He had read about the Nile, Euphrates, and Indus Valleys and believed the Central Valley, bounded by two mountain ranges, was these giants' newly come cousin waiting to be awakened. For millions of years wind and rain had scraped and scrubbed the Sierras on one side and the Coast Range on the other, depositing nitrogen riches on the vast bottom of that massive bowl. Rivers and streams flowed endlessly from the mountains beyond. Vast and ancient lakes had formed underground. The weather was propitious for the cultivation of crops: winter cold to make trees sleep deeply and summers devilishly hot to ripen their fruit. Frost, hail, and other hazards from above would come, but only now and then, like distant kin. Kearney believed that if the valley could be plumbed correctly, the bounty that would flow from it would know no equal.

He set up shop and began. He and his people scraped the land level, channeled water there, and laid out the roads. Trees and grape cuttings from Spain were shipped in. To orient buyers in the ocean-like expanse, four major avenues were named for the four poles of navigation: North, South, East, and West. In anticipation of their future farming glory, roads named Elm and Cherry and Chestnut and Walnut and Palm came next. He chopped the land up into twenty-acre parcels and advertised them at $1,000 a pop. With a mere $150 down and $12.50 a month interest-free until the debt was met, folks signed up from all over the state. There were four former schoolteachers from San Francisco. Accountants, haberdashers, and retired attorneys from Los Angeles. A handful of gold-rushers, flush with money.

Raisins. Kearney saw their future there. Thompson grapes grew like wildflowers on that dirt, and the flat valley floor was laid out like a factory to bake them. He produced them himself, and urged others to do the same. Soon, those twenty-acre parcels were turned into a nearly contiguous rack where millions of grapes, fresh off the vines, broiled undisturbed for fifteen days on wooden trays shaped like washing boards.

His dream got even bigger: that land would support a way of life all but vanished in America—a colony, peaceful and agrarian. It would have to be achieved by slow degrees and by banding together against the buyers and brokers who set one man against the next, eventually undercutting them all. A raisin cooperative was the only solution. In this way, farmers could speak with one voice. Over seven years, he cajoled and reasoned, drafted notes and agreements, and sent them back and forth. Every farmer thought his raisins were superior to the next and just couldn't see them tossed into a blind lot. They refused, agreed, and pulled out.

Finally, fed up with their stupidity, Kearney turned inward and envisioned an empire over which he alone would rule: the Fruit Vale Estate.

He purchased 5,000 acres, nearly eight miles square, and fashioned a master plan. At the hub of the immensity would be a 240-acre park, and in the middle of this park a home modeled after Chenonceaux. To design it he hired Maurice Hebert, a Frenchman who had fashioned for Charles Schwab of United States Steel a similarly styled Manhattan castle. With a footprint of 12,000 square feet, Kearney's would be the largest, most expensive home that corner of the world had ever known. The plans allowed for an entertainment hall and thirteen bedrooms, each with a bath and dressing room. Looking out through stained-glass windows you might let your eyes drift upon a manmade lake or delight in an Italian-style water fountain or English topiary gardens—just like those in London's greatest parks. During construction of the estate, Kearney temporarily quartered in a lodge on the park that he had built from native adobe bricks and furnished with the finest art nouveau that Europe had to offer—a taste of things to come. By 1909, excavation for the castle's foundation had commenced, and the grand park and eleven-mile palm-lined drive were complete. Kearney himself, however, never saw his plans come to fruition; he died at sea on a British luxury liner that same year.

What was it all about? Had madness gripped that Irishman? Could it all be distilled to simple vanity, revenge (toward those backward growers), or greed? Hadn't a similar madness driven his father to become the Watermelon King? Put Takahashi up to his contraptions, and turned Chamichian in one diabolical instant against his world-class trees? It gripped Andy too, he was forced to confess, that surplus of energy, that restless and immeasurable surfeit that refused to bend a knee, which all but said "no" to merely being a human being. "Enough is enough"—it also meant "enough isn't enough." Did everyone feel this way? Within each person was a similar epic drama unfolding? Was our human worth only confirmed when we had summoned an audience there to witness it—"Look at me!"—even if that audience was dredged from the dead? Why didn't life itself suffice? Why the need to prove that the four score we were allotted here on earth amounted to something rather than nothing? Who were we trying to prove it to? Did America do this to people, or did America attract people like Kearney who needed a place to do it?

This question had brought Andy to a near standstill in middle of that country road. The delicate winter light dazzled on the hood of his newly washed truck. He watched it dance. It brought him to. He shifted the truck forward, went uproad a little more, and left-turned down the drive.

The old man was sitting on the porch in a clamshell rocking chair, dressed up for the visit: cowboy hat, white shirt with blue stripes, a bolo tie.

"Don't bother," Andy said as he opened the truck door and limped up the steps. "I'm a little early."

"That's alright."

"Andy Demerjian."

"Tom Rider." He stuck his bony hand out to the side without moving his head. Andy took it more than shook it.

"How you doing?"

"*Comme ci, comme ça.*"

"It's a good piece of dirt."

"Go ahead and have a look around."

Rider waved a hand to show Andy that what was right there in front of him was what there was to sell.

"'Preciate it."

He threw a thumb over his shoulder. "There's couplea acre east end."

"Much obliged."

"Somewheres back there there's Junie, but don't mind her. She's 'bout as harmless as I am."

Andy guessed he meant his dog.

"I'll just take a look around then and make my way back here in a bit."

"Take yer time."

Andy went slowly down the steps, walked into the vineyard, and for nearly an hour studied it. The fifty-year-old vines were gnarled and knotted, the wire here and there burnt through from rust. There were gopher holes and dips in the irrigation rows. "Shabby" was the word that kept coming to mind. At one point he stopped and chuckled at the irony: nobody could say for sure where the foundation for Kearney's castle was intended to lay, but it might as well have been right there where he stood. He didn't really care to scout around the back of the house. He'd had enough of unleashed dogs for a spell, so he marched back through the dusty row and came up on the house.

"They need a deep drink right away," Andy told him.

"Just don't have the oomph anymore to do nothin'."

"You've done plenty enough. Don't you worry about it. How'd you get 'em off this year, if you don't mind me askin'?"

"I just 'bout give it away this guy, one of yer brethren, I believe. What's his name…"

"It don't matter."

"Kalabjian, is that it? Baladjian? Why you people got those names, I-A-N?"

"It's a long story. But basically 'Ian' means 'son of so-and-so.' Kind of like the Swedes got Peterson. Where you from originally, mind me asking?"

"Lubbock."

"Texan."

"Came here 1928. Farmed this here piece thirty years."

"No kin?"

"Nope. The wife she be gone, oh, seven, eight years gettin' on now."

"Lot of history locked up in this part of town. Kearney and all."

"Oh yeah. He was aimin' to make himself some heavenly earth. Didn't get halfway there."

"No. He was shy by a long shot."

"Only thing is, way things be, I can't be movin' nowhere."

"I understand."

"I ain't gonna be breathin' down yer neck er nothin'. Don't worry none about that part. 'Spect this here is where I'm gonna die."

"I was kind of hoping you'd help me come pruning time, frankly."

"Not a snowball's chance in hell, son."

"Four thousand dollars, huh? That's what you're askin'?"

"Yep."

"I think that's fair."

"Get my age, there's only two roads: hold on or let go."

"I hear you."

"Naw," he said, "I've had a good eighty-oddball years. I had five brothers, planted here and there across this country. Never 'spected to be scattered so. One by one they passed. I'm what's left. Though you never quite get old enough to watch young men die before their time."

"Hurts like the dickens, don't it?" Andy said.

The old man nodded.

"In terms of what you've got here, I think I can come up with half your four thousand right up front. The rest I promise you after the next harvest. You willing to carry a note for a year?"

"Damn shame this vineyard's such scruffy shape."

"Kind of what I was thinkin'."

"You go 'head then."

"Is that fair?"

"That'll do."

"I appreciate it."

2 0

VALENTINE AND ALICE, THE ELDEST SISTER, just driven in from
Oakland, were on the front porch smoking furiously. Kareen was in
the bedroom putting up her hair.

"Well, let's get going." Andy had poked his head in on her.

"One second, sweetheart." He liked to be fifteen minutes early
to every appointment, but when Kareen came along, he was always
fifteen minutes late. He looked at his watch and chuckled.

"All right, then." Andy stepped outside.

"Where is that girl?" Valentine asked.

"That hair of hers," Alice said.

"She's getting there. We'll be fine."

"He says that about everything," Valentine said. *"Inshallah!* It is
God's will!"

Alice laughed.

Arsen, Alice's husband, tall and dapper in a dark brown suit, was
leaning against his car.

Andy walked out to him. "Hey brother-in-law, how you holding
up?"

He stretched a kink out of his neck from the long drive down and
pulled a pack of smokes from his pocket.

"Have one."

"It's on your dime; why not?"

They lit their cigarettes and puffed in silence for a spell.

"You're a good man, Andy," Arsen said.

Andy did not feel its truth but neither did he feel the need to reject it. The matter, he supposed, belonged to God alone. He patted his brother-in-law on the back and said, "Let's both be chanting praises to the Lord."

"I'm ready," Kareen sang. She had taken one step onto the porch to see if he approved. Her hair was up in a bun. She wore green earrings, a peach-colored suit, and matching shoes.

Andy whistled. Valentine rolled her eyes.

Kareen got her two kids by the hand and led them down the steps, "Let's go then." They scooted into their cars and started up the road.

Thin clouds skimmed the sky, and the sun's heat was flickering, fragile. He took his wife's hand in his own and she squeezed back.

It was mid-November 1964, two months, a kind of purgatory, since he and Sammy had told the Italians to shove off. For the few weeks afterward, they'd recoiled like urchins whenever anything unexpected popped into the periphery of their vision. A car driving too close behind or a stranger asking them for directions was enough to get their hearts pounding. They phoned each other like teenage kids, every day, to make sure they were still alive. Sammy bought a revolver and set it behind the counter. One day at a time, they began to have a little faith, breathe a little easier.

If they were safe, the explanation was almost too bizarre to believe: the cops were the only threat to the Italians, and if, as Sammy suspected, they were taking their cut on the side, there was really nobody to fink to. The Italians had tied up all the constituencies so thoroughly that they'd reduced the threat to their operation to near about nil.

After the danger began to ease up, more than a few other questions swamped in. It was the second time in less than five years that Andy had blinkered his eyes from the stormy reality forming around him.

What the Italians had done to him was not all that much different than what his brother had.

Was he an idiot? Did Andy actually will this kind of deception upon himself? Did he give them a hand? Did he court the deception only to dodge it in the end, some strange game he staged to prove his prowess? Was he naïve? Did he partner with the enemy; did he blind himself to their lies because he lacked the courage to go at the world alone? All of these explained it in part, Andy supposed, but also, deep down, beyond his everyday awareness, he suspected that he had chosen to blind himself, to protect his faith in life, to protect life itself.

He had seen cynicism, the way it bled out from people and slowly ate away at the world like acid. "I can show you," it said, "how it all will end up before it has even had a chance. I will make you like a god." But, there was a price to pay. In exchange for that knowledge, your world would be emptied of magic, you would never again shake your head from amazement, or chuckle from wonder, or know the therapeutic hand of grace reaching out to you.

He remembered one afternoon, not long after he'd had that ugly conversation with the Italians ("Coon," they'd said. "We don't know about them coons"), he was out at the ranch. The sun had returned and the rain had washed the corn so that it glistened in the breeze. He leaned against the door of his truck, closed his eyes, and listened to their rustle until they were whispering to him, that sea of corn a sea of life taking him into its confidence, so much so that he walked straight into the field and stood listening some more.

Awe. That's what he felt, and he could link his hunger for that feeling clear back to when he was a kid. He remembered riding home on his bike from school straight into an oncoming storm, how the trees swayed and the leaves rushed past him, how the vast horizon bulked up with darkening clouds so that one side of the world glowed lavishly and the other side was swallowed up in shadows. The wind began to roar, bringing the whole chattering and neurotic nonsense of humans to a hush, the world of right and wrong, of that fact and the other, of the future and the past. It was maybe the first time he sensed that the world did not stop at the borders of the human, was not locked inside the judgment chambers of the brain. There is something beyond verdicts, bigger than us, and to know it is to free oneself, somehow, someway, and he wanted part of that bigger thing. He remembered peddling harder, to be a part of it, straight into the heart of it.

Maybe that feeling, that appetite, is what spirited him away from the farm. Abe had stolen that land from him, but in another way he had released Andy from it. Maybe they always knew it would come down to that. Maybe he and his brother had agreed, in the secret of their youth, Abe, you can take the certainty of the farm, all you can handle, and I will take life, with all its shabby uncertainty.

Even so, there was no excuse for Andy's stupidity. There was no way of getting on in the world without seeing things for the way they were. The more you dreamed, the more people believed you deserved the shock of reality when they emptied it at your feet. They seemed to say, "There is a price to pay for your dream." There had to be a middle ground, a third rail between yearnings for that awe and a cold, hard look at the facts. One had to be able to keep one's eye on the ground while simultaneously navigating toward a horizon.

"I think that's the one," Andy said.

They all watched a Pan Am jet slowly make a turn in the blue sky and then line up for arrival. Holding their breaths, they watched it drop and drop and then land on the tarmac roaring.

Valentine put her hands up to thank God.

The girls shrieked with excitement.

They watched passengers step out and make their way down the stairwell. Nairi appeared first, holding the hands of her two children, a girl and a boy. Asbed, her husband, was behind her. Andy saw him turn his head to take in his new home, the Sierras, the fields extending, it must have seemed, to the ends of the earth.

The girls rushed outside. Andy and Arsen followed behind. The sisters fell into one another, crying.

Andy shed a tear too. He wiped it away, went straight up to Asbed, and took him in. He was handsome and fit and happiness was overwhelming him.

In Armenian Andy said, "Welcome, brother-in-law. Welcome to America."

ABOUT THE AUTHOR

A SECOND-GENERATION ARMENIAN AMERICAN, Aris Janigian was born in Fresno, California, and currently lives in Los Angeles with his family. He returns to the Fresno area annually to work as a grape packer and shipper. He is the author of *Bloodvine* and the co-author, with April Greiman, of *Something from Nothing*.

HEYDAY INSTITUTE

Since its founding in 1974, Heyday Books has occupied a unique niche in the publishing world, specializing in books that foster an understanding of the history, literature, art, environment, social issues, and culture of California and the West. We are a 501(c)(3) nonprofit organization based in Berkeley, California, serving a wide range of people and audiences.

We are grateful for the generous funding we've received for our publications and programs during the past year from foundations and more than three hundred and fifty individual donors. Major supporters include:

Anonymous; Audubon California; Barona Band of Mission Indians; BayTree Fund; B.C.W. Trust III; S. D. Bechtel, Jr. Foundation; Fred & Jean Berensmeier; Berkeley Civic Arts Program; Joan Berman; Book Club of California; Butler Koshland Fund; California State Automobile Association; California State Coastal Conservancy; California State Library; Candelaria Fund; Columbia Foundation; Community Futures Collective; Compton Foundation, Inc.; Malcolm Cravens Foundation; Creative Work Fund; Lawrence Crooks; Judith & Brad Croul; Laura Cunningham; David Elliott; Federated Indians of Graton Rancheria; Fleishhacker Foundation; Wallace Alexander Gerbode Foundation; Richard & Rhoda Goldman Fund; Marion E. Greene; Evelyn & Walter Haas, Jr. Fund; Walter & Elise Haas Fund; Charlene C. Harvey; Leanne Hinton; James Irvine Foundation; Matthew Kelleher; Marty & Pamela Krasney; Guy Lampard & Suzanne Badenhoop; LEF Foundation; Robert Levitt; Dolores Zohrab Liebmann Fund; Michael McCone; National Endowment for the Arts; National Park Service; Philanthropic Ventures Foundation; Alan Rosenus; Mrs. Paul Sampsell; Deborah Sanchez; San Francisco Foundation; William Saroyan Foundation; Melissa T. Scanlon; Seaver Institute; Contee Seely; Sandy Cold Shapero; Skirball Foundation; Stanford University; Orin Starn; Swinerton Family Fund; Taproot Foundation; Thendara Foundation; Susan Swig Watkins; Tom White; Peter Wiley; Harold & Alma White Memorial Fund; and Dean Witter Foundation.

For more information about Heyday Institute, our publications and programs, please visit our website at www.heydaybooks.com.